A FATAL ENCOUNTER

An absolutely gripping classic British whodunnit

JANET NEEL

A Wilson and McLeish Mystery Book 3

Originally published as *Death of a Partner*

JOFFE
Ostara
CLASSICS

Revised edition 2024
Joffe Books, London
www.joffebooks.com

First published in Great Britain
as *Death of a Partner* in 1991

This paperback edition was first published
in Great Britain in 2024

Cover art by Dee Dee Book Covers

ISBN: 978-1-83526-013-5

For my husband,
Jim Cohen

CHAPTER 1

Detective Chief Inspector John McLeish gazed doubtfully at the plate before him. Having thought he was hungry, he now realized that actually he needed anything rather than the overflowing plate of cholesterol the canteen at New Scotland Yard had provided with such admirable promptness. Sleep would perhaps make more sense after thirty-six hours straight on duty, much of it spent with a sullen Jamaican who had killed his landlady and her three children in the crowded kitchen of a house behind the Westway. He took an experimental mouthful of fried egg and waited to see if it was going to suit him, then progressed to the baked beans, cautiously.

He finished the egg, all the baked beans and one of the sausages, but decided the fried bread was tempting fate and pushed the plate aside, reaching for his cup of tea, resting both elbows on the table. He lifted a hand off his cup in weary salute to one of his sergeants, a very dark Scot in a crumpled grey suit who was walking over from the counter, and the man altered course to sit opposite him.

'How goes it, Bruce?'

Bruce Davidson had accompanied McLeish from his last posting to C1, that division of New Scotland Yard concerned exclusively with murder, and they had now worked together for four years in the CID.

'Got that Tottenham case weighed off, nae bother. I hear you've finished the Westway job. Ye need to get your head down, John, you're looking rough.'

McLeish nodded. He had glanced in the washroom mirror and it had not been a reassuring sight. A big man, six foot four inches in his socks and a good fourteen stone, he always looked mildly untidy, and this morning, having worn the same clothes for a day and a half he looked like a football supporter after a night in the cells. At thirty-two, he was young enough not to look completely haggard, even after thirty-six hours with only the odd hour's sleep, but his dark hair was plastered to his head and the brown eyes were sunk back in his head and reddened with smoke and exhaustion.

'I'm going off. You too?'

'I'm waiting for Catherine — Sergeant Crane.'

Even falling asleep as he was, McLeish was amused at Bruce Davidson's hopeful, proprietorial air. Catherine Crane had joined the division three months ago, creating a major upheaval. She was a slight young woman of twenty-seven, whose dazzling, delicate, blond looks concealed a ferocious intelligence and attack. Every man in her vicinity had found himself putting his best foot forward, and she had done wonders for the sartorial standards of the notoriously uncaring C1 division. McLeish himself, though admiring, had been unaffected; he had been in love for over a year with a young woman only a little older, and even cleverer, than Sergeant Crane. His Francesca was a rising star in the Department of Trade and Industry, and they planned to celebrate her thirtieth birthday with a skiing holiday, due to start in two weeks' time. He smiled on Davidson, cheered immeasurably by the thought of getting on a plane with Francesca.

After chatting to Davidson for a few minutes longer, he went back to his office, looking for his secretary, a plumpish, infinitely competent, middle-aged mother of three. She was on the phone and he stood silently, filling the doorway, raising an eyebrow at her. She motioned him to stay.

'It's Francesca, John.'

'Thanks, Jenny. I'll take it back there,' he said, brightening, and she watched, with a little jealousy, as he hurried back to his desk.

'Darling. I've got a horrendous problem. Can you possibly duck out and have coffee in the caff in ten minutes?' The voice at the other end was slightly husky but very clear. 'It's Tristram. He's been arrested in New York. Better not talk on the phone, had we?'

'Oh, Christ. No. I'll meet you.'

He put down the phone, rattled. With his much-loved Francesca came her four younger brothers for whom, as the eldest child of a widow, she had always considered herself responsible. All four were talented musicians and difficult people, in varying degrees; Tristram, one of the twenty-four-year-old twins, had proved the most difficult, perhaps because he was not the most talented. McLeish gritted his teeth, and, trying not to consider the implications of what he had been told, made one quick phone call, then took the lift down and walked across the road from New Scotland Yard to the little café which was, as usual, full of workmen engaged in rebuilding the offices in the area.

Stopping to buy a paper, he caught sight of Francesca through the window, perched on one of the bar stools, totally unconscious of the table full of men next to her all eyeing her long legs. He stood and watched her, putting off the moment when, as he half knew, he would be asked to acquiesce in some lunatic scheme for pulling Tristram out of trouble, and saw her for a moment from a position of detachment: a tall young woman looking younger than her twenty-nine years, dark, with a long straight nose and arched eyebrows. She was looking particularly uncompromising today, tired and pale, her dark, short hair spiking up at the back. She had been crying, McLeish observed resignedly, as he pushed through the door.

'All right, tell me,' he said, as he sat down heavily beside her, and got a careful, measuring, sidelong look.

'I have to go to New York in a hurry and bail Tristram out. He was arrested last night, with one of the backing group and three of the band. They're all in the nick, charged with possession. Cocaine, as I understand it.'

'Jesus.'

'I know, I know, just when he was beginning to be a success like Perry. It simply went to his head — you know what he was like when he left.'

'Thought he could walk on water,' McLeish said, in irritated memory. 'Frannie, why do *you* have to go? He has a manager and a studio, doesn't he? What can you do that they can't?'

She sighed so heavily that her whole ribcage moved.

'I am to some extent on home ground there,' she said, reluctantly and not looking at him. 'Mike — Michael O'Brien — will help, but I need to be on the spot.'

McLeish held on to his temper, reminding himself that he was very tired. Francesca's much publicized affair with Senator Michael O'Brien was the reason that she had been sent home rather early from a tour of duty in the Embassy in Washington, over a year previously, just before he had met her in London. As one of Francesca's DTI colleagues had maliciously observed, it had been felt that fraternization with the American colleagues could be carried too far. Francesca herself had characteristically taken the line that the Foreign Office ought to have been glad that someone on the staff was that closely involved with the American political Establishment.

'What are you going to do with O'Brien?'

'Well, I'm hardly going to get back into bed with him after more than a whole year. There'll certainly be another incumbent by now. But he is the senior Senator, we were close when I was in Washington, and whichever way you slice it he won't want my brother being buggered or beaten up in a New York jail.'

Her classically good diction always became even clearer under stress, so that this statement emerged with the slightly metallic clarity of a dubbed film, and the clientèle of the small café was obviously appreciating every moment. McLeish decided that since she was unaware of her audience it did not become him to be self-conscious, and asked what she expected even a Senator to achieve in these circumstances?

'Oh, darling. The American legal system is so odd that I've been told I could get Tristram deported in my custody. It's a disaster, of course it's a disaster, he'll be banned from the US for ever presumably; but at least he won't be interfered with in some unspeakable foreign nick.'

'I thought he was off drugs?'

'Well we all hoped, didn't we? But evidently he isn't, and I must get him back.'

McLeish found himself on the verge of suggesting that a thoroughly unpleasant time in a New York jail might succeed in curing Tristram where all other methods, including exhortation, loving family support and a spell in a comfortable private hospital in Devon, had failed. He looked at his love's shuttered, miserable face and realized he would get nowhere along those lines.

'Why can't your Mum or one of the boys go?'

'Mum is in bed with bronchitis, as you would know if you had managed to get out of that place since last Friday.' Francesca, a true eldest child, knew how to score her points. 'Charlie's baby is due tomorrow, Perry is in Japan on tour, just like all the papers say. Jeremy *is* coming with me but he is too young to do this alone, and in any case I'm the only one who can deploy O'Brien.'

'How is the DTI receiving all this? You've got four rescue cases.'

Francesca sighed. 'They are as fed up with me as you are, but they won't stop me taking leave.' She stopped sharply, and blushed scarlet.

'Wait a minute.' John McLeish felt his blood-pressure going up. 'What about skiing, if you're using leave?'

She looked at him, wretchedly. 'I *have* to go. I really expect to get back in three or four days and I will try and hang on to the holiday. I know we need it, it seems ages since we went to bed.' McLeish scowled round the fascinated audience, returning the customers to their egg and chips. 'Anyway, it's been you who have been too busy for months.'

McLeish was too honest not to acknowledge the point. 'The more important, then, for us to have a holiday together.'

'I know. Darling, I am sorry, I really expect to be back inside the week, and I wouldn't go if anyone else could. I am trying — I mean I know I let the boys lean too much.'

He looked at her, defeated, and she saw that she had carried the point, but at a heavy cost.

'Do you still love me?' she asked anxiously.

'Not at the moment.'

An indrawn breath from the spectators unsettled both of them for a moment. Francesca nearly laughed, but McLeish's expression sobered her.

'Let's get out of here.'

She slid obediently off the bar stool, bidding a civil good-morning to the café owner who looked, McLeish observed, as if he would willingly have swept her into his plump Italian embrace, and they walked together to the gates of New Scotland Yard.

'I'll ring you when I get to New York.' She looked, worried, at his profile. 'You're furious with me. I'm sorry. I love you.'

'I don't think we can go on like this.' McLeish surprised himself as well as her.

'John.' It was an appeal and he was not proof against it.

He bent and kissed her. 'I am furious, and I want you back quickly. But good luck with it — ring me if you need help.'

The look she flicked him reminded him that this was one area where she would not appeal for his help; she had been more than careful to protect him from any involvement with a drug-taking brother. It was one of her many advantages that as a professional civil servant herself she understood the constraints of his career. She turned to go, head down. McLeish saw that she was crying again, but decided coldly there was nothing he was going to do and trudged wearily back to the lift, the morning's cheerfulness totally evaporated.

* * *

'I'm so sorry, Miss Morgan isn't in today. Would you like to speak to her assistant?'

The receptionist, like everything else in the glass-walled hall, was immaculately clean, glossy, highly fashionable and faintly reminiscent of an Italian restaurant. The young woman in the plain suit was not intimidated by it, nor by the hand-carved plate that proclaimed her to be in the offices of Yeo, Davis and Partners. 'But I'm having lunch with her,' she said. 'It was arranged some time ago.'

'If you'll just wait a minute, I'll ask someone to come and talk to you.' The immaculate receptionist's manner was fraying a little, discomfort with the situation showing like the edge of a petticoat. She looked across the hall and visibly relaxed as she saw a man moving swiftly down the staircase.

'Peter!'

The man altered course impatiently to deal with the interruption; just under six foot, he looked smaller because of the width of the powerful sloping shoulders which even good tailoring could do little to minimize. He looked sharply at the receptionist in enquiry, suppressed energy in his every movement.

'This is Miss Huntley who was supposed to be having lunch with Angela today.'

The tall young woman blinked as the man turned the full power of his attention on her.

'Have you talked to Angela this week?'

She stared at him. 'Well, no,' she said, 'but there was no need — I mean we had fixed up lunch last week. Is she not here?'

'No. No she isn't, I'm afraid. I'm very sorry she didn't let you know.' He was clearly preoccupied but Miss Huntley was not willing to let him go.

'You're her boss?'

'I'm the senior partner, yes. Peter Yeo.'

She had his attention back, and noticed how good-looking he was with those bright blue eyes and brown skin against the black hair. Rather heavy in the neck, but an attractive man. He looked back thoughtfully at her, taking in the brown eyes, the long, none-too-clean hair, and the patchy make-up through which broken veins in the cheeks were showing. Late twenties perhaps, but didn't make much of an effort.

'So how do I get hold of her?' the woman enquired, fretfully, voice rising out of control.

'Perhaps we should talk somewhere less public?' he suggested, and showed her hastily into his office.

'What has happened to Angela, then?' Miss Huntley asked anxiously, and he decided to make the best of a bad job.

'She hasn't been in at all this week.'

'And it is now Thursday. But she's very high up here, isn't she?'

He blinked. 'She's a partner, yes.'

'You must have talked to her family?'

'Well, I waited a couple of days. Then I talked to everyone. Her fiancé has now reported her as a missing person, I believe.'

'Giles Hawick? The Minister?'

'Yes. Sorry . . . but were you . . . are you close to her?'

'My uncle used to employ her. William Coombes. I do know her quite well.' She sounded indignant and resentful, and he slowed up deliberately.

'Ah. I have heard her speak of him.'

'Yes. He died two years ago.'

'I remember.' He was pouring coffee and she watched his thick, well-manicured hands.

'I need to see her.' Both of them were taken aback by the force with which she said it and she blushed red.

'I don't know where she is!' he admitted, reluctantly. 'I was disappointed when I found you didn't either. Oh, darling, hello, do come in.'

Since he now sounded flustered, Penelope Huntley looked with interest at the intruder: a good-looking, slightly overweight woman probably in her early forties, carefully dressed but uncertain.

'Darling, this is Miss Huntley, who was expecting to lunch with Angela today. Miss Huntley, my wife, Claudia Yeo. I've just been explaining that Angela seems to have gone missing.'

'I think everyone is probably making far too much fuss, and Angela has just taken off for a few days' holiday.'

Peter Yeo looked momentarily furiously exasperated. 'Giles Hawick is taking it seriously enough to have reported her as a missing person,' he said tightly.

His wife gave him a long level look with no liking in it at all, and Penelope Huntley watched, fascinated.

'Are we lunching, Peter?'

Peter Yeo jerked into action. 'Of course. Look, Miss Huntley, I'm afraid we are rather preoccupied. If you ring us tomorrow we may know more. I'm so sorry she isn't here.'

Penelope Huntley, who would very much have liked to have gone on with the discussion, found herself swept out of the office, and walked slowly down the road, flushed with a mixture of disappointment and excitement.

* * *

In New Scotland Yard John McLeish was trying, increasingly irritably, to clear his desk so he could go home. Bruce Davidson was making a meal of explaining a straightforward case essentially because he was trying to impress Catherine Crane. Not that he was succeeding; Sergeant Crane was sitting, legs crossed, only just not fidgeting, as Bruce Davidson wore on through a lot of unnecessary detail.

It was unprecedented for any woman to have that effect on Davidson, whose success in this field was legendary.

She was, of course, very desirable, McLeish conceded: reddish-blond hair above blue eyes, and a perfect, pale skin, lightly freckled. Her apple-green light wool suit reminded them all that spring would one day come. Indeed, she was a true beauty: straight, fine features, a long neck, a gently curved, slim figure. He found himself smiling gently as he sat and watched her, and pulled himself up sharply, realizing that the girl was annoyed by what was obviously a familiar reaction. He had looked at her papers three months ago, when the posting had been announced, and had noted how well educated she was. She had joined the Met with three A levels and a huge number of O levels as an eighteen-year-old, then worked her way over into the CID, and was now a Detective Sergeant and ready to move up, having passed the exams for Inspector.

His phone rang and he picked it up, reluctantly.

'John, sorry to interrupt. Commander Stevenson wants you, now.'

'I'll come. Excuse me, both of you.'

Catherine and Davidson were left in his office to carry on the conversation, and while Davidson was finding her some more coffee, Catherine turned the photograph on John McLeish's desk to look at it.

'Is she his wife?'

'No, no, that's Francesca. They're not married.'

'His fiancée?'

'No. No, I don't think you could say they were engaged. They've been together, oh, for over a year.' Davidson reviewed this explanation. 'They don't live together — I mean not in the same place,' he added conscientiously. 'She was married before.'

'What about him? McLeish?'

'No, he's not been married.' He gazed at her, earnestly. 'Fancy some lunch?'

Catherine Crane smiled back. 'Bit early for me.'

Davidson, taken aback, glanced at his watch. Twenty past eleven. 'Bit early for me too, sorry.' He stopped, uncharacteristically gravelled, got a quick entirely comradely look of amusement, and laughed.

'Come on, let's get out of John's office, he'll likely be a while yet.'

* * *

John McLeish, seated at the other side of a table from Commander Stevenson, would have agreed with this judgement. Despite the urgency of the summons, he had been kept waiting in Stevenson's outer office long enough to read the early edition of the *Evening Standard*. On page four, as he had feared, was a bad picture of Tristram under the headline 'Singing star on US Drugs Charge'. He skimmed the accompanying text, which added little to what Francesca had already told him, filling up the two columns with a recital of Tristram's career beginning with his legendary recording of 'Panis Angelicus' as a thirteen-year-old treble at St Joe's. As usual, much was made of the fact that he was younger brother to the wildly successful Peregrine, now in Japan on tour with his group. Indeed McLeish reflected, that encapsulated the trouble with Tristram — everything that he could do, Perry, two years his senior, could apparently do just that bit better.

'Come in John. Sit down.' Stevenson, a quick-moving, stocky northerner with a distinguished record in every possible branch of the Met, was rumoured to be going up to Assistant Commissioner just as soon as the present incumbent retired. 'I take it that's one of your connections in bother,' he observed, seeing the paper in McLeish's hand.

'I'm afraid so. Francesca is on her way to New York.'

'Why?'

'That's what I asked her.' McLeish hoped he was not sounding as defeated as he felt.

'You'll need to be very careful, personally, in dealing with an addict.'

McLeish sighed. 'They know that. Francesca wouldn't have him in the house when she knew he was on something.

They hoped they'd got him detoxed. She's got him booked in again at Cocaine Hall when she gets him back.'

'Will she manage to get him out of the USA?' Stevenson sounded startled and McLeish said, wearily, that Francesca had good contacts. Everywhere, he added sourly, thinking about it.

Stevenson considered him thoughtfully but decided there was little profit in going on. 'Not why I called you in. We've got another one to look at. Not necessarily for us yet, but we've been asked by Special Branch to take it on board. Missing Person.'

McLeish gazed at his superior. Most missing person reports do not end in a murder. Typically they are husbands or wives walking out to live somewhere else, or teenagers leaving home. He kept what he hoped was a bright and intelligent expression on his face and waited for enlightenment.

'That's how I felt,' Stevenson agreed. 'The problem is that the missing person was going to marry a junior Treasury Minister.'

'It's a girl, then.' McLeish blinked and looked apologetically at his superior.

'How long have you been on duty, John?'

'Thirty-six hours, sir. Sorry, I'll wake up.'

Stevenson considered him. 'You'll have to, you're all I've got at your rank. Go home, get a couple of hours' sleep, clean up and get back here. You're seeing Mr Hawick — who is Financial Secretary to the Treasury and has reported his fiancée, a Miss Angela Morgan, as missing. You're due at four-thirty at his office at the House of Commons after Treasury Questions, whatever they are. I'll send a driver for you.'

'Sir.' McLeish knew what Treasury Questions were, thanks to Francesca. Every afternoon in the House of Commons MPs could raise questions with Ministers about their Departments. These had to be answered, and answered well — or at least the first ten or so did — because the original questioner and other MPs were allowed to ask supplementary questions. Once you got down to Question 11, the questioner would get a deeply unhelpful written response which would, if the civil servants knew their business, leave no one any the wiser. Endearingly, Francesca herself was not good at drafting that sort of answer and usually had to enlist a more senior colleague to achieve the correct polished hand-off. And he knew that the Financial Secretary was the junior of three Treasury Ministers and did not sit in the Cabinet.

'Do you want me to talk to Special Branch, sir?'

'I've done that. Take a sergeant with you, assuming there is such a thing left in the building.'

'Yes, we got a replacement for Jameson . . . what? . . . three months ago. I've not yet worked with her personally, sir.'

'Ms Crane? I've seen her.' Stevenson's clean-shaven, tight-mouthed face relaxed in a ferocious grin. 'Wouldn't mind working with her personally, myself. Yes, take her — I'll check with Hawick's office that it's all right if you come mob-handed, but I've a feeling in my water about this one. I'd like to have a proper team together right from the start.'

'I'll tell her, sir.'

'Then get home for a couple of hours. Best suit to go and see Mr Hawick.'

John McLeish rose to go but was recalled as he reached the door.

'Anything we can do to help with young Wilson? I could ring up a colleague in New York.'

'She'd rather fix it herself if she can, sir, I do know that. But thank you.'

'Better for us to be involved than you personally, John.'

'I know that, sir. Thank you.'

He walked into the corridor, tiredness suddenly overcoming him with the prospect of a few hours off, and very nearly knocked Catherine Crane over in his preoccupation. He caught her elbow to steady her. 'Sorry, not looking where I'm going. I'm off home for the morning, but you're wanted to come with me to see a VIP about a missing person. Walk along and I'll tell you about it.'

He told her everything he knew, and made sure she understood where to be and at what time, talking with the speed of true exhaustion and repeating himself. He stopped, realizing what he was doing, and looked at her carefully to see if she had taken it in. She looked back at him and smiled gently, and he saw that she had been writing in a workman-like leather-bound notebook.

'Yes, sir. Got it.'

'Don't call me sir,' he said sharply. 'Everyone calls me John,' he added mendaciously.

Her smile widened, and she nodded, pleased but unsurprised. He rested his eyes on her, very conscious of the smooth skin and her flowery perfume. Gathering himself, he dismissed her and went down to the waiting car.

* * *

Four miles away, Francesca had already reached her own small Victorian house and was moving clothes from the dryer straight into a battered suitcase.

'Six pairs of knickers must be enough, mustn't it, Charlie?' she enquired of a tall dark-blond young man, unmistakably her brother, who was piling plates into a dishwasher and making two cups of coffee.

'Heap good laundries in New York, darling. How was John?'

'Oh God. Furious. And miserable. I felt awful.'

Charlie emerged from the kitchen and handed her a cup. 'I really am sorry. I would go instead of you but I can't, can I, with Mum sick and the baby due any day?'

'No, Charlie, of course you can't, we've been through that. And Jeremy can't manage on his own, he's just too young. It does have to be me.'

Her brother watched her, with love and anxiety, as she checked the contents of her handbag. 'Weren't you and John going skiing soon?'

'We were. We are. We have to get a week together. He's been so busy catching murderers we've hardly seen each other for three weeks. He never stops working.'

'You need to marry him. He loves you, he's a good bloke, you've been together for over a year. He's going up the ladder like a rocket, isn't he? He doesn't have time for all this.' Charlie watched Francesca's vivid face go wooden as she counted currency. 'He does still want to marry you, I take it?'

'Oh yes.' She spoke with dismissive confidence. 'It's always been me who said no.'

Her brother, closing her suitcase for her, regarded her with exasperation. 'You're nearly thirty. It's time you settled down and had children.'

'You've been reading Jane's magazines again.' Francesca silenced him, as she had meant to; his wife Jane, unlike his academically gifted sister, had done the domestic science course at her school. He jerked her case upright, tight-lipped, and put it by the door for her, but relaxed in exasperated pity as he watched her start to check her handbag for the third time.

'I suppose we are right to send you and Jeremy out to get Tristram rather than leave him to take the full consequences?' he said reflectively, as he loaded her and her possessions into his car and took the wheel.

'I couldn't possibly not go,' Francesca said, pushing a cassette-tape into the car recorder. 'It's Tris's demo-tape,' she said in explanation, and both listened, cut off in concentration, as a pure high tenor, singing 'Plaisirs d'Amour' filled the car. 'Listen to that top A. Better range than Perry, you know,' Francesca said, softly.

'Doesn't project like Perry does.' Charlie started quietly to sing with the tape, and his sister joined him, both stretching for the top notes. They looked at each other and laughed as they went for the top A and each found that no noise came out at all.

'I always think it's very nice of you not to mind being a baritone rather than a tenor, Charlie. I would give my eyeteeth to be a soprano, and to be able to get that high.'

'Or even higher. Tris has a reliable top C, which is more than Perry does.'

They fell silent, listening as the tape finished.

'He spits his final consonants out as if he were still at St Joe's,' Francesca observed with love and Charlie sighed.

'All right. You go and get Tristram out of durance vile, helped or handicapped by Jeremy — for the sake of his talent, if nothing else. And let's just hope your life is where you left it when you come back.'

CHAPTER 2

McLeish and Catherine Crane were expected and escorted quickly to the Minister's Private Office. McLeish knew roughly what it would be like from Francesca's description of her own Department, but he was still interested in the controlled bustle in the big untidy room. The Private Secretary, a dark, stocky man a couple of years McLeish's junior, greeted him, observing cautiously that they had surely met at Francesca Wilson's house? He then did a double take at the sight of Catherine Crane, who had been the object of the most careful attention from everyone else in the room from the minute she had arrived.

'The Minister is just finishing a phone call, then I must tell him one thing before he sees you,' he said, briskly, glancing at the miniature switchboard beside him which sat incongruously in the draughty, high-ceilinged, dingy room. A light flicked off, and he knocked and disappeared into his master's office, leaving McLeish and Catherine by his desk. A dazzled junior seized the opportunity to press tea on them both, his eyes never leaving Catherine, and McLeish, amused, accepted a cup.

'The Treasury exists to stand in front of the safe, shouting "Go away!" and making threatening gestures at any Department who comes

near it or them,' he remembered Francesca's clear, amused voice explaining the system. '*But in the end they get pushed over; they just manage to delay the bigger-spending Departments a bit. And they pop up again, good as new, the next time, like a row of skittles.*' The Private Secretary — Michael Marsden, he remembered with an effort — signalled them from the door and McLeish moved forward, keen to see what the kingpin of this row of skittles looked like.

His first thought, as he shook the hand of the distinctive dark man almost as tall as himself, was that Francesca must have got it wrong this time. Giles Hawick was not the sort of man you could flatten easily, and if you managed it, he would not pop up, bright, smiling and bearing no grudge, to face you the next time. If you injured this one, it would be as well to kill him before he killed you.

McLeish stepped back, surprised at the force of his reaction, and introduced Catherine Crane, watching Giles Hawick carefully. The high, arched eyebrows in the long bony face rose slightly in surprise, but no more. The immediate impression of directed dominance did not come from the man's physique, impressive though that was, McLeish decided as he accepted the offered chair and placed Catherine at the side of the room. Giles Hawick was a beautifully put together man, something over six foot without a spare ounce of flesh anywhere, the long lines in the face being particularly strong. Nor were the very deep-set dark brown eyes particularly hypnotic, as journalists occasionally suggested. It was the controlled, economical force that emanated from the man that was impressive, and the speed with which he absorbed information. In about two minutes he had established precisely which members of C1 he was dealing with and why.

John McLeish, himself a forceful character, felt as if he had been put through a wringer. He waited, out of long experience with dominant characters, until a natural break occurred and used it to ask for some background, starting with how long the Minister had known Miss Morgan. Giles

Hawick, looking surprised, sat more easily in his chair and started to marshal his thoughts.

'I've known her a couple of years. We met when she came with the chairman of one of the big contractors to lobby me about increasing the road-building programme, when I was a spokesman for Transport. She was working for Yeo Davis, where she is a partner now. A case of gamekeeper turned poacher, given that she had been a fast-stream entrant to the Treasury, much of whose function it is to resist that sort of demand.'

Francesca might have it right after all, McLeish thought, enjoying the turn of phrase.

'I liked the look of Angela and organized an introduction through a mutual acquaintance.'

Not being prepared to be beholden to those who were lobbying you, McLeish observed, considering the formidable professional across the table.

'My first wife died some years ago, as you may know. At the time I met her, Angela told me that she was involved with someone else. Women make their own minds up about what they want to do, I find, so I left it; but about a year ago she invited me to a party and indicated that whoever it had been was no longer around. I was very pleased, and we, well, we wasted no time. We intend to marry in April, immediately after the House rises.' He stopped and stared out of the window, across Horse Guards, looking suddenly weary. 'Have you talked to her family?'

'Not yet, sir.'

'They are very distressed. There are only two children, both daughters. Angela is the younger.'

'Is there much difference in age?'

'Four years. Jennifer has not married yet. She's a very attractive girl. In fact I took her out a couple of times myself when I found that Angela was occupied with someone else. I get on well with them all, actually. I think Francis Morgan feels I'm a bit old for Angela — I'm forty-three and she is twenty-nine — but he's never brought himself to say so. And

Sarah Morgan likes the idea of Angela marrying someone in the government.'

McLeish considered this cold and rational assessment. 'When did you last see her? Miss Angela Morgan, I mean.'

'Early on Saturday morning — about eight-thirty. I didn't expect to see her again until late on Monday — I went off to do some walking for the weekend and was taking an extra day. I rang her on Monday night and got no answer, but that didn't worry me. I was having lunch with her on Tuesday. She didn't turn up, so of course I then telephoned her office and found she hadn't been there that week. I rang her parents yesterday — Wednesday. I hadn't wanted to worry them before. Today I felt I could leave things no longer, so I had a word with a colleague in the Home Office. Perhaps I should have done it before, but I suppose one's always afraid of making a fool of oneself.'

McLeish decided it was unlikely that that sort of consideration very much exercised this cool customer. 'You have no idea where she might be?'

'I would not have called you in if I had, would I? Sorry, but I cannot imagine what has happened. What has usually happened when people vanish?'

McLeish took a minute to formulate his reply, and Giles Hawick got it at once. 'They've gone off with someone.'

'They've mostly gone voluntarily, yes, sir.'

'*That's* what your boss was trying to indicate.' Giles Hawick looked down at his blotter, lips tight with tension. 'Angela is a very attractive woman and also very forthright. If she'd wanted to go off with someone else, she would just have said so. Please, Chief Inspector, put that out of your mind. I want the police to look for her, not humour me. Where do you start?'

'With the hospitals and any reports of unidentified persons found dead.' McLeish decided there was no point tempering the wind to this competent and well-clad lamb. 'We'll also circulate her description, and if you have a good, recent photograph that would be very helpful.'

'We'd just had some done for our engagement. My Private Secretary will find them.' Giles Hawick suddenly looked tired and McLeish felt for him, as he promised to keep him in touch with their investigations. Not much danger of his Commander letting him slip up on that, he thought drily.

They rose to go, Giles Hawick with the politician's automatic competence escorting them to the lift and warmly asking Catherine Crane where she had trained and how she liked her job. He showed them into the lift, shaking hands with them both, and as Catherine turned away from him to press the lift button, he suddenly raised his eyebrows at McLeish in amusement at his own response to her.

* * *

'In what circumstances would an attractive woman of twenty-nine walk out on a fiancé without telling him or anyone else where she was going?' McLeish asked Catherine as they walked back through St James's Park.

'If she was frightened of him?' She sounded doubtful, but McLeish decided it would be possible to be frightened of Giles Hawick. He had the look of a man with a nasty temper if you got on his wrong side. 'But presumably the Commander doesn't think she ran away? I mean Special Branch has asked us to come in. They all think something's happened to her, don't they?'

She might sound diffident, McLeish thought, amused, but she wasn't, just more careful than his blunt Francesca about how she made her points.

'I agree. I don't like the sound of it at all. The best we could hope for is that she's had a brainstorm, and I don't know how often that happens outside of books. Anyway, we need to get back and get the procedures into place.'

All that took some five hours for very little result. By ten p.m. McLeish was reasonably satisfied that Angela Morgan was not lying unidentified in any morgue, nor in any hospital, unconscious or suffering from loss of memory. Tomorrow he would have to talk to her family and last known associates. Remembering that he had sent Catherine Crane to see Angela Morgan's employers, he decided to find out how she had got on; late as it was, he did not think she would have gone off duty without reporting to him.

He got halfway down the corridor and realized in irritation that he had no idea where she had been given an office. That small problem solved itself readily: one door stood open with Bruce Davidson leaning on the side in a careful presentation of a man who had just happened to be passing. He stood aside for McLeish, then took himself off, observing unnecessarily that he just had a wee bit of paperwork to finish up. Catherine Crane, installed behind her desk, gave him a slightly weary smile. She looked, McLeish observed, as immaculate as she had in the morning, but she was pale and her eyes looked huge.

'I've got some useful stuff from Yeo Davis — that's Miss Morgan's employers, sir, I mean, John. Her diary for last week and the week before. She had a lot of appointments, particularly at lunch. I've listed them.'

He peered at the long list. 'What does she do?'

'Yeo Davis advise on government and parliamentary affairs.'

'What does that mean they do?'

'Mr Yeo did explain it, but I'm not quite sure I see it, even so. He says they help companies to influence government decisions and legislation.'

McLeish decided he didn't understand it either but he wasn't about to discourage Sergeant Crane. 'OK, let's have a look at the list. Last Monday, appointment at the Ministry of Defence, lunch with Hugo Brett MP, afternoon date with Charles Council, drinks at the Reform. Tuesday, more of the same, except she seems to have met Mr Hawick at the House of Commons after work. Wednesday, she sees a chap who is one of the PM's advisers, or that's what it says — and what does she do for lunch? Blow me, I don't believe it!'

'What?'

'That Wednesday she had lunch with one F. Wilson, DTI. That's one person I know where to find.'

'Who is it?'

'A girl called Francesca Wilson, who is doing work that involves rescuing dud companies which employ a lot of people in difficult areas.' He hesitated, not sure why he was being cautious. 'In fact, she's my girlfriend.'

Catherine Crane smiled at him gently. 'Well, that is easy enough for you, isn't it? Are you seeing her tonight?'

McLeish scowled, reminded. 'No, she's in New York.' He glanced sideways at Catherine Crane's unchanged expression which showed merely courteous interest, and decided to sit down and talk. 'Francesca's got four brothers, see, two of them professional singers, two of them by the grace of God ordinary working stiffs in respectable offices.' He paused, trying to decide how to go on, noticing how dirty the walls of the small, dark office looked against Catherine Crane's neat, pale suit and bright blond hair.

'Is one of them Perry Wilson?' she enquired, visibly impressed.

'Yes. He's OK. Well, he's not, but he's not causing any difficulty just at the moment. There are twins at the bottom of the family and it's Tristram who's in trouble. Done for possession of Class A drugs in New York.'

'That *is* difficult.'

'And Francesca's there to try and get him out on bail.'

'Doesn't he have a lawyer?'

'Good question. Fran's gone to make sure no one lays a finger on a brother, that's what it is. They're like that.' He brooded for a moment, sighed, and reached for the list again. 'I'll be able to talk to her sooner or later, and it sounds as if she might actually be useful. She'll at least be able to explain Yeo Davis to us. Anything else on Miss Morgan?'

Catherine Crane moved one tidy package of paper, neatly tabulated, in search of an equally tidy pile, and McLeish watched with pleasure. Keeping the paperwork straight might not be glamorous but it was eighty per cent of the battle as he well knew, and he made certain his staff did too. It didn't look as if that particular conversation was going to be necessary in this case. 'Sorry, here we are. Mr Yeo sent us her CV — the one they send out to prospective clients. Only the basic facts, but useful. And some spare copies of the photographs that came out from the DTI this afternoon — we ran off dozens to send out to the regional forces, but I snaffled six.'

McLeish took the photographs and considered them. A lively, arrogant face, rather square, eyes wide-set, and a full, curving mouth. Dark brown hair, dark brown eyes, and slightly sallow skin which the photographer had not bothered to disguise or retouch, having understood that this was part of her charm. Not a true beauty, but the girl beckoned you off the paper; confident, sexy, that face invited you to join in if you could stand the pace. A handful, McLeish thought, but a lot of fun.

He reached for the CV while Catherine Crane busied herself systematically with her papers. Same age as Francesca, and had attended the same good North London all-girls' grammar school, for entry to which aspiring parents would have been prepared to pay blood-money had there been anyone in the austere intellectual governing body and teaching staff who would have taken it. They must have been the same year, for their birthdays were only two months apart. Even among perhaps a hundred girls in their year, they must have known each other quite well. Their ways had diverged at university — Angela Morgan had gone on to Oxford to read English, the fatherless Francesca, under more pressure to make a living, had gone to Cambridge to read law. A clever girl, though, Miss Morgan, an Exhibitioner like Francesca and a respectable second-class degree. He considered the arrogant, attractive, knowing face again and put the photo down, shifting his attention to Catherine's pale, classic beauty. He was about to divide up responsibility for checking Angela Morgan's last recorded movements when Bruce Davidson knocked and put his head in.

'John. It's Francesca, on the phone from New York, says will you hurry.'

McLeish jogged down the passage, overcoming irritation. Of course he had the sense to hurry when she was hanging on a line from New York.

'Talk more slowly,' he said, in exasperation, after the first few seconds. She was sounding strained, and as always when she was over-extended she was being unnecessarily bossy. Her sigh of exasperation reached him from 3,000 miles away.

'Sorry, but I've been at it all day.'

'Well, calm down. I need to talk to you, too.'

'What about?' Francesca sounded rattled and hostile, and McLeish gazed at the wall, wondering if he had really been in love with her for over a year.

'About someone called Angela Morgan whom you or another F. Wilson at the DTI had lunch with a couple of weeks ago. She's been reported missing and we're checking her movements for the two weeks before she vanished.' A dead silence ensued and he shook the phone. 'Francesca?'

'Sorry, yes. It *was* me. But why are *you* doing this, John? Do you think she's dead?'

Well, at least Francesca's mind appeared to be functioning on a subject unconnected with her damned brothers, McLeish thought grimly. 'Not necessarily. She was reported missing by her fiancé.'

'Giles Hawick. Does *he* think she's dead?'

'He hopes she is lying in hospital somewhere, having lost her memory.'

'And she isn't?'

'Not as of an hour ago, no.'

'She's gone off with another bloke, bet you anything.'

McLeish grinned at the telephone. 'I didn't think she was one of your mates. But you were at school with her?'

'Yes I was, but we were never that close. Different subjects for a start.' There was a pause while she gathered her thoughts and McLeish waited patiently.

'What do you know about her, John?'

'Bugger all, at the moment. I've got a photograph.'

'Then you know quite a lot, if it is a good one. Of all the women I know, she is by far the most successful with men, even though she isn't the best-looking. She is *the* original mantrap.'

John McLeish blinked at the telephone. Francesca's judgement was typically over-judicial and conscientiously unemotional, but this had real force behind it. He had never heard Francesca giving vent to feminine jealousy and on the whole he found the experience refreshing. 'You'd better explain to me what it is she does as a job. Hang on — I'll ring you back, the Yard can pay this bill.'

'That's all right, I'm in a mate's office.'

'Well, I hope the Senator can afford it.'

'I'm sure he can.'

A real advantage of his girl, McLeish thought grimly, was that she never lied if asked directly. She might not volunteer the truth all the time, but ask her and you got a straight answer.

'Angela is a lobbyist.' Francesca made it sound like someone who came to clean the telephone. 'That's not what Yeo Davis call themselves — I think they use some phrase like "government and parliamentary relations". They help clients to push the right buttons in government in the UK — and increasingly, of course, in the EEC. It's a perfectly respectable trade,' she added conscientiously. 'I don't *mind* lobbyists, I'd just rather they called themselves by their proper name as they do in Washington, rather than wittering on for hours about relationships with opinion-formers. Angela got up my nose as usual on this point over lunch, banging on about the importance of seeing that Ministers were properly informed and by the right people. As if the Civil Service spent all its time obfuscating issues and introducing Ministers to the wrong people.'

McLeish decided that it was probably not the moment to suggest to her that the real reason any civil servant disliked lobbyists must be that the chaps were paid to make sure Ministers got a view other than the Departmental one. 'Can you give me an example of what they do? I mean, why was Miss Morgan having lunch with you, or was that just for old time's sake?'

'No, no, I now rank as an important contact, a senior opinion-former, or so she flatteringly told me. It was quite a good example of lobbying, in fact. It's widely known — because the unions have publicized it — that the Department is looking at bailing out Huerter Textiles. Henry and I are doing it, as the resident textile rescue-squad. You just haven't heard about it because you've been too busy.'

Trust Francesca to get her points in while she could, McLeish thought irritably. 'And her firm is working for Huerter?'

'No, no, quite the contrary. *Her* firm, Yeo Davis, is working for Barton Mills, which is the other really big surviving textile company in the north-west. Their chief executive, Andy Barton, feels, with some reason one would have to say, that it isn't right that the government should bail out a competitor. The point *is*, darling, that in order to make sure Huerter has a future, we would have to put a lot of money in to restore a bombed-out balance sheet. Barton has heavy borrowings too, and to put it crudely, if they're paying interest and Huerter isn't, Huerter ought to be able to undercut them in the market.'

'So Miss Morgan was making sure you'd understood all that? I see where it annoyed you.'

Francesca was not amused. 'Yes, well, it is an offensively elementary consideration and one to which Ministers' attention had been drawn. Yeo Davis seem to have felt, nonetheless, that it was worth a lunch.' She paused. 'I'd have to say that given the change of government they ought to have a very good chance of preventing us assisting Huerter. I mean, this lot did come in, only six months ago, announcing that everyone would have to stand on their own feet and not be rescued, and face up to competition, and all that. But whatever they said, as you know they haven't actually done any of it yet

— they did rescue Fryers *and* Towyn Metals, using taxpayers' money, just like they said they wouldn't. Yeo Davis could have credibly warned Barton that, whatever the public statements, there was a real risk that Huerter would be bailed out.'

McLeish considered this. 'Are lobbyists well paid?'

'Yes. Not that Angela needed the money.'

'Rich girl, is she?'

'Very. She didn't earn it in any conventional sense: her last employer left one-third of his substantial fortune to her outright, and another third for life. His family — a sister and niece as I remember — was awfully cross. This was about two years ago.'

McLeish told Francesca to hang on while he got this down as a note, and stared at the result. It made a good reason for those excluded to dislike Miss Morgan, but it had been true any time these past two years.

'When you had lunch, how was she? I mean, it didn't sound as if she had plans to go off with someone else.'

In the silence at the other end of the line he heard Francesca think. 'No, she didn't come over like that, not at all. In fact, she was excited in an innocent way about the wedding plans. Reception at the House, all very grand and smart. And awfully good for her business, too.'

McLeish smiled to himself at the swift fall from grace in the postscript. Prodding gently, he got Francesca to run through the substance of the lunch-time conversation. It was clear that Miss Morgan's brain had been fully engaged on what she was doing, which was pushing a client's interest, and that such attention as she could spare from that had been centred on her forthcoming marriage. Nothing at all there, five days before her disappearance, to suggest she was planning to vanish. Francesca's attention would have been undivided as well, as that lunch had taken place before Tristram had managed to get himself so comprehensively into trouble. McLeish remembered abruptly Francesca's chief preoccupation. 'How are you getting on over there?' he asked, cautiously.

'Much fixing is going on. I'm basically just biting my fingernails and holding Tristram together. He has been bailed on several sureties and appears in court tomorrow.'

She was sounding terse and McLeish decided not to ask her any more details over the transatlantic phone. 'I've told them here I don't need the week after next off,' he said, as levelly as he could.

'Oh, John.' She sounded appalled. 'I'd managed to hang on to it. Why *ever* did you do that?'

'How was I supposed to know?' he said, instantly aware that he had acted too hastily because he had been so angry with her.

'Well, I said I'd call you. I ought to be home in three days and I've made a deal with Henry. That was just plain bloody-minded of you.'

'Coming from you, that's ridiculous!' A combination of justified annoyance, guilt and weeks of overwork blew John McLeish's temper to shreds instantly, and Francesca, seriously over-stressed and not one to duck a quarrel at the best of times, responded in kind. She banged the phone down a second before he did, leaving him raging.

Ten minutes later he had calmed down sufficiently to make himself a cup of coffee and write himself a note to check Angela Morgan's financial status. He bethought himself guiltily of Sergeant Crane, who might be assumed to be waiting to continue the conversation that Francesca's call had interrupted, and padded down the corridor. Her office was now marked by a frieze of officers, two lounging half in and half out of her door, a third a little behind, the attention of all three directed entirely towards her desk. Two of the three moved off as he arrived, with unconvincing references to waiting papers, but Bruce Davidson stood his ground, enquiring heartily how Francesca was and had she been helpful? McLeish considered him with something between amusement and irritation. Bruce was pale with the deep pallor that overworked CID tend to acquire in London in the dead of winter, seriously overtired and overweight. But he was alert and sparkling, his motor well and truly turned on by the presence of Catherine Crane, and he probably wasn't going to go home till he, or Catherine, dropped in their tracks.

'She was fine, and yes she was,' he said, dealing with Bruce's formal question. 'And it'll all wait till the morning. Go home, Bruce, or back to whatever your case is, and I'll have a word with Sergeant Crane.' He nodded decisively, and equally firmly walked into her office and closed the door on Davidson's hopeful face.

'Sorry, but that phone call was useful.' He ran, as dispassionately as he could, through Francesca's account of her lunch with Angela Morgan.

'So she probably didn't vanish voluntarily,' Catherine Crane said, in summary.

'It doesn't sound like it.' He looked unseeingly at the beautiful face across the table, hearing the echo of his quarrel with Francesca, feeling his mind still chuntering on in justification of the anger that had led him to cut off all possibility of their holiday next week. Well, he *had* been fed up, and why shouldn't he be? He was fed up with the whole situation, and all Francesca's family.

'Sir — John, is there anything more tonight?'

He came back smartly to the office and the desk on which he was leaning. 'No, sorry. Have you eaten since lunch?'

'A sandwich and lots of coffee which Sergeant Davidson brought. I'm fine.'

'I'm not. I'm going to get something at the pub on my way home. Come with me?'

'Thank you, I'd like to.' She smiled at him and he smiled back, cheered by the thought of a drink and something to eat in her company. He collected her as soon as they had both tidied their offices, McLeish maliciously enjoying Davidson's obvious chagrin as they said good night to him on the way out.

'A good man, that,' he said, guiltily, to Catherine as they went down in the lift. 'One of the best. I want to get him up to Inspector as soon as possible.'

'He has been very helpful.'

McLeish repressed a grin and bustled into the big noisy pub on the corner, receiving an instant acknowledgement from one of the bartenders, who all knew any member of the C1 hierarchy. McLeish carried over a loaded tray, and ate ravenously, noting with interest that Catherine Crane had an equally good appetite, though it was not obvious where she was putting it on that slim frame.

She caught his eye and laughed. 'I have to eat about five times a day, or I just stop in my tracks.' She licked her fingers and applied herself to her beer.

Like Francesca, McLeish thought, and irritably suppressed the reflection. 'Tell me about you. Did you do all your time in the Met, or did you start up north?'

'No, I came straight to the Met from school at eighteen.'

Left home as soon as she could, McLeish observed, instead of starting where she could work from home. 'Do you still have family in wherever it is — Stoke on Trent?'

'Yes, they're still there.' She was looking wooden, and McLeish decided to move off this point, but she forestalled him. 'It's my stepfather and mother and four half-brothers and sisters. My dad was killed at work when I was three.'

Doesn't get on with stepfather, McLeish noted mentally, listening to the colour in her voice.

'Where are you living now?'

'I've just bought a flat.'

McLeish asked whereabouts and discovered it was three roads away from his own flat, so they complained enjoyably to each other about the local council.

'You were a graduate entry, weren't you?' she asked as this conversation ran out, 'and in the Flying Squad?'

McLeish, warmed by the fact that she had taken the trouble to find out a bit about him, confirmed he had been at Reading University and had worked as a young sergeant in the Flying Squad.

'I always heard graduates weren't welcome there?'

'That's right. The guv'nor there, when he was offered me, wanted quite seriously to know what use I would be. It's changing now. But they took me in then because one of my mates in the London Scottish was in the Squad. They gave me a bad time — they'd all been in since they were seventeen and they were hard men. But I got by on brute force and ignorance till I learnt a bit.'

She gave him a quick amused glance, her head leaning back against the faded red of the alcove seat. 'The man who brought you in to the Squad must have been Alan Jones. He was my guv'nor in Tottenham and he said you were all right.'

McLeish beamed at her, more than pleased with this recommendation. 'How is old Alan?'

She settled down to tell him how old Alan was while he leant forward, listening with pleasure to the slightly nasal accent of Stoke on Trent. Her judgement of Alan Jones was both admiring and shrewd, and he asked about her own education, becoming aware that at least four other men were listening with great interest and that Catherine Crane was so used to this that she was unconscious of it.

'I came in with three A levels,' she said, matter of factly. 'I was at Queen Eleanor's and they urged me to go to university, but I wanted to be independent, so I came into the Met.'

McLeish nodded, his impression of family difficulty confirmed. 'What were your grades?'

'Three As. English, history and economics.'

'Better grades than mine,' McLeish said, impressed. 'Do the lads get at you, too?'

'Yes, a bit.' She laughed at him, the pretty mouth opening to reveal small, even teeth. 'But I don't have a posh set of in-laws like you do.'

McLeish, more sharply than he had meant, pointed out that he had a girlfriend but not a wife.

'This is a good pub,' she said, hastily, obviously aware of having trespassed, her gaze passing over the heavy plush seating and lighting on one of the barmen who was openly resting his eyes on her as he polished glasses.

'We use it a lot.' He followed her gaze, and the barman lifted his right hand in a drink-pouring gesture, nodding at the same time towards the clock which showed five minutes to eleven. McLeish indicated equally economically that no more drinks would be required. 'I've got my car in. Would you like a ride home?' he asked.

'If it's not out of your way,' she said, serenely, knowing that it wasn't, and McLeish got to his feet, savouring self-consciously the sensation of being whole-heartedly envied by the surrounding male drinkers.

He drove her sedately home. Getting out to open the passenger door for her, he noticed that, in contrast to Francesca, she expected this and accepted the courtesy gratefully.

'I'll wait while you let yourself in,' he said, in an attempt at sounding policeman-like, and she smiled at him.

'Thanks. And thanks for the ride.' She had her key ready and he looked down at her for a minute. She looked back, her eyes wide, and he found himself holding his breath. 'Good night, John,' she said, demurely, and walked up her front steps, turning to wave to him from inside the house.

CHAPTER 3

The boy and the dog skirted round opposite sides of the puddle, the boy, a light, tall fourteen-year-old, labouring in wellington boots too large for him, and the dog, a three-year-old Labrador bitch, picking her way reluctantly, with frequent pauses, as if her paws hurt. The boy, unlike the dog, knew that the mud did not go on for ever; beyond the bridge, the disused railway embankment along which they were walking became built up, so that water ran off it. He pulled the dog close to him to let a mixed string of horses and ponies go past, waving shyly to the lead rider, a pretty, capable girl an unbridgeable two years older than him. He watched her as she went past at a walk, the black Labrador and he both gazing wistfully, their breath steaming in the cold February morning.

He waited till the horses were well away and looked round the wide, flat landscape carefully before unclipping the lead.

'Way you go, Patty,' he said softly, and the dog was off, hurling herself along the embankment, all paws and flying ears, after a rabbit who had been sitting in a patch of sun but disappeared with contemptuous ease as she came close. The boy had been told unequivocally not to let her off the lead — the riding-school only used the land by grace of its owner and it was a shooting estate — but he hated keeping the dog straining at the lead and knew that she would always come to his call. He stood for a moment laughing at her as she cast furiously for the vanished rabbit, and walked on, to catch her up, along the raised embankment. The trees had grown up beside it in the twenty-five years since the railway had closed, and the boy stopped every now and then to watch small birds hopping around the top branches. He particularly liked this stretch; nothing but the odd tractor and the horses ever came down this embankment, and the birds were unworried by his presence.

After half a mile he decided to turn off the embankment and walk up the side of the next field and along the path at the top of it, following the horses whom he could still see in the distance. He called Patty to him. She didn't come, which was surprising; she was a docile creature and particularly devoted to him because he always took her for a walk when he was at the stables. He could hear her barking and looked down over the steep side of the embankment to the bottom of the trees. He called her again and again, but she would not stop barking at something he could not see. Probably a squirrel, he decided, and slithered down the side of the embankment to join her, scolding as he went.

Straightening up beside the dog, he looked where she was looking, and blinked. He saw a leg, uncomfortably wedged between sapling trees, swollen grotesquely, and gazed at it, stupidly, wondering if it was plastic. As his eyes focused he realized he was looking at a hideously swollen human body, and just then, as the light breeze shifted, he caught the stomach-turning odour of decay. He was a sensible and capable boy, an eldest child, so he moved closer, trying not to breathe, and stood steadfastly looking until he was confident of what he had seen: a body, must be a girl because it was wearing a skirt, lying face down, head towards the bottom of the embankment as if she had dived off the top.

He clipped the lead on to the dog with cold hands which would hardly function, and let her pull him up the slope as fast as he could make his legs move. He stopped on the embankment, shaking with cold and shock, to note the spot, then fled along the tractor paths, the dog running with him, to the stables where the ten o'clock children's ride was in its closing stages.

'Miss Williams!'

'Jamie, I'm teaching.' The thin, capable woman who was taking the riding-class looked at him in amazement as he leaned panting on the gate to the ring, the dog whining beside him.

'I'm sorry. Please, I've found something, I must tell you.'

She had known him since he was a very small five-year-old, perched like a mosquito on one of the placid beginners' ponies, so she told the class to carry on walking their ponies while she came to him.

'There's someone dead. Below the railway embankment.'

'Are you sure?'

The boy looked at her and uncontrollable tears suddenly filled his eyes. He was very nearly as tall as her, but she put an arm under his shoulders and supported him to the untidy room which served as the stable office, calling to one of the stable girls to take over the class.

'Patty found her. She's just lying there, but she is dead.' He scrubbed at his face with the handkerchief she offered and gulped for air.

'I'll ring the police.' She did so, casting an experienced eye over him. 'Sit down here, Jamie, and I'll make some tea. Mummy will come back in a few minutes, won't she, for Susie?'

'Not Mummy. Aunt Margaret is coming at ten.' The boy thought longingly of his mother, but managed to help Miss Williams describe the location of the body to a startled local station sergeant and to drink a cup of sweet milky tea without being sick. By the time his aunt arrived Jamie was so far recovered as to be able to refuse to go home and to point out, severely, that he would be needed, either to assist the police or to be lead rider in the eleven-thirty class, or possibly both.

He watched his aunt and Miss Williams wordlessly consult each other, but knew his aunt would do as she was told; successful solicitor though she was, she was ten years younger than Miss Williams and, as she complained, totally intimidated by her as she had not been by anyone since her late headmistress. He was unsurprised to find her packed off firmly to take his sister home, leaving him as a person of major importance in what he instantly assumed to be a real murder.

Miss Williams took him to meet the police Land Rover at the stable gate, a bone-thin, wiry woman in her late fifties, her expression sufficiently forbidding to prevent the parents, edging cars through the gate to collect children from the ten o'clock ride, from asking any questions. Jamie, through a renewed queasiness, just observed that the police driver was instantly reduced to half his age by Miss Williams's greeting.

'He was one of my boys,' she said in explanation to the CID sergeant who was leading the party as they bumped over the rough road, through the thick mud and on to the dry embankment. 'Like Jamie here.'

'Did you recognize the person you found, young man?' the sergeant asked, carefully.

'No.' Tears started into Jamie's eyes. 'She was all swollen.'

The sergeant's eyes widened, and he slid out of the Land Rover and stood back to let Jamie out.

'Very competent boy. Almost a professional singer, handles himself very well.' Miss Williams's natural pitch, well suited to reaching across a hunting-field, was discreetly reduced.

The CID sergeant thanked her gravely and went to stand beside Jamie who was peering down the embankment, looking pinched. 'We'll go down together, lad.'

'There isn't room. I'll lead.' He took a deep breath and headed down, the sergeant, two constables and Miss Williams in his wake. Soon they all stood side by side, one of the younger policemen coughing involuntarily.

'Oh dear, oh dear,' Miss Williams said on an indrawn breath. 'Sorry. Come along, Jamie, let's get you back.' She took out a handkerchief and mopped her eyes.

The police driver shot Jamie a look of enquiry which he missed, occupied as he was with guiding Miss Williams back up the hill. He had seen her weep before but only for a sick horse, and he was awestruck.

'Jamie, did you let Patty off the lead?'

The boy blushed to his ears and owned to it.

'You must not do it, Jamie, we'll be in trouble with Colonel James, I've told all you boys a thousand times.'

'He'll perhaps not do it again,' the sergeant murmured, and received the look that Miss Williams habitually bent on a child who was riding carelessly.

'How long had she been there?' Jamie asked, anxiously.

'A few days,' the sergeant said, grimly.

'How many?'

'Doctor'll tell us.' He considered the boy thoughtfully, and decided to take him back quickly. These teenagers were in his experience a lot less tough than they looked.

'Any idea who it could be?' he asked Miss Williams casually.

'No. But only a local would know to put a body there. If Jamie hadn't let the dog off the lead she could have been there much longer.'

The sergeant nodded, deciding it could do no harm to concede a point he had already taken. 'No one could tell who she was, surely?' Miss Williams said quietly to him, sounding shaky. 'She didn't even look *human*.'

The sergeant confirmed that that happened with bodies after a few days. 'We'll identify her, though,' he said, reassuringly. 'Somebody will likely have reported her missing.' He stopped, abruptly, as he remembered a conversation earlier that week, and lit a cigarette, thinking furiously. This could be the girl whom the Yard were looking for, and he had better do everything very quickly indeed, including finding his Chief, who would then want to find *his* Chief Constable and notify Scotland Yard. Presumably it would be the Yard who investigated this one, rather than the regional crime squad. He chewed his thumbnail as he walked, out of long experience keeping in mind the highest priorities: Ensure Body Not Moved and Ensure Next of Kin Notified before the Press got the story.

He posted the detective constable he had with him back down the path to join his colleague, armed with instructions to repel all attempts by anyone, however senior or armed with whatever authority, to go anywhere near the body unless he, Sergeant Black, personally accompanied them. Then he climbed into the Land Rover beside his two passengers and drove off fast, with the aim of abandoning Jamie to the custody of his aunt as quickly as possible. He could see with half an eye that the kid's aunt was going to be one of the confident, bossy, well-connected women with whom that part of Cambridgeshire was substantially over-provided.

* * *

John McLeish was in his office, Saturday or no Saturday, telling himself he needed to catch up on the paperwork. The phone rang and he picked it up, frowning. One of the pleasures of Saturday working was that the phone did not ring all the time. The voice at the other end was plainly over-excited and it took him a minute to disentangle what he was being told. 'Oh congratulations, Charlie. Sorry, what did you say it was again?'

'A little girl. Actually a very big girl as these things go, nine pounds. It's fantastic, John, there she is, a new person, lying on her face, sound asleep. I've just left them and I'm going back.'

McLeish repressed the malicious thought that this event might put Francesca's nose just a little bit out of joint. She had been utterly secure in her position as the only girl in the Wilson family and now there was another one.

'I've got another bit of good news. Frannie's going to be able to bring Tristram home pretty soon, apparently.'

McLeish expressed qualified enthusiasm and Charlie assured him he felt exactly the same about his younger brother.

'The difficulty is that Perry does everything that bit better than Tristram. Not that this is any excuse, John, I *do* know.' He paused, reminding McLeish irresistibly of a Labrador wondering how best to approach an acquaintance. 'I wanted to say, you see, that I know you thought Frannie shouldn't have gone, and that it's ruined your holiday plans, and, on behalf of us all, I'm sorry. I know the little boys lean on her too much and *I* would have gone if I could.' He coughed, embarrassed and a little pompous, very much conscious of his new status as a father, while McLeish remembered that he was a scant four years older than the delinquent Tristram. 'Anyway she should be back soon,' Charlie concluded.

McLeish thanked him gravely, feeling, as he often did with the Wilsons, that he was being enveloped in a large feather eiderdown, and, made restless by the call, went down the corridor to where he knew Catherine Crane was also in, getting her office in order. He stopped at the door and smiled at her. Wearing jeans and a blue shirt, she was tugging at a filing cabinet which was too large for her to embrace and which was threatening to over-balance on her. She looked about sixteen and beautiful. She let go of the cabinet, coughing in the dust of ages that appeared to be lurking behind it, and smiled back at him as the February sun shone through the small window behind her, throwing into sharp relief the patches on the wall where her predecessor had hung posters, and the ingrained dirt on the flaking paintwork round the mean, narrow, metal window.

'Where do you want that put?' McLeish advanced on the cabinet and shifted it authoritatively, ignoring the clip on the ankle dealt him by an unsecured bottom drawer apparently full of bricks.

'I should have unloaded it first,' Catherine Crane said, apologetically, 'but I just couldn't move in any direction with it where it was.'

'I'm here, just tell me if you want anything else shifted.' He hesitated. 'I'm going to do another hour, then have some lunch, if you want to come?' He was aware that he was not managing to sound exactly like a senior officer making a recent arrival feel at home, but decided not to add any further riders to his invitation.

'That would be very nice. Are we going to the canteen?'

'Not if I can help it. What about the pub?'

'If I'm allowed to buy my own.'

McLeish considered. 'That's fine on the food — I'll buy the drinks, I'm too old to get used to women buying my drinks.'

She laughed at him and said gravely that she would be happy to indulge him, and he went away, grinning.

* * *

Peter Yeo was also in his office, having told his wife he was lunching with a client. It was, he felt, just too difficult to be at home at all, with Claudia in a permanently bitchy mood and both his teenage children taking their cue from her and behaving intolerably. He wandered restlessly about, and decided that the lie might as well become the truth. Without Angela Morgan, at least two major clients were in danger of not getting the assiduous service they were paying for, and it would be well worth trying to see if one of them, whom he knew to be a fellow refugee from family life at the weekends, could be found. He was in luck, and fixed to meet Andy Barton at Brazzo's where Yeo Davis had a table permanently booked.

He had to admit that this particular client hardly added to the general decorative smartness of the place. Andy Barton, founder and chief executive of Barton Textiles, was almost as broad as he was long, virtually neckless, with incongruously long brown hair curling over his collar. His enormous hands dwarfed the elegant menu which he was studying in apparent disbelief, and Peter Yeo noticed again, as Barton without rising extended one massive paw, that though the fingers were an ordinary length it was the width of the palms that made the hands so large.

'I never see how they get the sales per square foot in these places,' Barton observed, without further greeting. 'I mean, they're not open twelve hours like my shops, and they aren't using the space.' His small bright blue eyes swept disparagingly over the minimalized black and white flooring, stainless steel chairs and black wooden bar.

'They make a huge margin on a smaller turnover, Andy, out of punters like us.' Peter Yeo was amused by, and respectful of, a man with an obsession.

'Angela not working today?'

Barton worked a sixteen-hour day, which began with careful, detailed consideration of the trading figures and key ratios for every one of his forty-three major shops and the output of both factories, and continued, usually by helicopter, with a detailed aerial survey of a particular area as the quick way of identifying new sites, interspersed with unheralded descents on the manager of any shop he took a fancy to visit.

Peter Yeo, who had known this particular juggernaut since he had his first small factory and two stores and dirt under his fingernails from shifting packing-cases personally, was not fazed by the question. 'Angela's taking a few days off — she hasn't been well,' he said, easily. 'I know she's been working very hard for you. I'm up to speed with Huerter, of course, but is your planning application in Leicester all right?'

Barton assured him warmly that Angela had done a great job and he was now confident of getting planning permission on the vast site he had wanted. Peter Yeo, who knew him in this over-candid, over-emphatic mood, decided to prod gently. 'Angela said the council wanted it for housing?'

'Yeah, some of them did. Silly buggers, it's jobs they want there first. Plenty of housing if those stupid farts at the council got round to repairing it and stopped their tenants tearing apart what they have got. My Mum brought up five of us in a flat far worse than what these immigrants complain about.'

Peter Yeo, who had personally persuaded Barton of the presentational disadvantage of using words like 'darkies', 'niggers' or 'wogs', decided that 'immigrants' even though used in the manner of one invoking a curse, was as good as he was going to get with this particular client.

'She's doing a good job on sorting this Huerter thing, too. Bloody ridiculous them blokes at the DTI pushing assistance for Huerter. I voted for this government because they said they weren't going to go in for that sort of rubbish. No one ever gave me anything and my business works. Still, Angie can fix the Treasury on this one, given her boyfriend, can't she? That's the reason I wanted you on this.'

Peter Yeo winced inwardly, but he was not going to tell Andy Barton that Angela was missing, or express any of his reservations about how much influence Angela could bring to bear. He smoothly changed the subject to the looks of the blond model, three tables away, and Barton agreed he wouldn't mind a bit of that; on the thin side, mind you, but tasty. The rest of lunch passed in similar diversion, interspersed with details of last week's turnover which were never far from Barton's mind, whatever other distractions offered.

* * *

Mrs Huntley was having lunch with her daughter. She ate placidly, acknowledging to herself with her customary good sense that, at the moment, as at any time since her brother William had died, she and Penelope were getting no pleasure at all from each other's company. Penelope was looking particularly discontented and disaffected, picking at her food. Her red suit was smart, but too bright a colour for her pale English pink and white skin, her brown hair could have done with a wash and her nails were ragged and bitten. She was frowning, deep lines appearing between her eyebrows, mouth drawn down at the edges so that instead of a classically good-looking slim English Rose in her late twenties, she looked faded, years older than her real age, and shrewish.

Mrs Huntley sighed; her brother whom she had loved, but knew to be self-indulgent to a fault, had done his niece real harm by leaving so much of his money away from the girl who had confidently believed herself to be his favourite thing on earth. Penelope, however, it had to be acknowledged, had made no attempt to rise above the blow she had been dealt by finding a dazzling girl of her own age favoured over herself in her uncle's will. At least, Mrs Huntley thought hopefully, she had stopped wondering, unbecomingly and stridently, how her uncle could have been fooled by Angela Morgan. It was Grizel Huntley's own view that her brother had not been fooled at all but had been charmed and diverted by a dashing girl thirty years his junior and had seen no reason at all why she should not have a share of his considerable estate when that left a very decent down-setting for his niece as well. Indeed, she had respected Angela Morgan for the straightforwardness with which she had tackled the issue when they had met at the lawyer's office. 'I'm sorry you're disappointed,' she had said to Penelope, 'but after all there's a lot of money, quite enough for both of us.' So there was, Grizel Huntley acknowledged, and it would be a great deal better if Penny could manage to think a bit more positively.

'If she has vanished, I'm going to see that solicitor about whether I can get her presumed dead.' Penny, sounding childishly, sullenly determined, broke into her mother's thoughts. Grizel Huntley looked across at her, shocked.

'I would wait a little if I were you.'

Penelope glared at her, turning an ungraceful scarlet, but Mrs Huntley held her ground. 'You are being silly about this, Penny. You are letting this disappointment — and that's all it is, you're still a very well-off young woman — get in the way of everything.'

Penelope choked on her pudding and started to cry, angry, uncontrollable tears. Grizel Huntley reached out to comfort her but she forced back her chair and fled, clutching her handbag and napkin, leaving her mother with the ruins of lunch.

* * *

Fifty miles north, Sarah Morgan had just finished serving a lunch that no one had done more than pick at. Her husband Francis had made a slightly better showing than her daughter

Jennifer, who was looking particularly ragged. Mother and daughter were very like each other, tall, dark, slim, pleasant-looking women with mid-brown curly hair and slightly snub noses. Francis Morgan, by contrast, was dark, almost black-haired, sallow-skinned, with bright brown eyes. Of medium height and packed with energy, even distressed as he was, he was bursting round the kitchen, hair still damp at the back from his swim.

'Let's go to the flicks. No point at all sitting round looking at each other. Come on Jennifer — or are you going out with Michael?'

'He's gone back to Australia, Dad. Last week.' Jennifer sounded defeated, and he looked at her sideways with familiar love and exasperation. She just didn't seem to be able to hang on to men, he thought impatiently, not like his Angie, wherever she was.

'Giles rang up,' his daughter volunteered, and he was uncomfortably reminded by something in her voice that Giles Hawick was one of the men Jennifer hadn't been able to hang on to — or not once he had seen Angela.

'How was he?' his wife Sarah asked, rather too quickly.

'Well, very worried. He said the police were talking to everyone Angie had seen in the two weeks before she . . . well . . . vanished, and so far had come up with nothing. I mean no one noticed anything unusual about her and she seemed to be full of plans for the wedding.'

'Well, I told them that,' Francis Morgan said irritably and his wife and daughter caught each other's eye in silent agreement that he hadn't told them that Angela was refusing point-black to be married from home and was insisting on the full London set-out, reception at the House of Commons, replying unanswerably when he had objected on grounds of expense that she could well afford to pay for it herself. A row of epic proportions had ensued, which he and Angela had evidently enjoyed but which had left Sarah and Jennifer sick with distress.

'I don't want to go out, Frank. Someone might ring.' Sarah Morgan was sounding diffident but resolute, and as

Morgan opened his mouth to protest in exasperation the doorbell rang. Both women looked at him in joint appeal and he marched to the door, pulling it open with unnecessary force.

He stood, door in hand, checked by something in the way his visitors, a man and a woman, were standing. The man, a stocky, greying fifty-year-old in a navy raincoat over a suit, his hair cut short, was attended by a uniformed policewoman, hair smartly set under the cap, her eyes watchful in the wide, flat, placid face, and both of them were standing square and stolid.

Francis Morgan stood and stared at them, and even before the man stepped forward steadily, hand extended, mouth opening to speak, he understood who they were and what they had come to tell him.

CHAPTER 4

'Catherine.' John McLeish, looking even bigger than usual, appeared in her office. 'The Cambridgeshire police think they have found Angela Morgan. They've got a body of about the right description and they've gone to see Miss Morgan's parents. We need to hurry but it'll take an hour or so and I don't want the papers on to it before the next of kin know. You got your kit?'

Catherine Crane wordlessly pointed to the back of the door of her office on which hung a neat suit. He looked round, and realized she had cleaned the whole office in the hour and a half since he had seen her. 'Looks a lot better. And only just in time. Meet you in ten minutes. I've got to change, then we're on our way. Sorry about lunch, we'll get a sandwich.'

* * *

'I'm sorry, Mr Morgan, but we can't move the body yet. There is a senior officer from Scotland Yard on his way, and our people, photographers and so on.'

'If it's my daughter I want to see her now, I don't want to wait.'

'I'm sorry, sir.'

Francis Morgan subsided abruptly on one of the uncomfortable chesterfields in the sunny, cramped, living-room and Detective Inspector Teversham shifted uncomfortably, wishing the phone call would come. The phone rang. He sprang to it and collected instructions in a room silent except for the sound of Mrs Morgan weeping drearily into her handkerchief. With one part of his mind he logged the fact that Mum had understood the worst immediately and must in some way have been expecting it. The deceased had been Daddy's girl, then — although it *was* usually the dads, where a daughter was in question, who fought against the realization of the truth. His WPC was looking at him anxiously for guidance, but he shook his head at her slightly and waited, standing squarely on both feet as he had done in many trying circumstances before.

'I'll come with you. Sarah and Jennifer, you stay here.'

Mrs Morgan made a movement of protest, but Francis Morgan looked to Teversham for support.

'I think that would be better, yes, sir,' he agreed.

'I must see her.' Sarah Morgan emerged from her handkerchief.

'Don't be silly Sarah, it might not be Angela,' Francis Morgan said, desperately.

'Sergeant Jennings here will make some tea, then she'll stay with you while Mr Morgan and I go over to the stables. We'll be back inside the hour. Perhaps we could have a cup now?' He watched, stolidly, as Mrs Morgan disappeared to the kitchen to show the sergeant what was what and considered, without watching her, the other Miss Morgan. She wasn't crying her eyes out. She was pale, but not as shocked as she might have been. Well, that was all right — she could look after Mum in the hour that was to follow while the identity of the body was established, and in all the grim hours after that, if the body was her sister.

He gently insisted that Francis Morgan got a cup of tea, with sugar, down him before he escorted him out to the waiting car. He sat in the back with him, for company, and chatted soothingly of nothing as the driver did the eight miles or so to Kirton and swept into the riding-school yard. Evidently a class had just finished and the place was boiling with ponies, small children, pink-faced with exertion in over-sized helmets covered with bright silks, parents urging them to hurry up and get in cars, and teenage girls bulging out of light jodhpurs organizing the whole.

A still point in this maelstrom was Sergeant Black, who had tucked himself between two of the sheltering twelve-foot evergreens planted to cut off the east wind from the ring. The man moved efficiently past a child who had succeeded in entangling her pony's reins with her feet and who was being blasted for it by a girl who couldn't have been more than sixteen but was sounding like a woman three times her age. Precisely who it was she was using for a role model became clear as a middle-aged lady, admirably slim in well-cut jodhpurs, erupted from some inner fortress to enquire, in tones that carried effortlessly across the yard, precisely why Caroline had failed to run up her stirrups, *how* long had she been riding? The tone was uncompromising but somehow neutral, and the child addressed, hastened to make the adjustment, rebuked but not embarrassed or crushed.

Teversham stopped where he was, saw Miss Williams notice him, and waited patiently while she dispatched four of the assorted teenagers to a distant meadow with eight ponies, and while the yard cleared of small children and their parents.

'Miss Williams? Detective Inspector Teversham. Mr Morgan is in my car over there.'

'I'll just have a word with him, Chief Inspector. I used to know him well.' She was white-faced but determined and the policemen stood back as she walked over towards the car.

'Decent of her,' Teversham observed, without moving his lips. 'Hang on a minute, who's this?'

A grey car, immaculately clean, was just pulling up at the gate and a big man in a plain grey suit was getting out to open it.

'Must be the Yard,' his sergeant observed.

'The bloke might be. But who is the popsy with him?' Teversham's terms for pretty women had been taken wholesale from his father who had been a young airman in World War II. The car drew up alongside them, McLeish having known them as policemen by the same process as they had recognized him.

'Chief Inspector John McLeish.' He flapped his warrant card in automatic greeting and waved a hand at Catherine who had also got out of the car. 'Detective Sergeant Crane.' He watched amused as both the Cambridge detectives shook hands gingerly, obviously taken aback.

'Father of the missing girl over there, talking to the good lady who runs this establishment and who has already seen the body. There's a man of mine on the spot. We think it's probably your girl — the ring on the finger fits the description and her parents are local.'

John McLeish considered this admirably succinct report and decided the competent bloke was bound to resent Scotland Yard intrusion.

'If this turns out to be the lady we're looking for, she was engaged to a Treasury Minister, who called in my guv'nor.'

'Oh, rather you than me, if that's who she is. And much better you have it from the start. My Super's already got his knickers in a twist.'

The reply was prompt and ungrudging and McLeish breathed easier. It was no fun at all working with an uncooperative and resentful local force.

'I've got a scene-of-crime squad coming, if that's all right. I've worked with them before, you see,' he added, in explanation and Teversham had just time to assure him he well understood and wouldn't himself like to work with anyone else's squad, before Miss Williams, tears in her eyes, and Francis Morgan, white with distress, bore down on them.

John McLeish introduced himself and Catherine in suitably subdued tones. Even through his distress, Francis Morgan was obviously struck by Catherine Crane's looks and as the party distributed itself into the big Land Rover he managed to sit next to her. McLeish, sitting on the other side of her, huddled on the uncomfortable bench-seating, could smell the faint perfume she wore and thought, with what detachment he could bring to bear, that one of the minor complications of this case was going to be the reactions of every man involved as suspect, colleague or witness, to this beauty he had managed to import on to his staff.

The Land Rover bumped along the track to where the young detective constable, looking chilled and tired, was waiting for them. As they decanted themselves McLeish managed to agree quickly with Teversham that, assuming the identification was confirmed, he would take Francis Morgan and Miss Williams back, leaving Catherine and himself at the site. He waited tactfully with Catherine and the young constable on the embankment, liking the sweep of the country as it spread out in the raw, cold day.

'Must be the only hill between here and Russia,' he observed to Catherine who pointed out it wasn't much of a hill, more a fifty-foot ridge, it just looked high in this dead flat plain. 'You must know Cambridge, though, John. Your girlfriend studied here, didn't she?'

'I didn't know her then,' he said, repressively, uneasily conscious that he had given Francesca no thought at all that day and didn't much want to think about her now. Catherine Crane fell silent, and he fished out the one-page note Teversham had handed him and read it, scowling. 'Good God,' he said, involuntarily, and Catherine looked at him enquiringly. 'I know the boy who found the body — I mean it must be him. He lives round here. Jamie Brett-Smith. He's a child star — a singer. Did the theme song for that TV thing.'

'It's a hymn tune. My Mum has it — I don't think she's ever bought a cassette before. How do you know him?'

McLeish hesitated, then said stiffly that he was Francesca's godson, and also something like her third cousin, or his mother was. He glanced down the slope and realized the party was returning. Francis Morgan white-faced and dazed, Miss Williams supporting his elbow, equally white and trying not to cry. Teversham, at Morgan's other side, nodded to McLeish in confirmation, pro forma. The small group struggled up the last piece of the embankment, Teversham necessarily in the rear and Francis Morgan stumbled almost on to McLeish's feet. McLeish reached out to steady him and the man looked up at him, unseeingly.

'Christ. Thirty years, and it's all gone. That's my Angie. It's her ring and I bought her that scarf.'

'I'm very sorry.'

Francis Morgan looked at him wildly as Teversham came up at his elbow, solid as a rock.

'It's your job now, is it?' he asked, earnestly. 'You'll catch the bastard who did it.'

'We'll try, sir.'

Francis Morgan looked from him to Catherine Crane, obviously hardly knowing what he was doing, in an agony of loss. 'How old are you, Sergeant?' he asked, abruptly.

'Twenty-seven, sir.'

'Almost the same age as her — Angie, I mean.' The bright brown eyes rested on her and you could see written all over his face the jealousy that this girl, daughter to some man, was still alive while his child was gone. Teversham and his sergeant closed round Morgan, shepherding him to the waiting Land Rover with meaningless gentle instructions to watch the step, up you go now.

McLeish glanced up the track to see, in the distance, another Land Rover swaying over the rough bits, and touched Teversham's elbow. 'That's my lot, I think.'

Teversham nodded in acknowledgement.

'Miss Williams, we'll find the road again if we go straight and turn left by the hedge, won't we?'

'Don't do that,' McLeish said urgently. 'Sorry, but if there was a vehicle involved it probably came from there. No tracks on this side, except ours.'

'Damn.' Teversham was unnerved by the nearness of the following Land Rover and irritated with himself for missing an elementary point. In the end it took ten minutes to get the Cambridgeshire police Land Rover turned past McLeish's squad and their vans, and away back up to the stable. Teversham had agreed to call the AC at the yard and report that the identification had been confirmed, so that he could go and see Giles Hawick. Francis Morgan would no doubt ring him too, but he was naturally so shaken that McLeish thought that small piece of insurance worthwhile. He watched them out of sight, then turned to his squad.

'Right, down we go. The corpse is at the bottom of the slope. Young woman, aged twenty-nine, dead about a week the local bloke reckons.' He glanced down the slope wishing he had brought boots; his shoes were already letting in mud. He looked at Catherine Crane's feet and saw she was in a similar situation. The sergeant from the scene-of-crime squad pushed past him, and advanced on Catherine Crane, holding out a pair of battered wellingtons with the air of the prince hopefully extending a glass slipper. 'They'll be too big, Sergeant, but maybe better than your shoes? We have some spare socks, too.'

McLeish watched her melting smile, as did every man in the group.

'Got anything there to fit me?' he asked pointedly, and a young constable reluctantly transferred his attention.

Kitted up some five minutes later with a pair a good size too small and with a hole in the right toe, McLeish led his troops into action. The smell hit them as they slithered to the bottom of the slope and McLeish resolutely took a breath before walking over to where the swollen body lay.

It was, as usual, not the person who lay dead but the shell in which the person had lived. The girl that was Angela Morgan had looked out of the photograph, whereas what lay on the ground, arms outstretched, could have been any young woman with dark hair. The well-defined features of the photograph had vanished, the face had swollen in death as had the exposed arms. Thank God it wasn't high summer, McLeish thought, stepping back almost on to Catherine's toes and reaching for his handkerchief; the cold, particularly at night, would have retarded decay. The girl had been missing for what — a week? — and off-hand he agreed with the local man's judgement that she had been here for most of it.

The sapling trees had grown tall in the twenty-five years since the Beeching axe had fallen on the single railway track, and, even leafless as they were, they effectively screened the view from the top. A thick hedge shielded her from the field which swept down towards the foot of the embankment. Whoever had brought her here must have known the place; you couldn't have picked it out in a hurry. The country is not as deserted as all that, as McLeish, brought up in a village in Leicestershire, well knew. There are always people about, in tractors, walking or riding; there is always an inquisitive dog. He stopped at this thought, wondering if dogs came along here frequently.

'Careful round the body,' he said unnecessarily to the sergeant in charge of the squad, who was matter-of-factly distributing heavy-duty surgical masks. He looked round for Catherine and found she had vanished.

'Back that way, sir,' one of the squad volunteered, barely intelligible through his mask, and McLeish saw her, twenty yards away, walking back slowly towards them, head bowed.

'All right?' he asked as she came up beside him and she replied that she was, thank you. She was very white, the freckles standing out brown on her skin, and she was blowing her nose.

'We'll go up and see if we can see how she got here. Carry on, Sergeant.' He plunged up the embankment, taking a grateful breath of fresh air, then turned and extended a large imperative hand to Catherine Crane and pulled her up beside him.

'Were you sick?'

'Yes, sorry.'

'Come on, let's get you up top.'

She stood on the embankment breathing in gulps of air as he stood awkwardly by her, then fumbled for a handkerchief and he saw that she was crying. 'Sorry,' she said, feeling him watching her and he fought back a violent physical impulse to give her a cuddle and take her away from all this. 'Happens,' he said gruffly, patting her gingerly on the shoulder, and striding down the track ahead of her. Behind them he saw a pair of horses, obviously having been warned off, turning to ride through a field, the colours of the riders' helmets very bright against the pale, cold, February sky. He tried to remember what the weather had been like in the last week and realized he had no idea; like many city-dwellers he had moved from flat to car to office without registering any variation.

'It's obviously rained a lot,' Catherine Crane volunteered, edging cautiously down the side of the track. 'That's a tractor, isn't it? I suppose they could have come that way.'

McLeish was walking the track, also keeping well to one edge, watching carefully. 'Still the same tractor. Hang on . . . here's car tracks. Faint, but there.' McLeish squatted unselfconsciously in the mud. 'No point me being clever.' He walked back along the side of the track and edged down to join the scene-of-crime squad. 'I want the whole track photographed and samples taken. Some car tracks, lots of tractor tracks, very deep.'

'Sticky stuff, this clay. Likely any car would have traces of it for a long time. Dyes clothes yellow, too,' the sergeant in charge volunteered. 'Is it murder, then, sir?'

'Well, have you noticed the head? It's out of shape. She's been missing for a week, was going to marry a rising Minister, successful career, everything coming up roses. Doesn't look like an accident. I'll get the doc to think on, when he arrives.'

'That's the Land Rover back now. I can hear it. Likely that'll be him.'

It was and McLeish greeted him with relief. This was a senior man whom he had worked with before, a fellow Scot, grey-haired now, slight, quick-moving and thorough. He went back down the embankment with him, telling Catherine to stay where she was and help with photographing the track. Dr Scott, from long experience, did no more than wrinkle his nose at the odour of decay, and spent twenty minutes there, mostly occupied with a careful consideration of the head.

'How long do you think she's been dead?'

'Rigor completely gone.' Scott gently lifted one bloodless arm, which fell limply. 'Subcutaneous swelling, decay. Six or seven days, I would say — I'll not be able to be more precise until the autopsy.'

'What was it, Doc?'

'Very nasty bang on the head for one thing. You noticed the skull is bulging — there, look. Done with something sharp-edged, and a lot of force.'

'That killed her?' John McLeish asked.

'Probably. I'll start as soon as you can get the body back. I'll ring you tomorrow or later tonight.'

McLeish thanked him, scrambled up the embankment, drawing in deep breaths, and walked carefully down the side of the track in the sizeable footsteps of his squad, explaining to them that they were looking for a sharp-edged weapon. He found Catherine Crane competently and tactfully assisting with operations, and as he came to stand beside her realized she was so cold that she was almost shuddering. He bustled her back to the Land Rover and raided the squad's provision box which he knew from experience would contain thick sandwiches and hot nourishing drinks. He pressed both on her.

'I'm sorry,' she said, when the shuddering had become only a shiver. 'I didn't realize I'd got so cold.'

'Well, you lost your breakfast and you never got lunch. We'll get a square meal, then we'll see the family. I don't want to spend too long — there's a lot else to do in London *and* I'd rather have the autopsy before I ask too many questions. Come on, we'll walk back to the car.'

Even in the twenty minutes it had taken to get some nourishment, the light had faded and the dull day was darkening into a cold night; the beginnings of a frost crackled under their feet as they walked briskly along the embankment. The long ridge to their left looked particularly bleak and lifeless, the heavy clay sitting solidly in the ridges where the plough had left it months before, no trace of last year's crop, nothing to indicate that this was good cereal country. The tops of the sapling trees, waist-high at the edge of the embankment, were leafless and still. A bad, cold night to lie out in. McLeish had to remind himself that the dead girl behind them would have felt none of this dank chill.

It was almost totally dark when they arrived in the stable yard and Catherine jumped involuntarily as something moved and rattled against the boards.

'The hunters will be in — only the rough ponies will be turned out,' McLeish observed out of childhood knowledge as he led her towards his car, looking very forlorn in the big parking area.

As he unlocked it, a light came on almost above his head. 'Who is it?' It was a clear, carrying command with no anxiety in it at all, and McLeish identified himself promptly.

'Ah. Will you come in for a cup of tea? I have James Brett-Smith, who found Angela this morning. He says he knows you and came back in case you wanted to see him.'

McLeish sighed inwardly. 'Of course, Miss Williams. Sergeant Crane and I would be glad of tea. Hello, sunshine.' This last was addressed to Jamie, who was peering round Miss Williams and was openly pleased to see him. Not every day you saw that poised, competent kid distressed, McLeish thought, resting a hand on his shoulder. It took a lot to faze a talented one like that, who had been a successful soloist for two years, managing with having a sick father and about one tenth of his mother's attention. He realized the boy had grown in the two months since he had last seen him and looked at him carefully, noticing the way his wrists poked out of the shirt and the slight roughness of the clear skin.

'Is Francesca still in New York?' the brat was asking anxiously, and McLeish, who had not wanted to discuss her in this company, found he had to reassure Jamie about her whereabouts and probable date of return.

'She's chaperoning for me on Monday next week,' the boy explained.

'I'd forgotten, but she won't have . . . Come and tell me about this morning.' He looked round for Catherine to discover that with admirable good sense she had asked for the facilities of the house, and was being issued with soap and hand-towels by Miss Williams. He took Jamie quickly through his story, finding him healthily excited by his part in it, but with an obvious undercurrent of anxiety.

'John,' Jamie asked when he had told his story, 'you won't leave her there, will you?'

'No, no, Jamie, that's the ambulance I can hear now, come to pick her up.'

The boy's colour came back and he looked shame-faced at McLeish. 'I know it's silly, I mean she's dead, but it's so cold and I couldn't bear the idea of her just lying there.'

Curious how the same thought had struck him, McLeish reflected, as he looked properly round the warm, untidy comfort of Miss Williams's sitting-room, which smelled cheerfully of woodsmoke and wet dog. A big black Labrador, catching his eye, thumped her tail and rolled on her side, looking up at him hopefully. She closed her eyes in ecstasy as Jamie flung himself on her, accusing her of being a flirt. McLeish looked past the boy to see Catherine Crane, colour returned, seated on an upright chair, drinking tea. He grinned at her.

'We'd best get on, Miss Williams, but could I use a cloakroom too? Is Jamie being collected, or does he want a ride home?'

'No, no, his aunt is coming for him. He's just polishing some tack for me.' So he was, McLeish observed, the devil plainly being given no opportunity to find work for idle hands.

He extracted Catherine a short while later and turned the car back on the darkened road which would lead them towards the A1. 'There were three dog leads and a packet of dog biscuits in the cloakroom,' he told her, grinning in the darkness.

'The hairbrush in Miss Williams's bathroom had Labrador hairs in it. Or it was the Labrador's hairbrush,'

Catherine Crane offered demurely, and McLeish burst out laughing, glancing admiringly sideways at her. He felt extremely comfortable with her already, he thought happily.

They followed Miss Williams's directions to the Morgan family, and knocked on the door, being let in promptly by the stocky WPC who had stayed in the house with the women of the Morgan family. Jennifer Morgan came into the hall; she had been crying and was looking white, but had herself in hand.

'Dad is lying down. He wanted to be called when you arrived. I don't know if you would like to talk to Mum and me first?'

'I'm sorry to trouble you now, but if you can bear it, it would help us to get some more information from you all. I had spoken to your father before on the telephone, when your sister was first reported missing, but we didn't cover all that much ground.'

'Oh, I'd rather talk about it now,' Jennifer Morgan said drearily. 'You've talked to Giles, of course?'

'When he reported your sister missing,' McLeish confirmed, leaping at the opening. 'I understand that you have known him longest of all the family?'

'Yes.'

'Do you know him well?'

She gave him a level look, understanding that he must be working, as they say, on information received. Quick, as her dead sister must have been.

'We did go out together a few times, yes, Chief Inspector. I liked him, but he and Angela are — were — better suited to each other.'

It must have been painful to have a man you liked appropriated by a younger sister, McLeish thought, but this self-contained creature was not going to tell him — or possibly anyone else — how it had felt. He considered her, as he went through the routine questions about when she had last seen her sister.

'We didn't meet very often in London unless it was at a party. I work in the British Museum, and my flat is quite close to it. I'm an Assistant Curator in the Middle Eastern section.'

McLeish blinked involuntarily, and she smiled faintly.

'I read Middle Eastern Languages, and spent a year in Turkey after Oxford, then came back to the Museum. I specialize in fourteenth-century ceramics.'

It was a less lively face than her sister's because it was more turned in, more contemplative, less concerned with the things of this world. Well, fourteenth-century Turkey must be pretty safely removed from the things of this world. He considered her good but unremarkable clothes, and wondered what she did for laughs. Or was fourteenth-century Turkey laughs enough, what did he know? He fell back on routine and asked Jennifer to confirm exactly when she had last seen Angela.

'I last saw her here, the weekend before she disappeared. She came up here for a night to see Mummy, to sort out some details about the wedding.'

'That must be a lot of work for your mother,' McLeish said, hopefully, and got another level, distantly amused look.

'You would have to ask *her* that. My impression was that since it was to be held in London, Angela was doing the work, with a good deal of help from colleagues at Yeo Davis. They have a lot of experience of large parties.'

Ouch, McLeish thought, not such a gentle, distant academic, are you? A very sardonic eye there indeed. 'We talked to Mr Yeo when your sister was reported missing. He obviously considered your sister a very valuable colleague.'

'She is — was — extremely competent, as well as very good at getting on with people, which is of course critical to jobs like that. I imagine she will be very much missed.' She looked sharply out of the window and produced a handkerchief which she held clenched in her hand but did not use.

'Miss Morgan, would you like to stop for a minute? Can we get you some more coffee?'

McLeish glanced at Catherine who was already on her feet, and Jennifer Morgan nodded in acquiescence. 'I'm sorry. I'll just go and tidy up.' She got up stiffly and went upstairs, holding blindly on to the banisters. McLeish joined Catherine in the comfortable modern kitchen where they foraged companionably for coffee and milk, waiting until they heard Jennifer Morgan come down again.

'I'm sorry,' she said, wearily. 'Where were we? My mother is coming in a minute.'

'We were asking about your sister's position at Yeo Davis. I think you had made it clear that Mr Yeo very much valued her. Would she have wanted to continue working there after she was married?'

Jennifer Morgan looked at him quickly and he realized he must have stumbled on something. But she knew her hesitation had given him a lead.

'She would have wanted to continue, yes. There might have been some difficulty there because of Giles's position, because of the conflict of interest. Yeo Davis exists to lobby government and Giles is a Minister.'

She sounded like Francesca when she talked about Yeo Davis, McLeish reflected.

'Did he want her to give it up?'

'Yes, he did. He found it awkward, but Angela was — naturally — reluctant.' Some colour had come back into Jennifer's face.

So he talked to you about it, McLeish thought, and saw Catherine register the same point. He decided to leave this one for the moment but logged the fact that Jennifer Morgan had still been interested in, and comfortable with, the man who had become her sister's fiancé.

A tap on the door made them all start. Catherine Crane went across to open it and held a murmured conversation with someone.

Sarah Morgan came into the room like a ghost, and McLeish drew breath as he saw her. She was deathly pale, the mid-brown hair flattened to her head, the lined skin without make-up except for a brave but mistaken line of smudged lipstick. She looked at him dumbly, and even McLeish's hardened investigator's nerve failed him. He glanced involuntarily at Jennifer Morgan who said she would make tea, which was what her mother preferred, and bore her off to the kitchen.

They returned with the tea accompanied by a bottle of pills — Valium, McLeish noticed automatically — and with Mrs Morgan looking more gathered. The buttons of her cardigan were correctly done up and the collar flattened neatly, the zip of the skirt was in its proper place at the side and her tattered bedroom slippers had been replaced with a tidy pair of court shoes, the wrong colour for the skirt. It was better, but not a lot, and McLeish who knew her to be in her late fifties decided any casual observer would put her at nearer seventy. Jennifer Morgan looked at him doubtfully, but he shook his head to her implied question; he preferred to conduct his interviews without members of the family present.

'Won't be long,' he said, reassuringly, just managing not to pat Jennifer Morgan on her beige cashmere shoulder.

He was extremely gentle with Sarah Morgan, as he had implicitly promised her daughter, but it was a desperately painful experience, and, he began to fear, not a useful one. She had not seen Angela since the weekend before the one on which she had disappeared, but had spoken to her twice on the telephone. Well yes, Angie had been very busy and preoccupied with the wedding preparations, naturally, but she had been happy. And no, they had not been expecting to see her that weekend, though with Giles away she had said she might come on the Sunday. But she would have telephoned first.

She seemed to be eased by talking of her daughter, and by the time she stopped, apologetically, and drank some tea poured for her by Catherine, she looked exhausted but less like a wraith. She pushed the Valium aside, observing that she did prefer *not* to take drugs, a reaction so typical of her age and class that McLeish decided he might after all be able to conduct a useful interview.

'I understand it was your older daughter who met Mr Hawick first?'

'Yes, she did, and I think she hoped something would come of it — well, so did I. But when he met Angela he was just bowled over by her. I was sorry for Jennifer but they had only been going out for a month or so, and not terribly seriously. And in any case, you can't do anything about these attractions, can you?'

McLeish agreed with her promptly and she raised half a smile for him. He waited, remembering Jennifer Morgan's obvious pain and wondering what her mother's views about it were. He watched her thoughtfully as she ate a biscuit.

'Angela must have been a very attractive girl,' he suggested, cautiously.

'Oh, she was,' Sarah Morgan agreed. 'But I used to wonder whether she was ever going to get married. She never seemed to fall for anyone her own age, they were always older.' She was talking with the ease of total emotional exhaustion.

'Was there anyone else who was important to her — I mean before she met Mr Hawick, of course?' he asked, vaguely.

Mrs Morgan took another biscuit and accepted another cup of tea.

'I did think that there was something between her and Peter Yeo — her partner — but nothing came of it. He has a wife and children and most men don't usually leave their wives, do they?' The question was rhetorical and McLeish waited. 'Anyway, Giles was perfect for her; fourteen years older and with his own very distinguished career. I was sure she was going to be happily settled.' She stopped, staring out of the window, her hands clenched together. 'And then this terrible thing happens. Who could have wanted to kill her?'

Francis Morgan did not bother with knocking at the door but walked in without apology. He was deathly pale and obviously still in the first shock of grief but it had taken him differently. He was wound up like a spring, furiously angry, unable to keep still or to prevent himself from fidgeting.

'Where's Sarah?' he demanded, and took in the scene in front of him. 'Why didn't you wake me?'

'I understand the doctor wanted you to have a sleep if you could, Mr Morgan,' Catherine Crane said briskly. 'Would you like some tea? We have only just started talking with Mrs Morgan.' She looked very young and pretty as she held up the teapot and Francis Morgan hesitated, then sat down, heavily, and seized two biscuits. 'Sorry,' he said, awkwardly, through a mouthful of Rich Tea. 'I can't stop thinking about her and wondering what happened.' He slapped both hands palms down on the table, slopping his tea and making them all jump, totally unselfconscious in his misery.

What, McLeish wondered acerbically, did he imagine his wife and surviving daughter were thinking about — or did he assume they had taken the death of a daughter and a sister in their stride? From under his eyelashes he could see Mrs Morgan was watching her husband with a sort of furious compassion, and was careful not to catch her eye.

The man was quite literally distracted, unable to concentrate at all. McLeish looked thoughtfully at Jennifer Morgan who had come in and was considering her father with what he was startled to recognize as dislike. This was evidently a family that was not going to be brought closer by grief. She nodded to McLeish and started gently to bustle her mother away. He settled Francis Morgan down as best he could and took him again through the events of the week before his daughter vanished. No, he hadn't seen her for a week before that weekend; he had missed her — this with a baleful glance towards the door — and had indeed got as far as ringing her up on the Saturday morning, hoping she would come up for Sunday, but had got no answer from her flat. 'It wasn't worth going down on the off-chance, or so I thought. But perhaps if I had . . .'

'You were close to your daughter, then?' McLeish asked hopefully.

'Yes. We were like each other; she knew what she wanted and she didn't mess around. I can't bear people who don't know what they want and dither.'

'So you were pleased that she was marrying?'

'Not particularly.'

McLeish did not manage to conceal surprise and Francis Morgan looked at him wretchedly, the restless brown eyes wide set, like the dead girl's, and very bright.

'He's all right, I suppose, Giles — for a politician. But he thinks he's the centre of the world and he was going to make it difficult for Angie to do what she wanted if it would affect his career. He likes all that, the cars and people calling him Minister, but he wanted her to be the good politician's wife, doing his entertaining. He didn't say so, mind, but I told Angie she would have to watch it after she married him. And he wanted her money, of course. These chaps don't have security of tenure.'

McLeish reflected that Giles Hawick was the classic example of someone who knew what they wanted and didn't mess around, and that that was what had attracted Francis Morgan's daughter. Perhaps he had not said to himself that in a marriage between two like this, someone was going to have to know a little less clearly what they had wanted.

'Was there someone else around you would rather she had married?' he asked bluntly, deciding it was that sort of conversation.

'No one in particular, but I thought she'd have been better off with a chap of her own age who would have wanted her to carry on where she was. Someone who would have known she was exceptional and have encouraged her.'

And been less of a direct rival to her dad, and all, McLeish thought, and stuck to his line. 'And there was no one like that in her life?'

Francis Morgan, calmer now, visibly bent his mind to the question. 'She had dozens of boyfriends,' he said, wistfully. 'I probably met them all. But they didn't seem to last very long. She didn't want to settle down, you see, and they all wanted her to.'

McLeish decided he was not going to get much more out of this and went on to check, gently, what Francis Morgan had done with the weekend. He appeared to have spent it blamelessly playing golf, dining with neighbours and at home doing some work. He would check it, if he needed to, but he could not at the moment see why Morgan would have wanted to kill the daughter to whom he had plainly been so devoted.

He managed to have another few words with Mrs Morgan also, who was looking much stronger. She apologized obliquely for her husband, and McLeish murmured that Mr Morgan had obviously been very much attached to Angela.

'So was I, Chief Inspector,' Sarah Morgan said evenly. 'And I was glad she was marrying an older man like Giles Hawick.' The emphasis on the 'I' was faint but definite and McLeish carried the echo away in his head.

CHAPTER 5

'I don't mean to sound ungrateful, but I'm starving,' Catherine said, as they reached the gate.

'Can you wait till London? There's a good place in Ealing — well it's a chippy really, but he has good steaks at any time you want them. Have a sleep if you want.'

She slept deeply while they were on the motorway, but woke as he came into London and had to stop and start in the heavy evening traffic. 'Better,' she said, smiling at him.

'Dinner's not far.'

Restored by a large steak, he explained to her as they ate that he liked to work very quickly on a murder case, pushing everyone to get an answer.

'I expect that means you do more cases than most?'

'I've been a bit lucky,' he said, modestly. 'I've ended up most of them with a full confession, once we'd worked it out. That way you know you've got it right.'

'Unless you're in Henley,' she observed with privileged acerbity and he laughed, embarrassed as every policeman had been by the revelations just made of Thames Valley's *modus operandi*.

'Eight cases withdrawn so far, isn't it?' Catherine asked.

'And more to come.' He smiled at her, thinking what a treat it was to talk shop with someone as beautiful and intelligent as this. She insisted quietly on halving the bill and he let her have her way, not wanting to jeopardize his chance of eating with her in the future. He glanced up as they completed this transaction to find the attention of the nearest two tables, both exclusively male, fixed disbelievingly on them. As three men slowly looked away McLeish received the uncompromising message that if any of them had been so lucky as to have dinner with Catherine Crane, none of them would have let her pay for herself. Indeed, he had a strong feeling that only his six foot four inches prevented one of them from saying so. He glanced at Catherine but she had obviously noticed nothing out of the way.

Outside the restaurant McLeish hesitated, not wanting the evening to end.

'A drink?' he suggested, hopefully, but Catherine shook her head.

'My flat is in almost as much of a mess as the office. I was in a chain, and I only managed to complete last week. I'd better go and get it straight. I haven't even got the curtains hung, or unpacked the kitchen stuff.'

'Let me come and help?' McLeish offered, cheerfully. 'It is the fault of C1 that you don't have today or tomorrow to get straight. I'll come and put in a couple of hours, so you can get a bit more comfortable.'

She hesitated, then said that she would like that rather than a drink, if he really wouldn't mind.

The flat was indeed in some disarray: immaculately clean, evidently she had done that first, but with most of its furnishings disposed in boxes on the floor. McLeish, naturally efficient and brought up by a mother with firm views on men's participation in the drearier household chores, took just over an hour to sort her kitchen to her satisfaction while she got the living-room straight, with all the books unpacked.

'That's marvellous. Thank you very much. Can I give you a coffee?'

'I'd like that. Then I'll be off so you can catch up with yourself.'

They fell comfortably into gossip about various parts of their experience until McLeish noticed she was looking tired. 'I'm off,' he said, briskly. 'I'll be going into the Yard first thing to work out what's to do. I'll not need anyone till about lunchtime so you have your sleep in, but I may ring you up after that. I find if you get the case started off quickly it all goes easily.'

She thanked him demurely, and he realized she was laughing at him. He looked down at her, about to kiss her goodnight as if she were one of Francesca's friends, and pulled himself up. This was a colleague, a fellow detective. As well take to kissing Bruce Davidson good night, he told himself, and got himself out of the door on this thought.

* * *

The telephone was ringing as McLeish walked into his own flat, and he picked it up to find his Commander on the other end of the line.

'So I've arranged you'll take a statement from Hawick tomorrow afternoon, then.'

'We haven't got the autopsy, sir, so I've no idea when the girl died, yet. I'll have to see him again when I do know. Wouldn't he rather wait twenty-four hours?'

'He's a busy man. Also, he wants to talk to someone, he wants to make sure we're doing our job. Don't give me a hard time, McLeish, just bloody do it.'

'Sir.'

'Don't be like that. Take that gorgeous sergeant of yours, give Hawick something to look at.'

'She's been with me in Cambridge all day — I told her she could have Sunday off.'

'Then tell her different. She with you?'

'No, sir. I left her at her flat.'

'Your girl's due back when?'

McLeish raised his eyebrows, taken aback by the transparency of his superior's line of thought, and primly gave him Francesca's projected timetable.

'Glad to hear it. Good luck with the Minister, and give me a ring afterwards. I like to know where the bullets are coming from. G'night.'

McLeish, shaking his head, rang Catherine and broke it to her apologetically that she would be required for the afternoon.

'Doesn't matter. We — you — would have had to see him soon anyway. Is the autopsy going to give us much idea when Angela Morgan died — I mean within a day or so?'

'Probably not,' McLeish conceded.

He went to bed to dream uneasily, and woke early as he always did in the early stages of a case before he had got the machine working properly.

At tea-time the next day he picked up Catherine at her flat, noticing that she was looking rested and pretty even if he was feeling jaded and disaffected.

They were received in the Minister's private flat in one of the narrow streets close to the House of Commons. McLeish remembered that this man's constituency was in Derbyshire. They took a tiny, cramped lift to the top floor of the building and were admitted by Hawick, who was wearing an expensive blue-green sweater, and slacks, the clothes sitting easily on his long, slim frame, the dark hair beautifully cut, a little too long, flopping on his forehead. Despite the elegance, it was a completely masculine presence, and he dominated the room as easily as he had his own office. He was grim-faced and looked as if he had not slept, but he offered them freshly made coffee and raised a smile for Catherine.

He saw her comfortably established at a table — 'I know you'll want to take notes' — and offered McLeish his choice of three big armchairs. 'I'm not sure some of the upright ones will hold you, Chief Inspector, I sit on them very gingerly myself.' Hawick chose a big chair by the fireplace in which a simulated coal fire burned merrily, emitting real warmth thanks to the gas which powered it. 'I'd prefer a proper fire, of course, but we made them illegal in this part of London some years ago.'

'We', McLeish remembered from Francesca, did not necessarily mean this administration but must mean one of the same political persuasion. Measures passed by those of a different political hue were described as the work of a 'previous government.' A good room to be in, McLeish thought, with its high ceiling and the Sunday quiet of London, and what was obviously a copy of every Sunday paper published lying tidily on a side table.

'It comes with the job,' Giles Hawick explained, following his eye. 'We read them all. There is nothing yet about Angela in any of them.'

'No, sir. We did not have a definite identification until late yesterday afternoon, in any case.'

'Poor Francis. He rang me last night, very kindly, principally I think to assure me that there could be no doubt. That it was Angela, I mean.'

'I'm very sorry.'

'Were you there too? Did you see Francis — Mr Morgan?'

'Yes, we were, although it was a Cambridge officer who broke the news because I didn't want any delay in case the Press got it. We were actually with him when he made the identification, though.'

'I've been to that riding-stable — Angela's sister Jennifer and I went hacking one day when I stayed the weekend there. It's an excellent stable — they produced a very good hunter for me once Jennifer had assured them I was safe. I can't remember it all, but I think we rode along the old railway line.' He bit his lip and looked into the remorseless, even flames. 'I was just following Jennifer's lead.'

'You only went once?'

'Twice. Angela didn't ride, though she had done as a child. I told you, I think, that I had met Jennifer first, some time ago.'

'Indeed.' Well, it was interesting, McLeish thought gravely, making an unnecessary note, that Giles Hawick had admitted unprompted to the local knowledge necessary for disposing of Angela Morgan's body in that particular place. But it had been the older sister he had gone there with, and had apparently abandoned in favour of the younger, more exciting girl.

He decided he wasn't going to get anywhere along those lines, or not yet, and went over again the details of when Hawick had last seen his fiancée. He found his account, as he would have expected, consistent, and considered the man carefully as he did so. For all his ambition, Hawick was obviously a man of strong passions and, for McLeish's money, well capable of murder. There was, however, no apparent motive, McLeish reminded himself, and he must not let his own uneasy conviction that Angela Morgan would have been more than capable of stirring up strong and complex emotions in those around her cloud his judgement. Time to ask the obvious question. 'We're at a very early stage in all this, Minister, but can you think of anyone who would have wanted to harm Miss Morgan?'

'Yes.'

McLeish blinked at him, startled.

'Yes, I can think of one or two people who might have wanted to harm her, as you suggest. None who might have carried that wish to the length of killing her. I take it her death cannot have been accidental?'

'Probably not,' McLeish agreed, thinking of the misshapen skull. 'Who had reason to wish her ill, then?'

'She was left a large legacy by an ex-employer. His niece, who is a little unbalanced, took this very badly, despite the fact she herself was a substantial legatee. She certainly made threats against Angela and has bothered her recently. This is a woman called Penelope Huntley. I've never spoken to her myself but I know Angela had found it necessary to get her solicitor to write.'

McLeish made a note. 'We haven't been able yet to speak to Miss Morgan's solicitor,' he observed. 'Do you know if she left a will?'

'Indeed she did. We both made new wills last week, in expectation of marriage. We each left the bulk of our estates to the other, with a couple of minor legacies — my old college and a couple of godchildren on my side, and her sister on hers.'

'Do you know what Miss Morgan's previous will provided?'

'No, I don't. But that will, of course, is the only one that's valid. We never married.' The wide mouth twisted. 'So the wills we made last week are irrelevant.'

He looked suddenly tired and old, the deep lines in his face intensified.

'There were probably professional jealousies in Angela's life, too,' he said, wearily, rubbing the patch between his eyebrows in a gesture McLeish recognized from his television appearances.

'You mean she could have run into trouble as a result of her professional activities?' he asked, cautiously.

'I hope not. I must say I was not totally happy about her going on at Yeo Davis, with me in the government. But she was very reluctant to give it up and there is a precedent. One of my Ministerial colleagues is married to a partner in a firm specializing in financial public relations where there are similar possibilities for conflict of interest.'

But maybe your Ministerial colleague isn't going right for the very top, McLeish thought with unreasonable conviction, and you were going to stop her working at Yeo Davis when you could. He glanced up and found the cool blue eyes on him.

'That being said, anyone will tell you that a Minister of the Crown needs a wife capable of supporting him. It's one of those jobs where the pay doesn't actually cover the cost of the lifestyle, and you can be out on your ear between one day and the next. But I think we would have tried to find her a job rather more removed from mine, over time.'

A very fair admission, McLeish thought admiringly, and made his standard speech about the need, if he might, to come back on various points as they occurred to him.

'Of course you must. Just so long as you are not intending to ask me not to leave London. I'm in Newcastle tomorrow and the day after, and next week I have several days in Washington. I have told you where I was already.' He hesitated. 'I'm assuming she was killed on the Saturday, of course, when she first went missing, as we now know. I hope so. I mean it would be worse if she had been — hurt — first.'

McLeish instantly understood the man's nightmare but realized he could give only qualified reassurance. 'She was probably killed by a blow on the head, Minister. We have not had the autopsy result.'

'Can you let me know?'

'Certainly.'

He and Catherine took their leave and crammed themselves again into the rickety lift.

It was another windy, sunny day, the brilliant February sun which has no strength in it but still gives the reassurance that summer will come and a sun will shine with real warmth again. Discarded papers blew in the narrow street as they walked back to the car.

'John, excuse me. Are we allowed to tell people involved in the case what the autopsy result is?'

'If that one's a murderer he knows what happened. If he isn't, it doesn't matter what he knows and he can go over my head any day he likes and make the Assistant Commissioner read him the whole report if he wants to. No point me being difficult.' He got a respectful sideways look, which he appreciated, and smiled down at her. 'Did you think he was a murderer, Catherine?'

'Well capable of it, if crossed,' she said, promptly. 'But I can't see the motive.'

'What about if Angela Morgan was involved with another bloke and he found out?'

'Yes, then. But not if he had time to think what it would do to his career.' McLeish grinned. 'He's too ambitious. He's one of these blokes where he comes number 1, 2 and 3, and anyone else comes nowhere.' There was real feeling in this judgement, McLeish decided, and tried to imagine what kind of man had decided to relegate Catherine Crane to fourth place in his scheme of things.

* * *

In a windy, cold field in Cambridgeshire, green with winter wheat, half a mile away from where Angela Morgan's body had been found, a small man with a narrow, turned-down mouth sat smoking his twentieth cigarette of the day at the wheel of a Land Rover. He arrived at a decision, threw the cigarette away, and turned towards a small depressing row of agricultural cottages. He emerged two minutes later with a bulky small man, and the Land Rover turned on to the Cambridge road, making for the headquarters of the regional crime squad. An hour later the phone rang in New Scotland Yard where John McLeish was sitting reading the scene-of-crime report.

'A what? Yes, sorry, of course I've heard of ploughs. My mind wasn't with you. Standing there, was it? Yes, I've got the scene-of-crime report, hang on — yes, deep tracks, evidently belonging to a tractor, plus other deep tracks, query agricultural machinery. Well, you can't blame them, Sergeant, they're like me, not used to the country, real townees. It was a plough, was it?'

He listened as the Cambridgeshire sergeant explained that the keeper on the shooting estate had realized he had seen the old plough there last week and had fetched the farmer in to explain where it had gone.

'He says he never saw a body when he moved it. He was very unhappy at having to come out at all, but I think he's just pig-ignorant rather than involved. Do you want me to send someone to look at the plough?'

'Have you seen it?'

'No. I'll go if I must, but we haven't got any forensic people here, it being Sunday. I can get them out, of course.'

'No, I'll send a couple of my blokes, as soon as I can. Could you do us a real favour? Make sure the vehicle is under cover so if there is anything on it, prints, whatever, that haven't already gone, we get them. I mean, don't let the farmer clean it, or anything dead stupid.'

The sergeant at the other end said grimly that the bloke was quite thick enough to do just that, so due precautions would be taken. 'I'll go myself in fact. No, it's no bother, it's on my way home. Give your blokes this number so they can arrange a visit, but I'll have a quick look while I'm there.'

CHAPTER 6

John McLeish was feeling justifiably pleased with himself as he walked into his office at eight o'clock on Monday morning. He had devoted Sunday evening to making a plan of action and knew exactly what he and everyone else he could press into service was going to be doing this morning. His schedule for the day was organized, thanks to some brisk telephoning the night before, and he would have Catherine Crane at his side all day, and all the days until this case finished.

He arrived at his desk, squinted at the offering tucked into his blotter and sat down to read it properly: a short, sanctimonious newspaper piece on the temptation and pressures on the successful young, Tristram Wilson being mentioned, with many a crocodile tear, as one of the recent casualties. It was presumably Bruce Davidson, who admired and was annoyed by Francesca in about equal measure, and therefore took an unremitting interest in all her activities, who had favoured him with this. McLeish threw it away and methodically sorted his notes; he was not going near a top firm of solicitors without a very careful list of questions, and his first port of call that morning was to be Huttons, who had been Angela Morgan's solicitors.

He and Catherine were ushered into the presence of Mr Timothy Hutton, who was housed in outwardly featureless modern offices in one of the little streets off Ludgate Hill. The view from the window featured a building site and a large collection of assorted earth-moving machinery and cranes, all displayed simultaneously. Even through double glazing there was a dull, continuous background noise, and the huge modern windows were dusty in the February sun. The furniture and fittings were ruthlessly modern, several steps beyond the conventional Scandinavian. Mr Hutton's desk was a shaped piece of black wood with a single file on it, and the heavily bound books that covered one wall appeared to be held there by the power of faith, no shelves being visible.

The owner was also uncompromisingly twentieth-century, a man of much the same height and age as McLeish but built like a string bean, with brown, short-cut hair and fashionable heavy horn-rimmed spectacles. He greeted them briskly and folded himself into a chair. McLeish noted enviously that Mr Hutton was a vision of elegance in one of this year's broadly striped blue and white shirts: he had tried one on himself recently, and had been forced reluctantly to the conclusion that he looked like a bouncer for an East End club.

'Dreadful thing about Miss Morgan,' Timothy Hutton said earnestly. 'We were all very shocked — I told my partners at prayers this morning. Sorry, that's what we call the Monday morning meeting where we discuss what's going on. How can I help you?'

'You can tell us, please, what Miss Morgan's property was and how her will distributes it. I understand that you are her executor.'

'I am, yes. With her father. I've just looked it up. I didn't, of course, expect to have to — not quite so soon.' He opened the file and considered it, unhurriedly and unselfconsciously, and McLeish had a sudden vision of an older Mr Hutton in a tailcoat and wing collar behind this modern facade. 'We have two wills on file,' Timothy Hutton said, reaching the end of whatever internal debate he had been having, 'but the second, which was made in anticipation of her marriage to Mr Hawick, cannot of course be submitted for Probate since that marriage did not take place. So it's the first will she made — what? — eighteen months ago, which is valid.'

McLeish said promptly that he would need to know the contents of both wills as well as details of Miss Morgan's estate, and Timothy Hutton considered him carefully.

'Yes, I see you do,' he agreed, 'and I'm not here to make difficulties. Look, I need to explain a bit of background. Angela was very comfortably off. Just over two years ago she benefited very considerably from the will of a chap called William Coombes, who was senior partner in one of the second-rank stockbrokers. They do all right, those chaps, even after taxes. She got about two hundred thousand and a life interest in another two hundred thou. The family wanted to dispute the will, and that's when Angela — Miss Morgan — came to us for advice. Well, Coombes was only sixty-two when he died — it was a heart attack, there was nothing wrong with his brains. The family didn't have a leg to stand on and so I advised. They caved in; I mean it was only a sister and a niece, and they'd both been provided for during his lifetime *and* the niece got a couple of hundred thou in his will. But the niece was very bitter about it — I had to write a letter to her solicitors a year or so later because she'd been bothering Angela long after the estate was settled.'

McLeish thought his way through this one, drawing a diagram on the edge of his notes. 'Miss Morgan got some of it just for life? Who gets it now, then?'

'The niece, the one I've been telling you about. Penelope Huntley. I can give you the address of her solicitors — Kenwards, two-partner firm in Kensington. I'll look for it. Go on asking me things.'

'How old is Miss Huntley?'

'Same age as Angela. I agree, she would not normally have expected the remainder to fall in and be useful to her, but of course if she had had children, it would have been valuable to them.'

'But if you were Penelope Huntley you might not have been consoled by the thought that your children would inherit after Miss Morgan's death.'

'No, I wouldn't. Nor was she.'

'Sorry?'

'That's what she kept writing to Angela about. Her lawyer had advised her that she could, by agreement with Angela, break the trust. They're both — were both — well over twenty-one, and they could have made a deal which essentially bought out Angela's life interest for a capital sum and then Miss Huntley would have got the rest.'

McLeish thought that it seemed a reasonably sensible plan.

'Is that very difficult to do?' he asked, cautiously.

'No. It's a routine valuation exercise based on actuarial tables. I don't think it would have done Miss Huntley a lot of good financially though, given that Angela was only twenty-nine and actuarially good for another forty years.'

McLeish considered him with pleasure. His last interview with a solicitor had been conducted in a language barely recognizable as English and it had taken over three hours and a reference to the Chief Constable to elicit the fact that the deceased had made a previous will in which the respective positions of his wife and his mistress had been exactly reversed. As McLeish had observed to a colleague at the time, he'd have understood the whole performance if the solicitor in question had been going to marry either of them, but there had been no question of that, it was just obfuscation for its own sake.

He decided to make sure he had this clear. 'So Miss Morgan would have got the lion's share of the other two hundred thousand even if she *had* agreed to break up the trust? Yes? Then why did she not agree to it? Or was she going to?'

Timothy Hutton stopped hunting in the file. He spread both hands on the table in an aid to thought and McLeish noticed how long the fingers were. 'Sorry. She wouldn't do it at the time, because she felt the whole issue ought to be allowed to settle down. It was very difficult, you know — Miss Huntley was bitter and there was an extremely unpleasant scene in Kenwards's offices. The partner there was terribly embarrassed, rang me up and apologized for hours afterwards, couldn't get him off the phone. So Angela didn't want to get involved — she didn't need the capital, after all — and she said to me she might do it in a year or so when Miss Huntley had calmed down.' He gazed at his hands, and visibly played this back to himself, then looked across at McLeish, and put his glasses on. 'Look, I'm not saying Angela actually refused. Sorry, I can hear how it sounds. She said — or rather I did, to her solicitors — that she would consider it again in a year or so when everyone was calmer.'

McLeish flipped back through his notes. Catherine was so quiet that she might as well not have been in the room and it occurred to him that he must train her to make some unobtrusive signal to him when she thought he was missing something.

'You said, Mr Hutton, that a letter had been written.' Her cool voice, with the slight nasal edge of Stoke on Trent, came from behind him, and Timothy Hutton looked up sharply.

'Did I? Well, yes, there was one. Not to me, to Angela, but she showed it to me.' His glance towards the file told them precisely where that letter was and McLeish asked for it promptly. Hutton extracted it with every evidence of reluctance. 'Bit hysterical,' he said, apologetically.

Yes, indeed, McLeish thought, working his way through the letter. 'Is this a copy?'

'No, no, it's the original. That's how it came. Penelope Huntley must have thought about it. Not exactly guaranteed to encourage my client to do anything.'

'What did you do?'

'Wrote a snotty letter to the poor chap at Kenwards — I rang him up first, of course, he was embarrassed all over again — asking him to ask his client to leave mine alone. I'll get you a copy.' He reached his hand for a bell, but Catherine's voice checked him.

'So, as matters stand, that £200,000 passes to Miss Huntley? It doesn't matter what Miss Morgan's will says.'

'Yes, that's right. It is part of William Coombes's estate and passes under his will.' He looked at her carefully to see he had made himself clear, then resumed his search through the file. 'You wanted to know what was in Angela's will — the one we're going to prove, that is. I'll get you a copy, but it's absolutely straightforward. It's left to her sister, after decent legacies for both parents and small ones to charity, and to her sister's children if the sister predeceases. Sorry, irrelevant now, of course. It's the sort of will young women without husbands or children do make. The second one — the one she made a couple of weeks ago — is a bit more complicated, but not much. Giles Hawick would have got £100,000 outright, her sister and various charities got small legacies, and the rest was to be in trust for children.'

'What if there weren't any?'

'Her sister Jennifer would have got it.'

'Let me see I have it right,' McLeish said, after a pause. 'If she had married before she died, the sister would only have got a small legacy. But Miss Huntley would still inherit £200,000 on Miss Morgan's death, whenever that happened.'

Timothy Hutton nodded and took his glasses off, and McLeish realized that he didn't actually need them. 'You haven't asked me what's in the estate, and I've got a list of assets here.' He passed it over the table, and courteously got up to give Catherine a second copy. The problem item appeared right at the bottom of the page, in what McLeish decided was characteristic legal style — you didn't hide it, you just put it last, after the long respectable list of £20,000 ICI loan stock, and 7,000 25p shares in Sainsbury.

'This is a loan of £100,000 to Yeo Davis? Her employers?'

'Well, it's the amount she was asked to put up when she became a partner last year.'

'Is that usual?'

'Difficult to say.'

Timothy Hutton was looking uncomfortable and McLeish said that it just seemed a lot to him. 'I mean, I imagine a lot of people might have difficulty raising that much?'

'Yes and no. She drew something like £30,000 from the partnership last year. People can borrow on that. But I did think it was a lot, and I tell you why: I can't really see what a group of professionals charging fees like that needs cash *for.* When we started here we only put in about £100,000 between four of us, to keep us going till the fees came in, and that was more than enough. And Yeo Davis charge a good deal more than we do, I can tell you. In some sense Angela may have been paying for the assets — they had assets valued at £600,000 then, most of it in the lease on the building. But you usually deal with that by giving new partners uneven shares. Say the profits come out at £500,000, then senior partner gets £200,000, second partner £100,000 and so on. It's not usual to make new partners put up a lot of cash.'

McLeish contemplated this and decided he would have to find out more about Yeo Davis's financial affairs.

'What happens to that loan now?' It was Catherine again and McLeish was mildly irritated by the way she seemed to be ahead of him.

'I'm looking at the partnership agreement now . . . trm, trm, trm, here we are — death in partnership — well, it dissolves the partnership, course it does, but what happens to the money? Ah yes, the partnership has a year to give it back. I remember saying this was a bit leisurely, wasn't it, but there was some apparently reasonable explanation, like no one gave any notice that they were going to die and the partnership could be a bit pushed to produce the cash if it was the wrong time of year. And of course none of us were particularly exercised about death as a real possibility. As executor, I'll ask for it back formally, but I won't hold my breath. It's interest-free, so I'd expect to get it in eleven months and twenty-nine days from giving notice.'

The phone rang and Hutton picked it up, glancing at his watch. 'Yes, yes I know. I'll be along as soon as I can . . . what, five minutes?' He looked enquiringly at McLeish. 'Fine.' He banged the phone down briskly and sat, clearly working out what else he could offer to get them to go. Amused, McLeish said that he would be happy to wait in an outer office for copies of the various documents, or to have them sent on.

'What would happen if anyone just wanted to get out of the partnership — I mean, without a death being involved?' McLeish asked, as they stood up.

'Six months' notice, both ways, and any loans repaid within that period. Pretty much a standard period. Lots of provisions against stealing clients subsequently, of course.'

As Timothy Hutton's attention was openly on whatever his next problem was, McLeish decided to leave, and to extract anything else he needed from the documents. He did now at least know roughly what was in them.

* * *

In the event, they went back to Scotland Yard so that McLeish could get to a phone and check with his secretary, and with Bruce Davidson, who was co-ordinating the evidence as it came in.

'Forensic rang,' Bruce reported dourly. 'The autopsy report is on its way, so they say, usual rubbish about typing difficulties. He wanted to speak to you but I said you had a string of interviews, so he coughed up to me, nae bother. Killed by a bang on the head from behind, massive bleeding inside the brain. Small contusion on the right cheek as well. He went on a while about the various tests but where he came out was that she'd been dead for at least five days, and seven was perfectly possible. Nae bloody use at all.'

McLeish silently agreed with that judgement. That left at least forty-eight hours from Angela Morgan's disappearance when, as far as the forensic evidence went, she could have been alive. It was in his experience difficult for most people to prove conclusively exactly where they had been for any forty-eight-hour period, members of the Metropolitan police force always excepted, and this was going to make his life very difficult.

'You find anything useful from the scene-of-crime report? I never got beyond page two this morning.'

'Not a thing. No weapon, no footprints, no fingerprints, all the bits of fibre caught on bushes came from the deceased's clothes.'

'A clever one. Car tracks?'

'Yes.'

'What do you mean, yes?'

'Lots of them. Traces of at least a dozen different cars up that wee track that leads back to the road, and of two or three heavy vehicles, all very deeply indented. The lads tell me it's a shooting estate — likely that's where people leave their cars.'

'Oh Christ.'

'Well, someone knew that, didn't they, John?'

'Yes. Yes, of course they did. We *have* got a clever one here. I'll be in later, after six. Hang on.'

He picked up his phone to find the Cambridgeshire sergeant to whom he had spoken the day before on the line. 'I only didn't ring last night because I couldn't find you, sir. Your blokes are on their way, but there are definitely bits of blood and hair on one of the metal parts of this thing — the truss, the bloke here says. Could she have fallen on it?'

'Jesus Christ. Well done, Sergeant, thank you very much. You haven't touched it — no, sorry, course you haven't. I take it it's not something a murderer could pick up? No, I thought not.'

The voice at the other end warmed. 'I was surprised too, sir, you know. I only looked for the sake of form. I took a picture last night and put a plastic bag on and told the farmer we weren't going to put him in jail here and now. He can account for his movements, as it happens. He was in Northumberland with the wife's mother for ten days, only got back three days ago. Well, she's been dead longer than that, hasn't she?'

'He still around?'

'Yes, that's the point. He's a bit upset, and he doesn't need to be. I'll tell him — I think that's your blokes now, I'll get them to ring you.'

McLeish put down the phone, heavily. 'She fell back on it, assuming it's her blood.'

'Accident?' Bruce Davidson said, and McLeish gave it thought.

'No. How did she get there? There must have been someone else around. Unless she crawled to the edge of the embankment — I suppose it's possible, but she can't have walked to the spot in the first place.' He gazed at his subordinate. 'This is silly. We'll wait for the lads up there to tell us about the blood and we'll read the autopsy report. What else can we do while we're waiting?'

'One of the appointments we found in Miss Morgan's diary was with a Miss Huntley. She was due to have lunch with Miss Morgan last week apparently — she is on the phone, I looked. Didn't want to talk to me, so I told her she'd have to wait.'

Miss Huntley? McLeish thought. Ah yes, the hysterical Penelope, niece of the late William Coombes. 'Now, her I do want to see. Fix a date for tomorrow, Bruce. Anything else?'

'Aye, a wee message from one of Francesca's young men at the Department. She's been delayed — she doesn't think she'll get back to London until Thursday, now. Sorry to bring you more bad news.'

McLeish grunted, feeling meanly triumphant that he had turned out to be right in his view that Francesca would not be able to sweep Tristram out of the hands of the New York police in quite the Napoleonic way she had assumed. And he had been perfectly justified, he assured himself smugly, in cancelling their holiday plans at once — she had never been going to get back on time. Feeling vindicated and far-seeing, he strode off to collect Catherine and finish his coffee.

CHAPTER 7

Over at the Department of Trade and Industry the news that Francesca would not be back before Thursday morning was being received with open dismay. Bill Westland CB, MC, the fifty-five-year-old Deputy Secretary responsible for both personnel matters and regional policy, cursed heartily. He summoned his junior, Rajiv Sengupta, a rising star of thirty-six who had the job of co-ordinating financial assistance to industry in the regions, to worry with him. He derived some comfort from Rajiv's habitual elegance; wearing a suit, shirt and tie that must have cost two months of his salary as an Assistant Under-Secretary of State, he was sitting at the other side of the large, uncompromising desk that the Department provides for its most senior officials, not a hair out of place and his black eyes alive with amusement.

'What are we going to do with Professor Thornton tomorrow?' Bill Westland appealed, hopelessly. 'You and I and Henry will be with the Minister at the Select Committee all afternoon, and we'll have to be on call to brief all morning. I was depending on Francesca to look after Thornton, and give him lunch and introduce him around, since she'll be working with him.'

'Why is Francesca delayed?' Rajiv asked.

'Some problem with the New York legal system. Or she's staying to thank O'Brien personally — I really don't know.'

'You don't seem to have much control of your goddaughter.'

'None whatsoever, as well you know, Rajiv. You're no use either, and you taught her for three years at Cambridge. Never mind that: at ten o'clock tomorrow we have Professor Thornton, distinguished economist, Oxford don and friend of the Prime Minister, here for five weeks to do a study on how effective regional assistance is, and we have no one to meet him. Now what do we do?'

'Send him to a regional office?' Rajiv offered.

'Without someone from here to look after him? Heaven forbid.'

'Give him to the Chief Statistician?'

'To *Gerhard*? Even if we get him to comb his hair, it'll be too much of a shock for Professor Thornton.'

'Oh come now, Bill, Oxford senior common rooms are full of people quite as untidy and generally as odd as Gerhard. Last time I dined at Balliol I sat next to the Regius Professor of Chemistry, aged around 193, who told me about his visit to Egypt before the war, probably the Boer War. His teeth didn't fit awfully well, so I couldn't be sure. Gerhard is at least intelligible.'

Bill Westland, grinned, sidetracked. 'You know the story about Gerhard, looking as he usually does, standing on the steps of Horse guards after a Cabinet Committee, when a kindly person sidled up to him and gave him a quid to buy himself breakfast?'

'I have always assumed it to be apocryphal.'

'Not at all, dear boy, I was *there*. Gerhard thought it a charming example of English eccentricity and placed the quid tenderly in the mince-stained pocket of whatever Oxfam-reject he was wearing. I suppose it's not a bad idea to get him to entertain Thornton.' He seized the telephone, and, ruthlessly disrupting Sir Gerhard's morning, imposed a guest on him for lunch.

'In the afternoon the good Professor Thornton can come and watch us and the Minister defending the assistance given to Willis Engineering,' Rajiv pointed out, eyes bright with malice, and Bill Westland winced.

'It is, of course, precisely what he ought to be seeing,' he agreed, reluctantly. 'As an exposé of the soft underbelly of our policy on regional assistance, Willis Engineering has no equal. I suppose so, Rajiv, I suppose so, but he is *not* to come to the briefing. Then what?'

'Well, by Wednesday I'm clear of the Committee, and I could take him to a Regional Office. If I must.'

'Yes, you must, but not Birmingham. After last week's announcement that its development-area status is being removed, the staff are all cowering under their desks while the population throw bricks through the windows. What about Manchester — virtually everyone there has applied for selective financial assistance? Can you keep him there overnight? Good, then Francesca can do the honours from Thursday and work for him thereafter. She's got the troops and it's right up her street, she can get on with anyone.'

'What age of man is he?'

'Mm, hang on. Fifty-two, married to an American, four children but three are steps, girls; his own boy is only eight. Fellow of Balliol, went to Harvard in his late thirties, came back five years ago. Lots and lots of long, distinguished, incomprehensible books on econometrics.'

'Frannie's maths was never any good,' Rajiv warned. 'This may be beyond her.'

'She'll find a way,' her godfather said, with perfect confidence. 'I just wish she was here now. I've got enough to worry about without Professor Thornton.'

* * *

Interesting that the offices of Yeo Davis should be very much less at the leading edge of modern design than the solicitors' which they had just seen, McLeish thought, and murmured as much to Catherine Crane, who laughed.

'It's like all the Italian restaurants used to be, isn't it? Lots of black and white tiles and plants and arches.'

McLeish was considering the possible relationship between design and organizational style when Peter Yeo himself came down to fetch them.

'Nice to meet you, Chief Inspector,' he said with automatic politeness, then considered what he had just said, decided it was beyond explanation and led them upstairs to his office. This echoed the prevailing Italian-restaurant theme, except for the large comfortable mahogany desk which featured reassuring and recognizable objects like drawers and blotters.

Peter Yeo himself was an old-fashioned and recognizable object, McLeish thought, seeing him against the rapidly fading light from the window. It had been Bruce Davidson who had interviewed Yeo before, when Angela Morgan had still been officially only a Missing Person and Peter Yeo, as her employer, one of the obvious people to talk to about where she might be. He considered him as he caused coffee to be produced and established them at the big table at the other end of his room. Given a choice, you would have taken him rather than Timothy Hutton for a solicitor. With his conventional double-breasted suit, carefully cut to disguise a distinctly stocky figure, and his watchful courtesy he was in sharp contrast to Hutton's hard-edged efficiency. The difference was partly generational; this man must be ten years older than Hutton. The real distinction however, McLeish thought in a flash of revelation, lay in their clients' expectations. Yeo Davis's business was concerned with representing people who did not know the ropes, or even that there were any ropes; Hutton's predominantly with fellow professionals in other fields who just wanted the best and swiftest way through. So Peter Yeo *had* to look reassuring and solid and a bit older, while Timothy Hutton could probably have come to work in striped organza without losing a single client.

He abandoned this line of observation and looked carefully at the man inside the suit. The impression of suppressed energy which he had received as he arrived was intensified; Peter Yeo could barely sit still and was discharging tension by moving papers on his desk, then fiddling with the Venetian blinds to prevent the sun from shining in Catherine's eyes. The bright blue eyes looked a bit bloodshot, and there was a flush of colour across the cheekbones. Yeo rubbed the back of his neck irritably, and reached for his coffee, downing two cups while McLeish and Catherine Crane were still passing each other milk and sugar. A thick weekend, McLeish decided, trying to think how best to establish what Yeo's relationship had been with the dead girl.

He started, as he had intended, from where the last interview had left off and went quickly over the ground again.

'Last Friday, yes, ten days ago, was the last time I saw her,' Yeo confirmed. 'Around five o'clock — she left early because she was meeting Giles. Giles Hawick, yes. She was spending the night with him before he went off for a walking weekend in Derbyshire. She didn't want to go with him because she had too much to do, what with the wedding. As I told you, I didn't particularly take in her plans for the weekend, you know how one doesn't, one just asks to be civil and doesn't listen properly to the answer.' He met McLeish's eye and blinked. 'That must sound remarkably silly to a policeman. Sorry, I'm afraid I'm still baffled by all this. What on earth can have happened? I understand she was found not all that far from her parents' house? But she wasn't planning to go to her parents — I know because I rang them on Tuesday when she still hadn't turned up.'

'I wondered if she might have come into the office on the Saturday?'

'Not while I was here. I was in . . . oh, from about ten o'clock to well after lunch, and I wouldn't have thought she would come in late in the afternoon. I mean, it's not a bad idea, Chief Inspector. She often was in on Saturday. We own the building and all the partners have keys, so unless someone else was here she *could* have been in and out without anyone noticing.'

'I see. You left at what time?'

'Well, about three. I was going to have lunch with a client but it got cancelled, so I just stayed here. There's a kitchen here, we have a girl who comes in and cooks lunch during the week and there's always cheese and things around. I killed a rather good bottle of Fleurie, as I remember it. I went to the flicks — I wanted to see *Some Like It Hot* for about the tenth time and it was being revived at Baker Street. I knew my wife didn't want to see it at all. Then I came back here to change, before I joined my wife at a dinner party. Angie wasn't here then, either.'

'What about Sunday? Did you go to the office?'

'No, I didn't. We spent the day with friends.'

That left a large space of time on Saturday where there was little possibility of establishing that Peter Yeo had been where he said he was. But the man himself seemed to be unconcerned about this.

'One or other of my partners is usually in the office on a Saturday. It happened that none of them were, last week. In fact it's so regular that Fiona — that's the girl who does our weekday lunches — is under instructions to leave something we can eat for Saturday lunch.'

'Do you tell her how many are likely to be here?' Catherine had decided to ask a question. Yeo thought about it.

'Depends — I mean, if I knew I had a team coming of course I'd tell her. But otherwise I just reckon there will be something around — or if the locusts have been at the fridge, well, I can always go out.'

'Can you remember what you ate?'

Peter Yeo considered her, as the reason for her question sank in. 'Actually I can. I had an enormous slice of quiche that was left over from Friday. I felt afterwards it would have been better not to make such an effort to finish it all. Fiona will probably remember.' He sounded mildly offended but not in the slightest bit rattled. 'I think *Some Like It Hot* started around three-thirty but I can't quite remember. I walked down — it's not far, and I was feeling rather full of quiche.'

That will check, McLeish thought, of course it will, someone just has to do it all. That means at some stage we may have to see Mrs Yeo. In fact, he decided, he would be interested to see a wife who accepted with such apparent equanimity her husband's absence on a Saturday. Presumably, however, the senior partner in Yeo Davis was hardly needed to do the odd household chore. Which brought him to consider the Yeo Davis partnership; how did it work? How important to it had Angela Morgan been? He decided to start as softly as possible.

'Groups like yours are a bit outside my experience,' he confided, 'and I need to understand a bit about what Miss Morgan did for a living. Could you tell me, perhaps with an example?'

He observed from the way Peter Yeo gathered himself and sat up straight that he was on familiar territory, and understood further that the general patter was well rehearsed. It was, for obvious reasons, a great deal less incisive than Francesca's summary, but the same skeleton was recognizable under the attractive padding placed round it by Peter Yeo. Much emphasis was put on the importance of identifying the key decision-takers and making sure that they had the right information — much was made of the necessity of their getting a balanced picture on which to take their decisions.

'Ours is not unlike the job of a good barrister,' Peter Yeo observed, reaching a peroration. 'We try to make sure the judge has all the facts before arriving at a decision. Mostly we do this by ensuring that our client gets to talk to the decision-takers. There is no point at all in *my* talking to those people, except on a preliminary basis; they're not that interested in my views. I do the background briefing but the clients have to do most of the work, and so I always tell them.'

McLeish decided this was good stuff from which, but for Francesca, he would have gained no clear idea of what a firm like Yeo's was really for.

'So you would, for instance, have lunch with people in government departments to talk to them about particular policies.'

'Yes, often that is the best way to start. We've got a lot of friends to whom we can talk about a policy generally, and where we can put a word in. Let me try and think of an example that isn't confidential. Yes. One of our clients is Andy Barton, who runs the biggest textile group in the north-west. Well, the DTI is at this moment considering giving money to keep Huerter, one of his main rivals, going. A Conservative government, if you believe their manifesto, ought not even to be considering putting money into dying private-sector firms, but Huerter employ a lot of people, many of whom voted for this government. One of the last things Angela did was to have lunch with an old schoolfriend in the DTI who is responsible for the Huerter case, to make sure the DTI understood the impact of such assistance on Barton's operations.'

'And did it?' McLeish asked.

'Oh yes, but Angela was clear that the civil servants were going nonetheless to recommend assisting Huerter. They've been rescuing companies for so long they do it automatically now, I expect. So that told us that we had better get a full-scale defence working immediately.'

McLeish, who had understood from Francesca's report of her lunch that she and her seniors were indeed going to push for assistance, was amused to hear that she had not succeeded in disguising her intentions from Miss Morgan.

'Can you tell me what you are going to advise your client now? I mean, what is a full-scale defence?'

'Ah, well it varies. I've got Andy Barton in to see the Minister responsible at the DTI. I'm keeping the Secretary of State — that's the top man — in reserve. And, of course, we are arranging to brief Treasury people, who will automatically be opposed to giving away public money; and we are working with the company on a memorandum on what assistance to Huerter would do to Barton, with a two-page bullet-point summary. Politicians don't have time to read screeds, so you have to give them short, pithy things to look at. We were doing all this anyway, of course, but the chaps at Barton, including Andy, are working on it much more effectively since we were able to say definitely that the DTI civil servants were agin them. These chaps, good blokes who've spent all their lives running businesses, believed the government manifesto and thought that if they shouted loud enough in the local paper, Whitehall would crumble and right would prevail. It's a bit more difficult than that.'

That lunch had, in fact, given a considerable spur to a campaign being waged against the policy Francesca and her colleagues wanted, McLeish observed. The point of Yeo Davis was now clear: they were there to inform, inspire, and orchestrate a client's efforts to get what he wanted, as efficiently as possible.

'I've read about people giving *MPs* expensive lunches,' he said, with interest.

'Waste of time,' Peter Yeo said briskly. 'The good ones don't have time for long drunken lunches, and you get better results by getting them to give you and the client a sandwich in a bar at six p.m. The ones you can get for lunch — there are plenty — will likely forget every word you tell them, and they certainly don't feel obliged to help.' He caught McLeish's eye. 'Sorry, but the fact is the average backbench MP doesn't know anything, unlike the average civil servant who really does know about his or her particular area. It's only worth using MPs to have a go at the government, and then you spoon-feed it to them.'

The man had come to life very considerably in discussing his job and a formidable personality was emerging. McLeish decided he would have to abandon any prejudice taken from Francesca about this trade; Peter Yeo knew his business and was obviously effective. And it was a good thing Yeo Davis existed; McLeish himself had often been quietly riled by the intellectual scorn which Francesca and her colleagues would bring to bear on criticism of some of their more sweeping policies. It might well have been necessary to invent Yeo Davis if they hadn't already existed. He reminded himself that he was talking to the inventor of the firm and decided to prod a bit further.

'How long have you been in this field?'

'I've spent all my life in general PR, but it was about eight years ago I decided that there was room for a specialist agency, not really a PR firm, which was concerned entirely with government relations. Government in the widest sense, including our masters in Brussels. I have — had — four partners, and we have another twenty people working for us.'

McLeish glanced at the clock on Yeo's desk and saw that he was running behind time, as tended to happen at this stage in an investigation when you needed to be in six places at once. He considered his notes; what he needed from this interview was to confirm that Angela Morgan had not been in the office on Saturday, and a statement of Peter Yeo's movements over the period within which Angela Morgan had probably been killed.

He also did need to understand the financial side. 'Was Miss Morgan about the same age as the rest of your partners?'

'No, no, she was the youngest by a good five years. She is — was — outstandingly able, that's why I asked her to join us.'

McLeish noted the absence of reference to the other partners. Yeo Davis, evidently, *c'est moi* as far as Peter Yeo was concerned.

'I'd like to confirm what the financial arrangements were. I mean how much did she get paid, and how much capital was she asked to put up, that sort of thing.'

'Yes, I suppose you do. Well, you understand about partnerships, do you? None of the partners here is actually entitled to a salary; in theory we split the profits in accordance with a formula that we fix annually and that takes account of age, and experience and what people are contributing in terms of work or clients. As a matter of practice, and because we've all got to live, we all draw about two-thirds of what we would have got last year as we go along, then share out the rest at the end of the year.'

McLeish contemplated this system and its possible application to the Metropolitan police force and felt imagination boggle. He himself would have been desperately pushed if he had had to manage on two-thirds of his salary until Christmas every year. A moment's thought told him that this system worked only because two-thirds of the expected total of a Yeo Davis partnership came out at an amount well in excess of his salary, or that of any public servant of his age. He asked what Angela Morgan had been drawing on every month and found his belief confirmed. Christmas must be worth having at Yeo Davis.

'What about tax?' he asked, still considering the mechanics of the system.

'All partners are technically self-employed but in order to prevent them from getting into a frightful mess we deduct a percentage from their drawings, so there is something put aside for tax. I'd have to say it's a great deal lower percentage than most employed people pay because there are all sorts of expenses a partnership can claim. If we seem to have got it wrong, we sort it out when we divvy up the profit.'

McLeish made a conscientious note, feeling that he had got himself sidetracked off the more interesting question of Angela Morgan's capital investment in Yeo Davis. Finding no way other than the direct question, he put it, and watched Yeo, unruffled, confirm that she had indeed put up £100,000.

'The rest of us had put up much the same, given that we had done it earlier,' he assured McLeish. 'It seems a lot, but we have employees, I can tell you, below partner level, who would be prepared to mortgage their children to get a partnership here. And Angela didn't need to borrow — I imagine you've talked to her solicitors? Well then, you know that she was pretty well placed.'

'I didn't know that a business like this needed much working capital?' McLeish said, in faithful imitation of Timothy Hutton.

'Oh, you'd be surprised. We live off fees, of course, but they can be slow coming in. And this is a short lease here — we have to provide for buying something or paying a hell of a lot more rent. No, that sort of money is needed, believe me.'

McLeish, who had a built-in prejudice, well supported by experience, against statements incorporating an appeal to belief, noted dourly that he might at some later stage need to get closer to Yeo Davis's accounts. That could wait, and he would possibly talk to Timothy Hutton again first. He wound up the interview and was rising to say goodbye when Catherine, sounding shy, asked Peter Yeo if she could possibly use their ladies' room.

'Of course, of course.' Peter Yeo was obviously delighted to do any service, however modest, for her and bustled her away, returning belatedly to ask McLeish if he would like a similar facility, which he accepted, obedient to the unwritten CID rule that you looked after your physical needs at any moment that opportunity offered, because you never knew when you were going to get stuck for hours without help. He waited what seemed to him rather an excessive time for Catherine, but decided, charitably, that you couldn't look as she did without pretty regular attention to the overall effect.

They were in the car, preparing to drive off, before she spoke. 'There's a nice little flatlet on the second floor. Bathroom, bedroom with double bed, kitchen off. I thought there might be.'

He looked at her sideways; she sounded both smug and irritated. 'You think it's misused regularly?'

'I'd put money on it.' The response was so swift and unhesitating that McLeish was taken aback, and drove much too close to the car in front.

'Sorry. You thought he was that kind of bloke?'

She was silent, and pink across the cheekbones — and McLeish, who like all good policemen depended heavily on intuition, understood suddenly that experience was speaking here. She laughed shortly, obviously annoyed with herself but determined to make her point.

'Well, let's say that I've heard of married blokes who always had to go to the office on Saturdays, and it usually wasn't office work they were doing. It sounds all right, and if the wife gets suspicious and rings up, well he's there, isn't he?'

'Not so good if the wife decides to drop in,' McLeish offered, with interest.

'Well, you have to keep the office door locked on a Saturday, don't you? So you've got warning,' she said dismissively, and McLeish let himself, briefly, wonder who the bloke had been who had introduced Catherine to this experience. He abandoned speculation firmly and concentrated on the implications for the present case, since he was plainly being offered expert testimony.

'Could be that any of the other partners used it?' he suggested.

'The place isn't run like that. Mr Yeo is the boss, isn't he?' So she too had observed Yeo's imperial command of the partnership.

'No, I agree. So he was maybe with a girl on that Saturday?'

'Maybe. I was wondering about him and Miss Morgan. I mean, he likes women, and she operated by sleeping with the boss.'

McLeish found himself shocked by this piece of feminine sharpness and must have registered something because his sergeant blushed.

'I don't mean that like it sounds — she didn't do it to get on, or not like that.' Her hands moved, in frustration as she tried to explain. 'I think she might have done it as a quick way of finding out how the business worked. Because she was obviously both clever and ambitious.'

'Mm.' McLeish found himself receiving this with reluctance and wondered why, since it made sense. He glanced at her, being taken aback to find her looking strained and as near plain as anyone with her looks was going to. Her profile was very sharp against the gathering darkness.

'What is it, love?' he asked, anxiously, falling into a term of his childhood, and she jumped.

'Sorry, I'd drifted off. I was wondering about Peter Yeo. Suppose they had been having an affair, and *she*'d dropped him?'

McLeish considered this. 'When she met Giles Hawick?'

'Well, that's possible, isn't it? If you remember, Hawick said — and he's not silly — that there was someone else on the scene when he first asked her out. Perhaps it was Mr Yeo? And she decided Hawick was the better bet, particularly since he wasn't married.'

McLeish pondered this, eyes narrowed, driving fast but carefully. 'Perhaps there isn't all that much fun in going around with a married bloke, after all?'

'She could still have wanted him but got tired of waiting — decided he wasn't going to leave his wife.' Catherine was sounding tough and rational, but something in her voice made him feel this whole discussion was uncomfortable for her. He sneaked a look at her, and found he had an excellent view of the back of her head; she was staring out of the passenger window at the darkening vista of St James's Park. He looked again, cautiously, and saw that she was blindly extracting a crumpled paper handkerchief from her neat navy bag. He waited thirty seconds before glancing sideways again, and found her dabbing at her face, trying hard not to sniff. He flicked up the left-hand indicator and stopped the car.

'I need some tea and I've got a thermos here,' he announced, getting out of the car without looking at her and opening the back door on his side to find the thermos which he had filled before starting off. He got the top off and a cup poured before lowering himself gingerly back into the driving seat and passing it over to Catherine. Then he glanced quickly at her. It was nearly dark outside but the dashboard lights cast a faint greenish glow. She was still sitting with her head partly averted, so her face was hidden. He poured himself a cup of tea and drank it, self-consciously, very aware of her sitting tensely beside him.

'Thank you, John. That was nice.' Catherine sounded suddenly exhausted, and as she gave him back the cup she turned towards him, letting him see that she had been crying, but without looking him in the face. Looking down at the curve of her cheekbone, still wet with tears, he suddenly wanted her, quite overwhelmingly. He sat frozen in his seat by surprise, so blocked by his own consideration of duty, honour and the right way to behave to junior staff that in the end it was she who moved towards him, and touched his cheek.

He slid his cheek against hers and, moving with delicious deliberate slowness, he kissed her on the lips. The sheer pleasure of it swept him up and it was a full minute before he pulled back and looked at her, amazed at how happy he felt.

'Jesus, Catherine. Another minute and I'll be inviting you into the back of the car.' He watched her smile, happy and comfortable with him, secure in the pleasure they shared.

'If you like, or we could go back to my flat?'

For McLeish the rest of the journey had the quality of a dream. With one part of his mind he knew he was getting the benefit of the backlash from an experience in Catherine's past, but with another part he didn't care about any of that, there was no reality beyond her.

The feeling of dream-like ease persisted when they arrived at Catherine's flat. He opened the car door for her, hugged her as she got out, and they went up to her flat, his arm round her shoulders. He took off her clothes for her, while she undid as many of his buttons as she could, and after that it was pure, undiluted, uncomplicated pleasure until they fell asleep in each other's arms.

CHAPTER 8

Either Bruce Davidson always sounded like a Speak Your Weight machine when he was delivering a prepared statement, or the answerphone stripped all character from people's voices. McLeish had rung his own flat to collect messages; he could see Catherine just waking, and waved to her to indicate that he was on the phone. He realized that he was getting cold, clad as he was exclusively in a rather small towel, but decided to stick it out and pick up all of Davidson's message.

There were two key pieces. The first was the news from Cambridge: the samples of blood and hair collected by his long-suffering team were confirmed as a match to the dead girl's. The indentation in her skull also matched. She had either fallen or been pushed on to a spike on the plough; the level of her blood alcohol gave some credence to the idea that she had fallen. The doctor who had done the autopsy, however, had scotched, promptly, any suggestion that she could have moved thereafter. She had died instantaneously, or pretty nearly so, without first getting up and crawling down the embankment, or for that matter getting up and riding a bicycle. Someone had thus moved the body, and it had to be assumed that it was the same person who had pushed her on to the plough.

'Doc says the best bet, given the mark on her cheek is that someone slapped her one and she fell back. He'll put it in writing tomorrow,' Davidson summarized succinctly.

The second key piece of information was that Angela Morgan's car had been found in North Kensington, not far from her flat, and was now cordoned off and being crawled over inch by inch by a forensic team hastily dispatched by Davidson. Did McLeish want to come and see it, *in situ,* because they would have to move it when Forensic had finished?

A detailed inventory of Bruce's day followed, and McLeish understood that having Catherine Crane working on this case had rattled Bruce in several ways. Right at the end, as McLeish's teeth were starting to chatter, Davidson confirmed that Penelope Huntley would meet him at eight next morning and he hoped that that wasn't too early, sorry, but the lass had been difficult to tie down to a time. McLeish glanced again at his watch — eleven-thirty p.m. Just as well someone had rung Catherine half an hour ago, or they'd both still have been asleep, and he would have had difficult questions to answer in the morning about why he had been, uncharacteristically, out of touch with everyone since leaving Yeo Davis at six.

He rang Davidson to confirm that he could make the eight a.m. appointment.

'We have a date at eight o'clock,' he said redundantly to Catherine.

'I heard. I've put the heating on. Why don't you have a bath, you're cold?'

'I'd like that. They've found her car, too — I'll have to go and look at it before they take it away.'

'I'll come with you.'

He hesitated. 'Nothing I'd like better. But they're all going to wonder why I dragged you along at this time of night. I mean, what have we been doing?'

Catherine looked downcast, and McLeish felt uneasy. 'Sweet, it's you I'm trying to protect.'

'And yourself.'

McLeish acknowledged the point promptly. 'Both of us need protecting. Old Stevenson would go spare if he knew, and I'm not certain whether he'd try and get me moved as a danger to junior staff, or you moved as a wicked woman. But he'd shift one of us. His staff do not have private lives and certainly not with each other.'

She looked at him carefully; wrapped in a sheet, with her blond curly hair ruffled, she looked like an advertisement for almost anything.

'Sorry, you're right,' she said. 'It would be me he'd try and shift, too. He's not got much of a reputation as a feminist.'

'The Met's a bit short of those,' McLeish agreed. 'Look, you get some sleep. I'll go and see the car and get back to my flat, and I'll pick you up at seven-thirty tomorrow. All right?'

'You'd like to get home?' She was perfectly secure in her own attractions and amused, and McLeish was disconcerted.

'No, I mean . . . no. I just thought you wouldn't want to be woken up again.'

'I don't mind being woken up.'

He found himself avoiding the street in which Francesca lived as he drove for North Kensington, calling ahead on his car phone to make sure that the forensic team was still there. He arrived to find them just finishing and asked hopefully if any prints had been found.

'No prints on the steering-wheel or any of the doors. Somebody's been over it with a duster. They probably wore gloves, too. We've got some smudges but that's not a lot of use.'

McLeish left them to it and walked away to consider exactly where he was. It was a cul-de-sac off Ladbroke Grove, with two restaurants and two large pubs at the top of it. The pub was orthodoxly darkened and shuttered, but a few diners were still left in the restaurants. It was a road on the way up, this Malplaquet Terrace, as McLeish, a Londoner by adoption, observed. The two large pubs, the little Indian grocer, and the shabby peeling premises which offered dry-cleaning were relics of an earlier era, but both restaurants, on the other hand, were new and forbiddingly smart. One was Italian, one French; both were separated from the street by extensive terraces and were distinctly expensive. He peered at the menu displayed with accompanying admiring press comment outside the Trattoria San Giorgio, and decided you'd be lucky to get out of there under £20 a head. La Bretagne looked even pricier. Next to these was a small antique shop, window lights on, even at this hour, displaying elegant white china dogs and small pieces of Victorian furniture, and next to that an estate agent. It would only be a matter of time before the pubs, the little grocer and the dry cleaner's were replaced by some establishment selling something on which an enormous mark-up could be obtained.

As he walked back down the cul-de-sac McLeish found a demarcation line, so precise it might have been achieved by running a tape across the road, where the commercial element stopped and flat-fronted, early Victorian terraced houses, took over. Further down yet, the terracing ceased and became pairs of large semi-detached houses set well back from the road with the front gardens mostly paved and dedicated to parking space. It was possible to see the same sort of divide as at the commercial end: every second house had been restored and repainted, with extensions sprouting in the gaps between them. Most of the others seemed to be in the process of renovation. McLeish counted, out of interest, ten separate sets of scaffolding. People would still be living here who had been in residence since before the war and were holding on to controlled tenancies until dislodged by offers of cash or other accommodation, but they would not be there much longer.

He had arrived back beside Angela Morgan's car, and stopped to contemplate it. A blue BMW, neat but not gaudy, not souped-up, but a fast, useful car. On her money she could well have afforded something grander, like a Porsche, but evidently she had decided against ostentation. It was the sort of car that a successful young man bought for himself, not a woman's car in the generally used sense of the phrase, nor a car that a man would choose for a woman. It was neither the sensible shopping-basket that men bought for their wives, nor the flashy jobs rich men bought for their mistresses. He looked at the number plate and realized that he had found the sole piece of ostentation Miss Morgan had allowed herself: she had been Angela Jane Morgan and the car was AJM 563. She must have had to pay a bit for that.

The car was parked neatly between two patches of off-street parking, in one of the very few parts of the street that was neither metered nor dedicated to residents' parking. Not put here by chance then; someone had known this street. Assuming the car had gone missing at the same time as Angela Morgan, it might have been there for over a week; it had only been found that evening by a uniformed constable who was keeping his eyes open. Evidently, people in this street were used to strange cars being parked and nobody had thought it worth while to ring the police, despite the fact that the doors bristled with Neighbourhood Watch signs. Perhaps the car had not actually been there since Angela Morgan disappeared, but that seemed unlikely. He asked the forensic team leader for his views and the man shook his head.

'I would think it's been here for several days, sir. It's covered with dust and the road's dry underneath, although we've had a lot of rain.'

'Anything useful?'

'We've got some tiny samples from the tyres. It's been in the mud somewhere. We'll compare it with what we took up at the site.'

'Could be the murderer used this car?'

'He cleaned it first, then, before dumping it, sir. Nothing on it, just a few smudges. Probably put it through a carwash. The inside has been vacuumed recently, too. We're not getting much here, apart from the samples off the tyres. We'll take it apart when we get it away from here, of course.'

Both men stood aside to let a big dark-green Jaguar edge carefully round them on to the forecourt of the house immediately to the left of where the BMW was parked. A small bouncy couple in their fifties got out, staring at the lights and the screens round Angela Morgan's car, and came over to them with all the confidence of the middle-class member of a Neighbourhood Watch scheme.

'Can I help? That car's been parked there over a week, and I was just beginning to wonder about ringing the police. Lots of people from the restaurants park down here in the evening, but I only just realized, talking to my wife, that it had actually been there all day as well. Stolen car, is it?'

McLeish, tired as he was, fell promptly on this witness and accepted an invitation to coffee. The Masters had been out to dinner and were well mellowed, wide awake and disposed to chat, but sitting in their quarry-tiled kitchen-diner, with thousands of pounds' worth of elegant cabinet work and expensive machinery around him, McLeish managed to extract a coherent story. Mr Masters was quite clear that he had first seen the blue BMW late on the Saturday evening, ten days before, pointing out that, while you couldn't exactly complain, it had made access to his own forecourt space a little difficult, or at least when there was already another car on the forecourt, which there mostly was, that being Mrs Masters's runabout. He was sure it had been there every night since, and Mrs Masters turned out to be equally confident that it had also been there during the day. They had looked at each other, disconcerted at this apparent lack of liaison, but McLeish had been reassuring: very natural that they hadn't compared notes, extremely useful that he now knew how long the car had been there.

'Was it stolen, Chief Inspector? I mean, do chief inspectors look at stolen cars? We've never seen much above a detective sergeant in the road before?' Mr Masters, mellow or not, had gathered his wits. He was a small bright-eyed, balding, active man, interested in everything around him.

'Not necessarily. We've been looking for this car as part of a murder investigation. It belonged to a Miss Angela Morgan, and you may have seen the death reported.'

'What's the matter with me?' Mr Masters enquired, smiting himself on the forehead. 'I saw it in the papers, I even noticed that the car was missing, and it was a BMW. I just didn't put it together.'

'You would have, sooner or later,' McLeish said, liking the man. 'That's what happens, something ticks away in your mind and you suddenly realize there's a connection. We'll have to send people round all the houses in the street, see if anyone saw the person who left the car here.'

'Could have been the girl herself?'

'Yes, possibly.'

McLeish decided not to expand, and rose to go, conscious that it was one-thirty a.m. And that he had an interview at eight in the morning. He found at the edge of his consciousness the wish that he was just going to his own flat to crash out rather than back to share Catherine's warm bed.

* * *

At eight a.m. it was pouring with rain, and very cold, as the partners of Yeo Davis straggled in through the neat entrance, their footsteps echoing on the tiles. It was far too early for the immaculate and highly paid receptionist to be in; in fact, no one below the level of partner was present. Peter Yeo, accustomed to leading from the front, had arrived at seven-thirty and personally made the coffee and brought in croissants, so that the reassuring presence of food greeted the other three partners.

'Sorry to get you here so early,' he said, 'but Angela's death means we have to reorganize the entire workload, and I wanted a longer meeting today. There's a lot going on. Tim, I'd like you to report on administrative matters first, to get that out of the way.'

Tim Reagan, a gaunt forty-year-old, who was a genius with trade unions as well as being an accountant and Peter Yeo's right hand, moved swiftly through the secretarial problem, which was one of shortage of same, and seemed, as Peter Yeo observed pleasantly, to have been exactly the same difficulty any time in the last two years, to a discussion of building security, in which no one was much interested either.

'The next problem is fees,' Tim said, noticing sardonically that his partners' level of attention rose sharply. 'As you all know, we billed £400,000 for our success fee to Regina Securities a good eleven months ago — they were one of Richard's clients.' He paused and the meeting observed a thirty-second silence in honour of Richard Fairley who had left the partnership a year previously for considerably more than a handful of silver, taking with him Regina Securities' main reason for being interested in paying Yeo Davis's bills.

'I've written, Peter's written, the solicitors have written. Absolutely nothing has happened. We need to decide whether to put in a writ or what.'

'Have we tried lunch?' the next most senior partner enquired hopefully, invoking what all felt to be the partnership's most powerful weapon.

'Oh God, yes.' Peter Yeo roused himself. 'Brady and I lunched, and we've talked several times. He's been all sweetness and light, promised nothing and done ditto.'

'Do we *have* to sue?' the questioner pressed, unhappily, and Tim Reagan considered him wearily.

'Mike, that £400,000 sits in our last year's accounts as an asset — a debt someone owes us. It's in this year's draft accounts too, but we have people called auditors who are going to recognize this bill, and ask all sorts of boring questions like why it has not been paid, whether it is likely to be paid, and if so when. And if we can't produce some pretty credible answers then they won't allow that £400,000 to sit in the accounts at the full value. Either we'll have to take a very heavy discount on it, or we'll get our accounts qualified. The other even more pressing reason is that we need the cash; we're running an overdraft and that's not funny with these interest rates.'

Peter Yeo, who had been watching his partners, realized that he and Tim were not carrying the other two and decided to make another effort.

'The reason the auditors will give us trouble, Mike, is that they have to certify that our accounts give a true and fair account of the financial state of the business. And if we have £400,000 in there which isn't really £400,000, then the accounts don't tell you what's going on.' He watched grimly as Mike Laister, easily the best man with any drinks company, grasped the point.

'The business isn't worth what we thought it was, that's what you're saying?'

'Right.' Tim Reagan was obviously relieved. 'Or it *may* not be, but we won't know till we sue them.'

'It'll take a long time in the courts, won't it, though?' Mike Laister was still clinging to his point of view.

'What we hope is that a writ will make them settle, Mike, at some level.' Peter Yeo sounded soothing.

'It'd better,' Tim Reagan said. 'The administrators of Angela's estate are going to ask for her £100,000 back. They're not going to get it till the end of the notice period, which is twelve months, but we need the cash. And we are behind with tax.'

'We've got more than enough time to worry about *that*, Tim, and I'm sure the bank will cover us.' Peter Yeo spoke hastily. 'But do we now all agree that we should issue a writ against Regina? I honestly don't believe there is any alternative.'

His partners, brought to the sticking point, agreed, somewhat reproachfully, and passed on firmly to the question of who was going to take over which of Angela's clients.

'I will of course remain responsible for Barton, since I know Andy well,' Peter Yeo said, firmly. 'But I'll need some support if I am to give him the service he wants. Angela was doing a very good job there, taking him round the MPs he had to talk to.'

Tim Reagan stirred. 'I did say to her that the man Andy should see was Giles Hawick himself. It will in the end be a Treasury concern, and if the DTI is really going to be allowed to spend millions propping up Huerter, now that it's a different government, it's very much in Hawick's area. Maybe she felt it was too awkward? Or maybe she felt she could do the briefing personally, as it were? Did she do anything about that?'

He observed with interest that his partner Peter Yeo was looking extremely uncomfortable.

'She would have, of course, but I don't know if she did.' He considered, scratching the side of his jaw. 'It's a good point, though, Tim, thank you. I'll see what I can do with it. There's a lot of work to do on that case — can I have Susy Harvey to assist?'

Two of his partners protested promptly that the said Susy was fully deployed on their cases, and Peter Yeo settled down to reorganize the workload, emerging after ten minutes' hard negotiation with more or less the conclusion he had wanted.

'I can't do that thing on Saturday,' he said apologetically to Tim Reagan, who, having sacrificed one of his staff in the arrangement, was mildly suggesting a reciprocal deal. 'I've promised to take Claudia away for the weekend, and she's not going to let me off it even though we're so short-handed. Can't blame her, really; there's never any time.'

Tim Reagan, who would not have dared to give his French wife as little time as Claudia Yeo got, murmured that this was of course important and good luck to them, indeed.

'Something else I wanted to mention, Peter,' he went on. 'If it turns out that £400,000 really isn't there, then perhaps we charged Angela too much for her partnership share? We were acting in good faith, of course, and I can't imagine that anyone is going to be difficult now she is gone. Just thought I'd mention it — the auditors may say something like it.'

'Let them,' Peter Yeo said, angrily. 'Angie had nothing to complain about — anyone would have been glad to put up £100,000 to get in here. That Regina fee is just a blip — we're on to a £500,000 success fee from Barton, and we'll get that.'

Tim Reagan raised his hands in mock submission, surprised by his partner's vehemence, and followed him out of the door.

In the hall sat Claudia Yeo herself, evidently waiting for her husband, and Tim stopped to say hello to her. She looked as if she needed that weekend away. She was overweight, overtired, distinctly anxious, her hair was untidy, and both her suit and her shoes were in need of a clean. Not what one expected of the wife of the senior partner, Tim observed, thinking smugly of his own immaculately turned-out Patrice, who would refuse to eat if she put on even an extra pound and who would as soon leave the house naked as without make-up.

'Oh, Peter, there you are.'

His senior partner was not at all ravished by this incursion into his working day, Tim observed maliciously, as he faded tactfully away. Peter Yeo bustled his wife into his office calling automatically for coffee. 'Claudia, I've got a meeting in ten minutes, then I'm booked solid through the day. What is it? Can it not wait till tonight?'

'What do you mean, tonight? Eleven-thirty or later, as usual? Perhaps I ought to ring Dawn and make an appointment if I want to talk to you? You never see the children either.'

They glared at each other across the table, two people in early middle age who had had the same quarrel in the same words many times. By mutual consent they desisted, and Peter Yeo took a deep breath.

'Sorry,' he said, grimly. 'What is the problem?'

'I've had the police round, asking about Angela.'

Peter Yeo breathed deep in exasperation. 'Type of police? Bobby in a helmet with a notebook, was it?'

Claudia considered him with open dislike and lit a cigarette deliberately. 'No, dear, a CID sergeant from Scotland Yard. A Scot. I asked to see his identification. And his assistant's.'

'I'll find you an ashtray. *Don't* put it in the saucer, Claudia, for God's sake.' Peter Yeo felt a headache starting, and felt the familiar pressure just above the right eye worsen with the realization that in precisely five minutes he would be needed in a meeting. 'What did he want to know?'

She didn't answer immediately but looked down at the table, then up at him. 'When I come to think about it afterwards, I don't know quite what he was after.'

Peter Yeo controlled the impulse to shout at her, realizing that his wife was badly rattled. She might exasperate him, but she was fully as intelligent as he was and it would be as well to get to the bottom of this.

'Did he say why he had come to see you?'

'He had a perfectly good reason. They had checked Angela's diary for the two weeks before she had gone missing and were talking to everyone in it.'

'Including the clients?' Peter Yeo sat bolt upright, appalled.

'Oh God. Well, I suppose so.'

They stared at each other, momentarily united in recognition of the difficulties.

'I'll call them all, personally.' Yeo jabbed a finger on a button on his phone. 'Dawn, please get Angela's diary for the two weeks before she went missing — and last week — and list every date she had. Now, please, in the next ten minutes. Sorry, but this is a crisis.' He returned his attention to his wife. 'I didn't realize you had seen Angie quite recently.'

'We had a drink together.'

Peter Yeo rose abruptly and went to straighten a picture on the wall opposite him, his wife watching him warily.

'Why?' he asked over his shoulder. 'I didn't think you were all that friendly.'

Claudia Yeo closed her eyes and forced herself to speak to the empty space behind the desk. 'I suppose I wanted to make sure she was going to marry Giles Hawick.' She dragged on her cigarette, listening for any movement from her husband behind her, and jumped as he walked round to stare out of a window.

'And she said she was?' he asked, into the silence.

'Yes, she did. But she also said Hawick wanted her to give up her partnership here and she didn't think she could bear to.'

'She'd have talked him round, surely?' Peter Yeo was still looking out of the window, and Claudia glanced at his familiar back, too short and too broad despite the most expensive tailoring, with real anxiety.

'You don't honestly think that, do you, Peter? People like Giles Hawick don't get talked round.'

He turned, and they regarded each other steadily across the room. 'She was definitely going to marry him. And I suppose we might have lost her in the long run, but not just yet.'

Claudia Yeo nerved herself for a final effort. 'And you'd really accepted that they would marry?'

He hesitated, then became angry. 'Of course I had, Claudia, what do you mean?'

'I know you two were very close, as the papers say.' Claudia Yeo was feeling sick, but knew she was on secure ground. 'I hoped that she had really decided to go for Giles Hawick instead.'

Peter Yeo opened his mouth to speak, and found nothing useful to say.

'I didn't tell the police any of this, of course,' she said. 'I just said that I was having a drink with her to ask her what she would really like as a wedding present from the firm, because men are no good at that sort of thing.' She paused and looked at him sidelong. 'I thought that was rather clever.'

Peter Yeo's mouth quirked involuntarily. He reached for Claudia's hand and held it, looking steadily into her face. 'She was a good mate and a very able, ambitious girl. I'm not sure Hawick was right for her and I'd have been sorry to lose her, but that's beside the point. She was going to marry him.'

She tightened her hand on his, and they sat holding hands for half a minute before Peter Yeo caught sight of his watch. 'Darling, I must get on. We are in chaos here until we get all Angela's work redistributed, we're all of us doing five things at once. Thank you for coming to talk to me, and why don't you come with me to this thing this evening? It's not a riot of pleasure, but we'd be there together.'

She returned his kiss, but declined firmly to join him at the Allied Steelmakers' annual dinner (carriages eleven-thirty), saying she would actually rather go to the cinema with a girlfriend, and tripped out of the office looking considerably less harassed than when she had arrived.

* * *

At New Scotland Yard, John McLeish was spitting feathers, as one of his staff graphically put it. He had arrived, pale and markedly short of sleep, at seven-fifty and at eight-thirty had rung Penelope Huntley's flat to find her barely awake, bad-tempered, vague and professing not to have made an appointment at all. Furious but civil, he had offered to go round to her flat to see her, an offer which she had declined with the first sign of decisiveness she had been heard to display. She had offered to be at New Scotland Yard by nine-thirty and it was now nine forty-five.

'She's playing hard to get, isn't she, John?' Bruce Davidson suggested. 'She agreed eight o'clock when I spoke to her yesterday, after I'd offered her every other hour of the day. She's a nutter, maybe; there's always one in a case.'

'Mm.' McLeish decided to get some work in. 'Tell me about Mrs Yeo. Was her husband playing around?'

'I'd say so. She's a good-looking woman, but she's jumpy and she does'na have the confidence. Let herself go a bit — ye get that with women whose men are giving them a hard time, and who hav'na found a way of getting their retaliation in first.'

McLeish considered his local expert on women narrowly. 'It's not evidence.'

'You didna ask me for evidence, John, you sought my best judgement, and you have it. I'd have been glad to give a wee helping hand there myself, and I'm sure one was needed.'

Some of it was instinct with Davidson, of course, but most of it was solid experience, starting, as Davidson had once told him, with his being seduced by the school-dinner lady at the age of thirteen in his native Ayrshire. 'Och well, John, there's not a lot else to do up there in winter,' he had observed, radically changing McLeish's views of the activities available to schoolchildren in country districts. McLeish reflected uncomfortably that he would have to be very circumspect in his dealings with Catherine, with this beady-eyed observer around the place. On this thought, Catherine put her head in, politely excusing herself to Bruce Davidson, and said that Miss Huntley had finally got here.

'She can damn well wait for a minute,' McLeish decided. 'Bruce, why did the good Mrs Yeo want to have a drink with her rival? All girls together, did you think? No hard feelings, darling, *so* nice you're getting married?'

Bruce Davidson considered his notes. 'She said to me that the partners in the firm couldna decide what to give the lass for her wedding and had asked her, as wife of the senior partner, to have a wee word. It's possible, John.'

'Yes, it is,' McLeish conceded. He signed. 'We'll have to see her again, Bruce — if Yeo was having it off with Angela Morgan, both he and his missis have to be in the frame. And you think that's likely?'

'I told you that I formed the impression that Mrs Yeo was not secure in her husband's affections,' Davidson said, primly.

McLeish grinned at him and told Catherine to organize Penelope Huntley, hoping he had struck the right brisk note. He was not reassured by hearing Bruce Davidson in the passage cheerily observing to Catherine that she was looking a bittie pale; was it just the London air, or had she been burning the candle at both ends? He let a dignified minute pass before going out himself, collecting Catherine, and dispatching Bruce to supervise the house-to-house interviews in Malplaquet Terrace, to see if anyone could be found who had seen the blue BMW arrive or caught sight of its driver.

* * *

McLeish stopped at the door of the interview room and looked in through the spyhole, wanting to get some feel for the evidently hostile and, by all accounts, neurotic Penelope Huntley. His first sight of her was reassuringly normal: a tall, dark girl dressed in a good grey suit of the type favoured by Francesca, which acted effectively as a uniform without doing much for her. An expensive handbag lay on the table, and she was reading the morning paper in a perfectly ordinary way.

But as she lifted her head to greet them, McLeish decided the first impression had been false. Her hair was lank, her skin blotchy and spotty. She was evidently a heavy smoker for the first two fingers of her right hand were stained with nicotine, and, now that he looked, the nails were bitten and the cuticles chewed raw. She looked as if she had just got out of bed, and McLeish had a sudden vision of a dark basement flat with greasy mugs on every surface. She looked both wary and defiant; well, people often did, faced with the police, but it was an unusual combination to find in a girl from the confident middle class.

'Is it not warm enough in here?' he enquired by way of greeting, seeing her clasping her jacket round her. Penelope Huntley let go of it anxiously and said no, that it was perfectly fine, she'd just been cold outside. McLeish took her briskly through the course, making the now familiar speech about Angela Morgan's death being treated as a case of murder, which meant taking statements from everyone who had been associated with her and might be helpful. Penelope Huntley sat silent through this speech, chain-smoking, her eyes downcast. In the end he stopped talking and watched her till she looked at him, sideways and warily.

'In the course of this process we have talked to Miss Morgan's solicitor, who told us that she was the life tenant of a substantial estate, and that you are what they call the remainder-man.'

'That is the correct term, yes. It was my Uncle Bill's money.'

Well, that woke her up, McLeish thought, watching the restless fingers. The sight of a young woman alternately smoking her head off and chewing her cuticles left a lot to be desired. 'I understand that a substantial part of his estate was left to Miss Morgan?' he enquired, with a strong feeling of throwing petrol on to a fire.

'Yes, it was. We both got legacies, and she got the bulk of the estate for her lifetime. She was his mistress, of course, although she was over thirty years younger than him.' She ground a half-smoked cigarette into the ashtray, and McLeish was left with the feeling that she would willingly have done the same to the live flesh of Angela Morgan, if available.

'How do you feel about that?'

Her head came up and she looked him in the eye. 'Well, it was his money, wasn't it, and I was only his niece. I was disappointed of course, but I got over it.'

A good, prepared speech, McLeish thought, with not a word of truth in it. In fact, he realized, she had simply adopted the words other people must have said to her over and over again. He wondered whether she had always been quite so uncaring of her appearance or whether it had been grief and rage at Uncle Bill's defection that had started this off. Not a very easy question to ask.

'Were you close to your uncle?'

'Till *she* came along.' The answer was like a rifle shot, full of pent-up rage, and McLeish sat back.

'You felt she displaced you — with him, I mean?'

'Well, she had all the advantages, didn't she?' Penelope Huntley was destroying the remaining cuticles on her left hand, a finger pushed savagely against her teeth. 'I mean, she could go to bed with him. He wanted her, and he was getting old and silly.'

'I understand that he was sixty-two when he died,' McLeish said, drily. 'It's not all that old.'

'He was idiotic about her. Completely OTT. She didn't really care about him at all, she just wanted his money.'

McLeish decided it would be a waste of time to suggest that it would have hardly been reasonable for Angela Morgan to expect to inherit a quick fortune from a man of sixty-two. 'They had no plans to marry, then?'

'Of course not. Or *she* didn't. She was just stringing him along.'

'Even though she would have been a rich woman had she married him?'

Penelope Huntley looked momentarily disoriented, but any recognition that a valid point had been made disappeared and she went back to chewing her cuticles.

'You now, of course, come into possession of a substantial sum, following Miss Morgan's death,' McLeish observed, sounding as accusing as he could, and she stopped chewing and gave him her full attention.

'Yes, I do. Not anything like it would have been if Uncle Bill had left it to me in the first place, because it will pay duty twice.'

'But more than you would have got if Miss Morgan had agreed to your suggestion of splitting the fund up between you.'

'How did you know about that? Solicitors, I suppose — if it was mine I'll find new ones.' She glared at McLeish, who looked deadpan. 'Yes, I wouldn't have got all that much, but she wouldn't even agree to that, greedy cow.'

The sudden descent into abuse took McLeish by surprise and he realized he must have shown it, because the girl literally got a grip on herself, folding her arms and hunching over the table.

'Well, you've got it now,' he said crudely, and watched with fascination as the corners of her mouth tucked in smugly.

'I'd like to go over your movements with you for last Saturday, Sunday and Monday week, please,' he went on crisply. Penelope Huntley looked at him in amazement, with dawning understanding. More human than she'd looked all morning, he thought, realizing he had taken against his witness at least partly because she was alive and the amusing, lively, feminine creature that had been Angela Morgan was not. Uncle Bill had been a wise man to leave the money to Angela, who had enjoyed it, rather than to this grudging, bitter, scruffy young woman.

'I didn't kill her, if that's what you mean. I thought of it at one time, but I knew I'd make a mess of it.' She bit savagely at her cuticles again, and McLeish had to fight back the urge to yell at her to stop, for God's sake.

'Could you tell us where you were and what you were doing on those three days, please?' he said, instead, levelly and she gave him another sideways, calculating look. 'Including, please, names and addresses of anyone you spent time with,' he added pleasantly and saw her understand that he was serious and she had better get her act together.

It seemed to take an unreasonably long time and much bad temper, evasion and deliberate obfuscation, together with consultation of a diary that appeared to be alternately blank and covered with scribbled hieroglyphics. And the narrative extracted with such difficulty was not helpful. Miss Huntley claimed to have spent the Saturday by herself in and around her flat, doing a bit of shopping and cleaning before meeting a few friends — only one of whom appeared to have an address — and going on to a party around ten o'clock at night. A large party, in and out of which people had evidently flowed like water circulating in a swimming pool. Sunday was not much better; Miss Huntley had not risen from her bed until one p.m. and had not left the flat until five, then only to go to the cinema. On Monday she had gone to her job — improbably she appeared to be a supervisor for a market research firm — as usual, and could be vouched for by colleagues there. Well, two colleagues anyway. No, she did not own a car — could not afford to — but she did have a driving licence. Uncle Bill had run a car for her on his company while he was alive but of course that had all stopped when he died.

McLeish, who remembered that she had been left £200,000 outright, received this as further evidence that the young woman had gone into a massive sulk after her uncle's unexpected death. It was difficult to tell, of course, whether she had always possessed an unattractive, aggressive, sullen personality, or whether rejection by her uncle in favour of Angela Morgan had tipped her over into this behaviour. Perhaps she would brighten up now that she had another substantial amount of cash to spend.

He asked her to come back as suited her to sign her statement, and she made all kinds of difficulties about when this would be possible. He finally dealt with that by saying briskly that one of his staff would come to her place of business. She opened her mouth to argue further, being plainly in the mood to announce she was leaving her job rather than allow any arrangement to succeed, but something about McLeish's expression checked her and she agreed meekly.

McLeish saw her off and returned to confer with Catherine.

'You get all that? It'll all have to be checked — you've got Donalds and Ridley to do that.' He gazed at her bent head as she read through her notes, and she looked up and smiled faintly at him. 'Shall I do it now?'

'Not yet. What did you think of Miss Huntley? What a bitch, eh?'

Catherine considered him thoughtfully. 'I was sorry for her. Her dad died, then her uncle went off with someone else. And left his money away from her.'

'I hadn't quite seen it like that,' McLeish acknowledged humbly, remembering that the beautiful woman in front of him, whom you could not suppose ever to have encountered rejection in any form, had lost a father when young, and had been so little attached to her stepfather that she had left home at the earliest opportunity. 'She is in the frame, though?' he suggested.

'Oh yes. What was it she would get on Angela Morgan's death — about £120,000 after taxes? And I suppose she feels she's won. I mean she's alive, isn't she?'

McLeish observed soberly that £120,000 and the death of a hated rival seemed a prize well worth playing for. 'She's got a nasty enough temper — I just don't myself see her as clever or organized enough to cover her tracks. Well, perhaps you'll find she hasn't — it's not much of an alibi, is it?'

'No. Gaps all over Saturday and Sunday — you reckon Angela was killed then, rather than Monday?'

'I reckon Saturday. We've got no sighting of her after first thing Saturday morning.' Catherine Crane looked at him carefully, and he grinned at her. 'Come on, I know that look now. What am I missing?'

She blushed. 'It's just that the only person who saw her on Saturday was the Minister — Mr Hawick.'

'Why would he be lying?'

'Only if he was the murderer and had actually killed her earlier.'

McLeish sighed. 'I'd not forgotten him, but I just couldn't see why he'd want to kill her. He didn't get any of her money if she died before they were married.'

'It could have been jealousy. Mrs Morgan did think there was, or had been, something with her boss. And Mr Hawick didn't seem to me the kind of chap who'd put up with that.'

McLeish nodded, not entirely convinced, but unwilling for a variety of reasons to discourage Catherine. 'We need to check what he was doing those days, anyway — I didn't try too hard when we were last there, because I hoped the autopsy might give us something. As it did. I'll get Jenny to fix it.'

She nodded, and he sat looking at her until she looked back at him. He glanced up at the spyhole and grinned. 'Let's get some lunch. I can't face the canteen but there's a trattoria round the corner. I never see anyone from this place there.'

They ate in the small crowded Italian restaurant which was, as he had promised, free of their New Scotland Yard colleagues. It was also free of DTI civil servants as he had quietly ascertained while they waited for their lunch to arrive.

They walked out into a cold, bright day, into one of the labyrinthine streets by the side of Westminster Abbey, straight into a column of knickerbockered children chattering hard and sweeping all before them. As they stood patiently in a doorway waiting for the column to pass, Catherine turned to say something to McLeish and he looked down at her for a long moment.

'Better get back.' Smiling to himself, he looked idly across the road and saw Francesca, who should not have been back till Thursday.

She was not looking in their direction, her head was turned to say something to whomever she was with, her short hair blown straight up by the wind as they went into the little newsagent's, leaving McLeish a clear run to get Catherine back to the Yard. He walked heavily beside her, trying to convince himself that Francesca had not seen them. But she had, of course she had; that was why she had fled.

He got back to his own desk and sat, looking at his hands, unable to decide whether to ring her up, or what to say.

CHAPTER 9

If this was the rising star who had been going to elucidate for him the mysteries of selective financial assistance as performed by the Department of Trade and Industry, one might well wonder what their less capable staff looked like, David Thornton thought, exasperated. This Francesca Wilson, whose name had been called in aid whenever he had asked for any information, and whose return had been so keenly expected, was not impressing him at all.

He had known from the moment he arrived in the Department that as a personal friend of a Treasury Minister he was unwelcome. All the officials he had met had conceded, with every appearance of good will, that of course the Treasury, on behalf of the taxpayer, was right to be seeking some analysis of the effect of the substantial amounts of aid going to the regions. He had understood, out of long experience, that this signalled that he would receive the treatment characterized as 'all assistance short of actual help', but he had been willing to give them the benefit of the doubt. They had explained that they were attaching to him for the period of the study their brightest and best at Principal level; she would of course have to keep her regular work going, they had caveated, but she did have staff who would assist them both. Now it was Thursday, here the girl was, and it was quite clear that she was not actually listening to a word he was saying. No one else at the small meeting was either; Bill Westland, Rajiv Sengupta and Gerhard Bukowsky were watching Miss Wilson, and Sir Gerhard was all but patting her hand.

'Miss Wilson, how would you suggest we might best initiate the analysis of the cases I have suggested?' Thornton asked briskly, deciding he had had enough and would much rather be back at Oxford doing some real work. He was unsurprised not to receive an immediate answer and waited out the pause with an expression of courteous interest. The girl looked momentarily totally disoriented, but concentrated for a minute, then spoke.

'As you suggest, Britex provides a particularly good example. Crudely, rescuing Britex cost £6.3m, but against that there were the benefits of not paying 1400 chaps unemployment benefit. The problem — and I take it this is what Treasury are hoping to emphasize — is that there is some evidence that many of these 1400 would have been deployed to greater benefit in other local firms who can't get the labour. The evidence is anecdotal, and sweeping assumptions would have to be made, but that could be done, I imagine. We know where to look for such information as there is.'

Aha, David Thornton thought. One of those people who carry an invisible tape-recorder inside their heads and can reel it off afterwards, even if they weren't listening at the time. He regarded her thoughtfully, noting the careful use of Civil Service impersonal. Not a convert to the use of cost-benefit analysis but a conscientious, intelligent operator, who had given a neat exposé of the politics that had placed him in this position — of course the Treasury wanted to cut back the DTI's apparently unlimited powers of dishing out cash.

Francesca looked back at him, just perceptibly smug, aware that she had surprised him and David Thornton revised his first estimate of her. Not plain, not with those wide, dark-blue eyes, slightly reddened by what he assumed to be jetlag, but equally not making any effort: hardly any make-up, hair spiky and untidy, and clothes neat but well short of inspiring.

'That is more forthcoming than your colleagues in the Regional Offices felt able to be,' he observed, watching Bill Westland stir uneasily.

'Well, they're a bit close to it. And very hard-pressed. I'd suggest it would be counter-productive to ask them to do more than produce their statistics and whatever anecdotal evidence they feel like offering.'

'I got a lot of the latter and not much of the former,' he murmured, thoughtfully.

'I can never remember which is which, but if you mean they didn't chip up many figures you don't surprise me. They're about eleven months behind, or were when I last looked. Those numbers would have to be dug out.'

David Thornton blinked at her, noticing that Bill Westland was resting his head on his hand. 'The former is the first object mentioned, and the latter the second,' he said automatically, as the strikingly elegant Rajiv covered his mouth with his hand, and young Miss Wilson nodded impassively in acknowledgement. He waited to see what this lot were going to do next.

'I think', Bill Westland said, heavily, removing his head from its resting position, 'that the most useful thing would be to leave Francesca with you so that you can get out a plan of work.' He bent a warning glare on his subordinate who had returned to whatever internal consideration had been preoccupying her, and Thornton remembered that he had been told Bill Westland was the girl's godfather. The other two senior men in the room, taking their cue from Westland, scrambled to get out of their chairs, Sir Gerhard administering a passing, anxious pat on young Miss Wilson's shoulder.

Left alone with David Thornton, Francesca contemplated him through the fog of tiredness, misery and rage that had enveloped her since she had seen John McLeish from across the road after Tuesday lunch. He knew she was back and he had not rung in answer to her call. His failure to do so was more eloquent than anything he could have said, and perhaps indeed it was meant to be. But it was not like him to avoid a necessary confrontation; perhaps he was in a state of confusion and if she sat tight, like the books said, all would be well.

She abandoned speculation, grimly, and bent her full attention on David Thornton. A bit moth-eaten, she had thought when she first saw him, but she now realized this was a little hasty; he was an attractive man who paid very little attention to his appearance, burly with faded, blond good looks, hair rapidly thinning from the high, well-shaped forehead. An eclectic mixture of clothes, not in Sir Gerhard's class, of course, but very much the outfit of a man who didn't believe in wasting time on these things — a pale-grey checked suit worn with a blue shirt and heavy brown walking-shoes. And he was a good thirty pounds overweight. She watched him as he walked round the room adjusting the blinds and reorganizing the coffee cups, finding something comforting and familiar about him. She had been taught at Cambridge by distinguished academics and recognized the type, as well as the absolute authority which good people, absorbed in their subject and not interested in personal promotion, can convey. There would not be a lot of point standing between this one and a hypothesis, and she might as well identify what his position was.

'I take it that you start from the belief that regional assistance is a distortion of the economic process?' she said amicably.

He turned to look at her with interest. 'Not necessarily. Some government assistance is a useful economic weapon, loosely known as defensive investment. Have you read my book on its application in Belgium?'

'No, but I could.'

'I don't expect it of you.' He grinned at her, amused. 'It does, however, seem to me possible that the politically inspired, high-profile rescue cases may be distorting competition in the broader sense, and in particular competition for labour.' He considered her professionally deadpan expression, understanding that he was on a Departmental corn. 'Or I may be wrong,' he offered, 'in which case my work will give Treasury more confidence in the programme.'

'I can't imagine anything giving Treasury confidence in a DTI programme.' Francesca dismissed this overture. 'Treasury can't bear most DTI spending programmes and DTI of course always wants to spend more, so there is a running battle, rather like the Hundred Years War. Every now and then one side gains a few hundred yards of territory, only to cede it the next year.'

'You are suggesting that I am this year's Treasury harquebus?'

'That's another thing I can never remember what is,' she said promptly, and ungrammatically.

He smiled at her, enjoying himself and noticing that she was looking much better than she had first thing that morning. 'Tell me about the Regional Office statistics,' he said, hopefully.

'I'd have to look up precisely what it is that they collect — one of my people is producing a list now — but the short point is that every six months someone thinks of a new set of numbers it would be nice to have, or decides they would like the old ones sliced up another way. The result is what you would expect when the people are well-intentioned public servants with no particular mathematical or statistical training, and there aren't enough of them. Eleven months behind, I believe, states the most favourable position.'

'And that is why you — the Department — have never done any cost-benefit analysis?'

'One of the reasons. The main reason is that no one here at head office, as it were, has any time either. And we are short of economists — as I expect you know.' She considered this statement. 'Never mind economists, right now in London we're short of people who can read and write.'

'So I'm not really going to get any help?' David Thornton decided he would do well to remind this articulate creature where he came from.

'Of course you are.' The girl looked amused. 'This bit of the Department is very politically attuned. Most civil servants are, but we are particularly so — how should we not be? And I agree in principle with getting some analysis of whether we are doing more good than harm. But it's not a normal exercise and we do not have enough people. This wing of the Department has a half share in a graduate economist, which we will yield, and I'll tell you who to ask for the other half. I can offer you additionally about half an HEO — High Executive Officer — chap who came in six years ago with two A levels, and the best of my executive officers, who does have A-level maths.'

Thornton considered her carefully, and decided that this was not obstruction; she had acknowledged his political card and offered up what there was to offer.

'Will it be difficult if I bring in one or two graduate students, given that you don't have the people?' He offered this suggestion mildly, and watched the confident face become uneasy. Very simple to read, this one, once you had got her out of whatever gloom she had been in.

'It'll cause all kinds of difficulties.' Francesca decided to come clean. 'But then having you around at all, questioning policy, brings its own difficulties. The offices are pretty prickly and defensive.'

'Resenting interference with their patronage?'

'Not quite fair. Most civil servants have this quaint belief that we have a duty to inform the public what is happening. Very difficult to do that if policy keeps taking violent swings.'

'The present government has stated its intention to draw back from intervention, and this study will not necessarily cause a violent swing.'

'You will not convince anyone in this Department that that is not the intention of the Treasury.'

David Thornton nodded and reflected wearily that it was familiar ground; in fact the politics of his own college were probably more Byzantine than these. 'What do I do about staffing this study, then?'

She gave him a wary look, declining complicity. 'Talk to Bill, explain it to him, he's the head of personnel — we call it the Principal Establishment Officer.'

'I'll do that.' He caught her glance unobtrusively at her watch. 'Just one more thing for now. I have been asked to consider, specifically, the Department's recommendation on assistance for Huerter Textiles. I understand it's your case?'

'It is. I have, however, been out of the office for over a week. There is a meeting and it's starting in five minutes. Can I talk to you afterwards, when I am up to date with what we are doing?' She hesitated, watching him. 'We have been — are being — heavily lobbied on behalf of Andy Barton Ltd, Huerter's major rival. The lobbyists have been talking to Treasury, too — I don't know if you knew?'

David Thornton met her eyes. 'Giles Hawick, whom I taught as an undergraduate, asked me to do this study six months ago, when his party was returned to government, but I was then finishing a book. I know the Huerter case is arousing a great deal of feeling, and I have been asked to look at it while I'm here.'

That's why they are all so prickly, particularly in the North-West Regional Office, he realized, undisturbed by this perception and hoping that his statement would prove mildly soothing. At the same time he decided he had probably been a little naive himself: the timing of Giles Hawick's urgent renewal of his invitation to do this study *was*, of course, connected with the Huerter case.

'The Department is recommending assistance to Huerter, I take it?'

'On balance, having taken full account of the effects on Barton.'

'Mm.' He doodled for a moment and looked up to find Miss Wilson watching him suspiciously. 'You've got a meeting, I'm sorry,' he said pleasantly. 'Do go to it.'

The girl considered him. 'Gerhard is giving you lunch, yes?'

'Yes, indeed. And Bill Westland is taking me to an interdepartmental meeting after that, so I am being well amused.'

'I'm not sure that was their intention.' She rose and collected her papers. 'I'll come by later and see what else you need.'

* * *

Quarter of a mile away, John McLeish sat at his desk contemplating the telephone. He recognized reluctantly that he simply wished Francesca were still in New York. He didn't want to see her and he didn't want to hurt her; he would just like her not to be there while he explored his affair with Catherine. He considered offering Francesca a statement that he wanted some time on his own, and immediately remembered Bruce Davidson sympathetically but firmly advising a colleague that when lasses said they wanted some time on their own, what they actually meant was they had another bloke they wanted to go to bed with. So it was either tell the truth or take the easy route: keep his mouth shut and let her draw her own conclusions. And that treatment she did not deserve.

To his unconcealed relief his secretary buzzed him and told him Commander Stevenson wanted him.

'You getting anywhere with this Morgan case?'

'We've done a lot of work. It's complicated.'

The Commander faced him with a basilisk glare that indicated that a subordinate should not try his patience. 'Who's in the frame, John?'

McLeish decided that even at the risk of explosion he had better expose some of the difficulties.

'It could have been an accident — she actually died by falling backwards on to the sharp edge of a plough, but someone hit her first. Contusion on the cheek. We don't yet know, within about forty-eight hours, when she was killed. She was missing from early on a Saturday through till the next Saturday. The doctor says she'd been dead at least since the Monday, so it could easily have been since the Saturday. He won't put it closer than that.'

'He's probably right not to.' The Commander's attention had been hooked, as he hoped, by the technical problem exposed to him.

'The motive is just as difficult. There are two women who benefited financially from Miss Morgan's death — her sister and a Miss Huntley who is the niece of the older bloke who left Miss Morgan his money when he popped it two years ago.'

Stevenson considered him, slitty-eyed. 'So a man or a woman could have done it? Bit of a goer, wasn't she? All this comes back to me now, John. Well, what about these girls?'

'Miss Huntley I'd put very definitely in the frame, on motive alone. And she is a bit round the twist. And she doesn't seem to have much of an alibi for a lot of Saturday and Sunday. Sergeant Crane's out checking up now.'

A smile spread over the Commander's brisk military features. 'How is Ms Crane getting on — I practically got crushed in the passage when I put my head in her office the other day. What a popsy — I really can't believe she's a sergeant.'

'She seems very effective, sir,' McLeish said firmly, fixing his mind on the next point to make about the Morgan case.

'Good. So this might be straightforward.' He considered McLeish. 'No?'

'There are other possible suspects. The bloke Miss Morgan worked for — Peter Yeo — doesn't seem to have been happy about her projected marriage. He may have been having an affair with her before Hawick turned up.'

The Commander, trained in the basic tenets of domestic life, sighed. 'Bugger. I never like these cases with ex-lovers around. What about Yeo's wife, where's she in all this?'

'She's next on my list to talk to, but I wasn't so bothered about her — I mean, the girl was going to marry someone else and presumably had given Mr Yeo back, as it were.'

'Any more exes about?'

'The only other one we know about is dead. Bloke who left her most of his money, William Coombes.'

The Commander brooded for a minute, scribbling a diagram on the pad in front of him. 'There was another girl who stood to gain when Miss Morgan died. Her sister?'

'Jennifer Morgan. Yes, that's right. There's also a hint of a secondary motive. Mr Hawick — the Minister — was taking her out when he met her sister, and switched over.'

'She got an alibi for the weekend?'

'I'm seeing her again, too.'

'I see what you mean about complicated.' The Commander put his pen down and looked at him across the table, shoulders squared. 'You haven't mentioned Mr Hawick. Is he in the clear?'

McLeish, who had been waiting his chance, seized it. 'No, sir. He has no alibi for either the Saturday or the Sunday, or doesn't seem to have. He went walking, by himself, not fifty miles from where Miss Morgan was found.'

'Did he have transport with him?'

'No sir, he said he took a train from St Pancras on the Saturday. It's a good line, about ninety minutes each way. And we do now know that Miss Morgan's own car transported her to where she was found, and it then came back to London.'

The Commander looked at him, openly worried. 'Bloody hell, John.'

'I was trying to get a bit closer to the times, sir, before I told you. It may all come together — I mean, we may be able to eliminate Hawick. But we can't yet.'

'What would his motive have been?' The Commander, as always, was prepared to look an unpalatable fact squarely in the eye. 'Apart from jealousy?'

'I don't know, sir,' McLeish acknowledged. 'He lost money by it — she'd made a will in his favour, but it was conditional on their marriage. If he'd wanted cash he could have waited until after they were married.'

'He shouldn't be pushed for cash. His first wife left him a good bit when she died.' Stevenson soaked up facts like this.

'That was a car crash,' McLeish offered. 'She was thought to have fallen asleep at the wheel. Drove into a tree. I looked it up before I went to see him the first time, trying to keep my feet out of delicate subjects.'

'Hang on, John, let's not get run away with. He wasn't married to Miss Morgan, and so her money went to a sister and to this Huntley girl. Why did it go to the Huntley girl?'

McLeish explained the passing of the life interest.

'She wasn't a friend of his? No, but the other Morgan girl was, wasn't she? And *she* gets a decent lot of money, since her sister died unmarried.'

'I've thought of all this, sir,' McLeish said carefully, 'and that and the fact that I can't place him those two days make me unhappy. But there's nothing proven. Even if she had had an affair with Yeo, she was actually going to marry him, Giles Hawick. I mean, he'd won.'

'If she really *had* given up Yeo. And if there wasn't anyone else.'

The Commander was gloomily contemplating the 10" × 8" glossy print of Angela Morgan on his desk. 'I knew a girl like that on the Force. Went straight through two of my DIs and a DCI in a year. Bust up two marriages and put the third bloke into Friern Barnet for six months. I'd better have a word with the AC. He can work out what to tell the Home Office, if he has to say anything. But you get this lot sorted, John, and bloody quick. Do you need any more help?'

McLeish, who that morning had counted twelve officers variously deployed, said unhopefully that he could use another team to work on Hawick's movements. 'DI and a sergeant?' he suggested.

'What do you want, John, blood? You'll have them by tomorrow.' His superior looked him in the eye, daring him to comment on the way scanty resources were being directed to a case in which the Home Office was interested.

McLeish rose to go, resolved to get out of the room while his luck was holding, but was checked on his way.

'John? I hear your girl got home safe, with her brother.'

He turned reluctantly. 'Yes, sir. I haven't seen them, they only got back yesterday.'

'Resourceful young woman.'

'Sir.'

An incoming phone call enabled him to make his escape.

McLeish got back to his office and checked his messages, both relieved and oppressed to find that there was nothing from Francesca. Catherine was still out checking Penelope Huntley's story, and McLeish decided to wait for the promised manpower to check Giles Hawick's story. Claudia Yeo and Jennifer Morgan had to be interviewed, in random order. He found Claudia Yeo at home and asked if he could come and see her.

'You met Sergeant Davidson yesterday,' he told her as soothingly as he could. 'I'd like to bring your statement round to get it signed and perhaps ask you a bit more about Miss Morgan. Or, of course, you could come here, if you would find it easier.' He listened, interested, to a variety of anxious excuses as to why today was impossible, and extracted a date for the next day, his every nerve alerted. It was not obvious why Mrs Yeo should be so agitated; she was not of a class to be rattled by the need to give a statement to the police. Tomorrow ought to be interesting.

'Any luck, Jenny?' he asked, walking into his outer office.

His secretary waved to him to be quiet. 'I think Chief Inspector McLeish is free this afternoon,' she was saying. 'May I just check his diary?' She pressed the cut-off button. 'It's a secretary at the Treasury, John, wanting you to meet Mr Hawick.'

'Tell them, yes, now if he likes.' He stood, towering over the desk, wholly intent, while she confirmed the time.

'Good,' he said, feeling in his briefcase for papers he had meant to leave with her that morning. His searching hands encountered the dirty shirt, pants and socks he had shoved in that morning. It was over a year since he had found it necessary to carry clothes around with him; Francesca's efficient daily help did any washing he left behind and returned it to a drawer clean and ironed. He stuffed the clothes into a plastic bag which he hid in his desk, hoping that Jenny was not drawing any conclusions.

'Find Bruce for me — I'd like him in on this interview.'

He waited impatiently while Davidson was extracted, and the two of them went down in the lift, McLeish hastily bringing him up to date. They walked briskly through the crowded streets to the Treasury entrance in Great George Street and found themselves in the crowded Private Office. The Private Secretary nodded to them across the room from where he was murmuring into a telephone, and a younger man with the same crisp efficient manner led them towards a closed door and knocked deferentially before standing aside to let them through.

'No calls please, Peter. Ring David Thornton — he's over at the DTI somewhere, try the PEO. I'd like to see him around six if he can spare the time. Tell him it's about Huerter Textiles, will you? Sorry, Chief Inspector, how are you? A different assistant today?' Giles Hawick shook hands with Davidson, who said amicably that senior officers had to take turns to have that wee girl take notes for them, leaving McLeish's rather stiff explanation of Catherine's position and responsibilities withering on his lips.

'There's something I should have told you, Chief Inspector, but it had totally gone out of my mind.'

Despite his brisk approach Hawick looked profoundly uncomfortable and McLeish felt the back of his hands prickle.

'I was only reminded by the fact that it has happened again. Or rather it actually happened for the second time about two weeks ago, but my constituency secretary has been ill and has only just caught up with the backlog.' He stopped, and McLeish patiently maintained an expression of gentle interest.

'What was it, sir?' he asked, when the pause had stretched itself quite long enough.

'An anonymous letter. I mean two; this is the second one. I really put the first one out of my mind.'

Absolutely not true, McLeish thought behind his courteous exterior, and Davidson's cough only went to confirm his view. You just weren't going to tell us about it, were you?

The Minister glanced at him sideways across the huge desk. He was wearing a good grey suit which emphasized his elegant height, and seemed desperately tired and worn. He looked at McLeish for a long moment, then his mouth quirked. McLeish cursed himself for being unable to conceal his disbelief. 'I destroyed the first one — but this last one — here, you'd better see it — is very much along the same lines. My secretary — my constituency secretary, that is — will confirm that. She wouldn't read my private mail of course, but this was only labelled "strictly private and confidential", and, as I'm sure you know, everything including the statement that you have already won a prize in the *Reader's Digest* Special Draw is so labelled. So she opened both — this one isn't long, but neither was the first one.' He handed a sheet of paper encased in a plastic folder across the table and McLeish peered at the message.

'We'll need to take your fingerprints, sir, and your secretary's, so we can eliminate them,' he observed without looking at Hawick.

'Yes, of course. We put it in a folder before it could collect any more prints.'

The letter was on plain paper, composed of block capitals cut from a newspaper, and was indeed short, but to the point: YOUR ANGELA STILL FUCKS HER BOSS AT THE OFFICE.

'When did the first letter arrive?'

'About three months ago.'

'And you assumed that it was Mr Peter Yeo that was being referred to?'

The poised man behind the desk looked humanly surprised. 'Oh yes. Angela had told me she had had an affair with him — in fact he was the reason she stood me off a bit when we first met.'

McLeish hesitated, but there was no option but to ask the question. 'Did you believe that letter?'

'No.'

'Did you tell Miss Morgan about it?'

'No. Since I didn't believe it, I didn't see why she should be bothered.' He broke off, eyes narrowed. 'Come in,' he called, annoyance only just concealed. 'Yes, Michael?'

It was the Private Secretary who had taken it on himself to interrupt the Minister. 'I beg your pardon, Minister. Professor Thornton can come at twelve noon but not about six tonight. You are free.'

'Yes. Yes, ask him for noon, will you? If we haven't quite finished here I'm sure he'll wait a few minutes.'

Not an unwelcome break for his interviewee, McLeish thought irritably, and it had destroyed his own train of thought.

'When did this letter arrive? Have you the envelope?'

'Under the letter — Jane, my constituency secretary, had the sense to keep it. Postmark is two weeks ago, I told you. Jane's been ill.'

McLeish remembered that the Whitehall machinery, embodied in the large and efficient Private Offices provided for Ministers, draws its skirts away from anything connected with party politics, and a rigid division is kept between constituency business and the affairs of the nation.

'If you'd got this when you were meant to, what would you have done?'

Hawick looked at him, his face suddenly all straight lines, the mouth set and tight-lipped. 'That is a hypothetical question.'

'You don't need to answer it, sir. This is new information for us, and I'm trying to work out what the writer was trying to achieve.'

'Since I didn't believe the allegation before, I wasn't going to believe it this time.'

You did before and you would have this time, McLeish thought out of total inner certainty. You'd have reckoned, knowing your young woman, that there was something in it.

'I'll need to take this away and see what it tells us,' he said, calmly. 'I would also like, if you have time now, sir, to go over your own movements on last Saturday, Sunday and Monday. The doctors are clear that she died no later than Monday evening, and of course you yourself saw her on Saturday morning.' He waited out a pause and watched the man deciding whether there was any point in being angry.

'You're asking everybody, I take it?'

'Everybody close to her or who saw her shortly before she went missing, sir.'

'I said goodbye around nine a.m. — well, I must have, I got the nine-thirty train. I never saw her again.' He paused and McLeish waited, silent. 'I got to Derbyshire about eleven o'clock and started off — I'll show you the map. I ate lunch about here.' He turned the map. 'And then I walked on and reached the climbing bit — here — about nine in the evening.'

'Did you meet anyone?'

'I met — no, I didn't exactly meet, I passed two couples on Saturday, and two men, not together, on Sunday. Not all that many people walk in February. I was in a climbing hut for Saturday night, but no one else was there, it's early in the season. And in a hotel on Sunday.' He gave them names and details of that.

'Do you remember anything about the people you met walking?' McLeish asked as casually as he could, and watched, expecting an explosion, as the man put his hands convulsively flat down on the desk. There was a long silence while the Minister gazed out of the window, communing with some invisible auditor.

'The first couple were young, and the boy had bright red hair. That is literally all I can remember about them. I can't remember anything at all about the second couple — oh, wait a minute, they had a dog with them, a Border terrier.' He looked both pleased and surprised, and McLeish murmured that that was helpful. About the two he had met walking on the Sunday he was almost totally blank, except that he remembered that he had thought the younger man poorly equipped. 'He was wearing sneakers, and a rather light jacket, and I thought him not well dressed for bad weather.

He had a northern accent — I remember now, though he didn't say more than it was a grand day.'

That'll be fun, McLeish thought, sourly, dredging up that lot. You might find the walkers if you advertised on national TV, but if it came to it, someone well senior to McLeish in the hierarchy was going to explain to Hawick the necessity for this procedure. He looked up to find the Minister watching him.

'Not very easy to check on.'

'No, sir.'

The man continued to watch him. 'What are you going to do?'

'Get Forensic to have a look at the letter. Someone wanted to upset Miss Morgan's applecart.'

Hawick perceptibly relaxed. 'That's true, isn't it?' He hesitated. 'I assume you now know all about the fuss over Bill Coombes's will? Yes? Not for me to tell you your business, but I was actually quite concerned about his niece Penelope Huntley's behaviour.'

'Do you think she sent the anonymous letters?'

'I don't know, Chief Inspector, but I honestly can't think who else could have.'

McLeish suppressed a small shock and felt Davidson shift in his chair. It had been Francesca who had pointed out gleefully, as they watched the tag end of the coverage of a party conference, that the use in political circles of the words 'frankly' or 'honestly' or 'truly' should cause sensible men to examine very carefully the content of any following statement. So, McLeish reckoned, the Minister not only at least half believed the allegation in the letters, but thought he had a good idea who had made it. And he would not have told the police anything about the earlier letter, had his hand not been forced by the inopportune arrival of another.

Deciding that he had asked all the questions he wanted answered for the moment, he thanked Giles Hawick demurely for his help and listened to Davidson ostentatiously closing a notebook and gathering up pencils. The Minister was looking both subdued and uneasy; a highly intelligent and intuitive customer, he had realized that the two policemen were treating him with some reserve.

'You're working on several avenues of enquiry, of course?' he asked hopefully.

'Yes, sir.'

'To any result?'

'It's early days yet, sir.'

The Minister winced slightly as he opened the door, recognizing a hand-off, however civilly administered. 'Where is Professor Thornton?' he demanded. 'In the waiting area? I'll collect him.' He escorted the policemen punctiliously to the lift, then stopped to look towards a man sitting in one of the group of chairs in the lobby. McLeish glanced across too, his attention caught by the man's absolute concentration. He was absorbed in reading a typescript, the noise and bustle of people continually going past making no impact on him at all.

'David,' Hawick called to him, and he looked up, focusing slowly. 'With you in a minute.'

The man nodded and went back to his papers like something going back into the sea. McLeish watched him covertly, remembering that this was the Professor Thornton who had been summoned on something to do with Huerter Textiles. And the dead girl had been pushing the rival interests of Barton. Remembering grimly that his best source of information was not at the moment available, he decided he would have to ask the man he had to hand.

'Minister, we are also of course talking to people who worked with Miss Morgan, and a name that keeps coming up is Huerter Textiles. I know it is the DTI rather than your Department which is principally involved.'

'A decision on assistance to Huerter Textiles lies with the government as a whole not with any particular Department.' This was said with an audible snap, and McLeish guessed Hawick had been saying something like it to several different audiences.

'I see. Has a decision been taken? I'm sorry, I don't know a great deal about the process,' he added mendaciously.

'No.'

And that's all I'm going to get, McLeish thought, as the lift arrived and the Minister extended his hand. He looked back past the Minister at the unconscious David Thornton, filing him for future reference: older bloke, bit heavy now, but probably handy in his time. Looked like a nice peaceful life, being a professor.

CHAPTER 10

'So he hasn't got an alibi at all, and he didn't tell us about an anonymous letter. Jesus wept.'

McLeish had taken Davidson with him to report to Commander Stevenson, so that he could have the benefit of both men's opinions if he wanted them.

'Did you think he believed the letters?'

The question was addressed to McLeish, who hesitated. '*I* thought so, sir. But he's one of those people who would have trouble accepting anything from that kind of source.'

The Commander considered him, and silently transferred his attention to Davidson, who was emboldened to speak. 'Letters like that would get up his nose, wouldn't they? I mean, he'd wonder, and then he'd keep his eyes open.'

'Would he have hit her?'

McLeish and Davidson had agreed on the way back that it did, unfortunately, strike them as perfectly possible that that cool, canny customer, if driven by sexual rage, would kill violently. McLeish, as senior officer present, took it on himself to convey this joint view to Stevenson.

The Commander shifted in his chair, giving a clear impression of a man with his back to the wall. 'So if he's so clever, why hasn't he an alibi?'

'Better no alibi than one we can break,' McLeish suggested, boldly.

'Mm. Mm. I'm not very happy with all this.'

We're ecstatic, of course, enjoying every minute, McLeish thought sourly.

'I'll have to talk to the AC. Dear, dear, dear. McLeish, I want a full report on the investigations so far on my desk by the end of the day. No point looking like that, we'll need it for the AC.'

True, McLeish thought fair-mindedly, as he removed himself and Davidson, but it made a maddening delay when he needed to see Jennifer Morgan. Galvanized by necessity, he dictated a rapid first-draft report, gave the tape to his secretary, and sat back and thought. Writing the report had made him realize that he really did not know enough about Jennifer Morgan. She had inherited a substantial legacy on her sister's death and it was possible that she hoped to inherit her sister's fiancé as well. He needed to know in detail where she had been over the weekend when her sister had gone missing.

Davidson put his head round the door. 'The Minister's fingerprints are on that letter, plus several sets the same — they'll be the constituency secretary's — but we're checking. Nothing else at all. The cut-out letters come from the *Daily Telegraph*.'

'Do they now? When did we take Hawick's prints?'

'Didn't have to. Special Branch had them.'

'That was useful.' McLeish, slightly shaken, was considering this as Catherine Crane appeared beside Bruce.

'Hello?' he said, trying not to light up like a lamp. 'Any luck? Come in both of you and we'll pool what we've got. Bruce and I had to go and see the Minister.' He brought Catherine quickly up to date.

'Well, I went off to see if I could find out where Penelope Huntley was those two days,' she said. 'Her statement seems to check. Her friends are a bit peculiar.'

'Not reliable witnesses?'

Catherine thought about it. 'Well, I don't believe they were lying deliberately. They're just not very reliable people, they don't have much idea of the day of the week at the best of times. They agreed, you know, that they had been out with Penelope late on Saturday and that she had turned up to see them on Sunday, but they're vague about the whole thing. I'll write it all down, but she was apparently in her own flat by herself till at least nine p.m. on Saturday, and from around two a.m. until two p.m. on Sunday.'

'Plenty of time to murder Angela and dump the body. No?'

'I can't see her or any of that lot being well enough organized, John. They'd have left tracks a mile wide.'

'Druggies?'

'Not seriously. I could smell hash and there were a lot of windows opened in a hurry when I got there. No sign of anything stronger — no kit around, the place was quite decently furnished and reasonably clean. I'd like to ask the local station if there's anything known, but I'd be surprised. Someone's probably drawing the dole when they shouldn't be, but it's that sort of level. Messy rather than serious crime. You know, half-dressed, hair not combed at eleven-thirty in the morning, everyone a bit sulky.'

'Middle-class?'

'Oh yes. Knew their rights; not particularly rattled once they realized what I was. I mean, basically educated enough to see that if I was asking about a murder, I wasn't going to bother about a dole fiddle or some hash being smoked. They were also quite forthcoming about Penelope, once we got talking. They all reckoned she had a fixation about Angela Morgan, couldn't talk about anything else, she always came back to that and how badly she'd been treated under her uncle's will. The bloke who owned the flat then got a bit worried, said no one was suggesting she would have killed Angela — so I did the bit about all evidence being important and several lines of enquiry being followed.'

Bruce Davidson swallowed his coffee noisily. 'Would Penelope have been sending the anonymous letters?'

'Could easily be. She is a bit round the twist, even her friends say so. I'd like to see her again and face her with the letters — I wish we'd known about them when we saw her yesterday.'

Both of them looked at John McLeish, who was hunched over his desk, elbows squared, looking too large for it and rather as if he was about to leap across it. 'That's important. If it was her — or if Hawick thought it was her — then he probably *didn't* believe what the first letter said. He knew she was a bit unhinged, he's a shrewd bloke.'

He looked sideways at Bruce Davidson to whom he deferred, though not always consciously, on all matters of sex, and was disappointed to see him looking openly amused.

'It worried him all right, John, you could see that, nae bother. He's one of those blokes who goes a lot on instinct.'

As the most successful politicians must do, McLeish silently agreed. The ones who concentrated entirely on policy, doing it all in their heads, or the ones who boiled around too busy with the noise going on inside their own skulls to listen — those were the ones that came unstuck and ended up either at the centre of a massive row or as disappointed old men with their memoirs. Rather the same thing happened to policemen who lost touch with their instincts, come to think of it — which was why he was going to talk to Jennifer Morgan this afternoon, whatever anyone else thought he should be doing.

McLeish turned Catherine and Bruce out of his office with instructions to Catherine to keep on with Miss Huntley, and Bruce to get his notes in order. He managed to find Jennifer Morgan in the fastness of the British Museum and arranged to see her later. After this he sat quietly, watching the telephone, trying to force himself to pick it up and talk to Francesca rather than just leaving the whole thing in limbo. The phone rang sharply, making him jump, and he looked automatically towards his secretary's office before realizing she must be out at lunch. He picked it up, apprehensively.

'Yes, thank you, will you hold for Perry Wilson, please? Thank you.' The voice, ruthlessly chirpy and strongly Caribbean-accented, brooked no argument and McLeish waited out a series of clicks and half-heard snatches of conversation, understanding immediately that Francesca had elected to use the brother to whom she was closest as an intermediary.

'John? Christ, you must be fed up with us — I'd not have let Frannie go if I'd been here, but I couldn't argue effectively from backstage in fucking Tokyo. Anyway she's got back, I'm back, and I'll deal with it from now on. Tris doesn't get out of that loony-bin he's in until he's signed out. And if there *is* a next time, he stays in jail, wherever he is — I've told him.'

'Must have encouraged him enormously.'

'You still pissed off, John?'

McLeish, considering his answer to that question on the assumption that it would go straight to Francesca, realized that he was boxed in. 'I haven't seen her yet, Perry. I was just ringing her when you came through.'

The momentary silence at the other end of the line told him that, whether he had meant to or not, he had put the brotherhood on warning.

'I'd have been *very* pissed off if I'd had a holiday booked,' the confident, slightly husky voice conceded. 'I guess I'm just telling you that Charlie and I at least know it was a diabolical liberty and we won't let it happen again. Busy, are you?'

McLeish agreed that he was, and asked civilly about the tour in Japan, finding himself unwillingly doubled up with laughter at Perry's sharply focused observations on Japanese policing methods as applied to rock-concert audiences.

As he put the phone down, having avoided any more personal questions, he found himself thinking that he would miss Perry, bloody nuisance though he was. He rang Francesca's office, now clear that he must get to her before her envoy reported.

'What about a drink around six? I'm working flat out.'

There was an anxious pause during which McLeish thought, meanly, that she was probably doing something with one of the brothers. This flash of self-righteousness died away as he recalled what was actually happening in his own life.

'Fine.' Francesca was grimly putting a line through a meeting with colleagues that had been convened at a good deal of trouble and expense. I am still reasonably sane, she thought, I know where my priorities are. 'How is it going?' she asked, politely and nervously. 'I am now sorry to have spoken ill of Angela — I mean, when we last talked she was only missing.'

This all too human piece of reasoning eased the tension. McLeish momentarily forgot his difficulties in the interests of getting a piece of the puzzle straight. 'It's bloody complicated. Look, you can tell me: would the fact that Angela's firm was lobbying for Barton be embarrassing for her fiancé as a government Minister? It didn't occur to me to ask last time.' He listened as he had so often before to Francesca thinking her way through a question.

'The short answer is yes, it must be — have been — embarrassing. But it's in the detail that it gets interesting. I went back from that lunch with Angela and reported up to Ministers so that they would know where the pressure was coming from and who was doing it. And I reminded them that the particular lobbyist for Barton was going to marry a Treasury Minister. I didn't *need* to remind them that Treasury would be opposed to assistance to Huerter, because Treasury is against assisting anyone, ever.'

McLeish made a note, thinking as he wrote. 'Were you warning your Ministers that Treasury might be more likely to win the battle in this case, since their hired lobbyist was engaged to the relevant Treasury Minister?'

'Quite the contrary. I was handing them a weapon. Very useful for my man to be able to wonder aloud whether it was not the firm to which Giles's fiancée was attached that was advising Barton.'

McLeish, who never ceased to be surprised by the lengths to which public servants would go to get their own way, drew a diagram thoughtfully. 'That would have got right up Mr Hawick's nose, wouldn't it?'

'Absolutely. He's a proud man. He was in the DTI, you know, when they were last in government, as a Parly Sec. Said to be OK then, but of course the Treasury will now have got at him.'

'What would he have done, Fran? Made Angela resign from Yeo Davis?'

'Long term, I'm sure he would. He wants to be PM, you know.'

'And in the short term?'

'This is where it gets difficult. Even if she'd resigned last week, my man could still have teased him with her Yeo Davis connection.'

'So Hawick would have had to think of something else. Some other way of covering his back?'

'That's right. That's what I've just seen.' Francesca sounded reluctantly amused. 'But I'm having problems telling you about it. You could ask him, surely? Hawick, I mean.'

They had always accepted the boundaries of each other's jobs and their professional secrets, and McLeish would normally have taken this as a signal not to press further. But now a light suddenly switched on in his mind. 'When I saw Hawick this morning, he was fixing a meeting about Huerter. With someone called David Thornton, who is part of your lot? Old bloke, looks like a boxer dressed as a professor.'

'*Not* part of our lot.' The protest was automatic and immediate. 'Wished on us by Treasury.' She laughed. 'All right, you've got it. The chap you saw is Professor Thornton, distinguished econometrist, erstwhile tutor to Giles Hawick, however many years ago he was at Oxford, and he's the Treasury's insurance policy. If his advice comes out that assistance to Huerter will screw up the economy in the northwest, then Treasury is on secure ground and can claim that their opposition is rooted in Pure Research. Anyone mentioning the machinations of Yeo Davis will be held to be suffering from sour grapes.'

McLeish considered this, carefully. Even if Giles Hawick had found a way of neutralizing any embarrassment caused by his prospective wife's trade, the man Francesca described would have resented having to take that sort of measure. And would have held it against his fiancée, in the sense that it would have made him more determined to get her to change jobs. Both she and Peter Yeo, by all accounts, would have resisted this fiercely. Equally, it wasn't a motive for murder: on this occasion Giles Hawick had found a way round whatever embarrassment she might cause him.

'Why is this Thornton with your lot, then?' he asked, surfacing.

'So that we can provide him with the facts and figures to use against our policy, of course.'

'Ah.' McLeish was on familiar ground. 'Like being told off to help the Chief Constable from another force when he is investigating your lot.'

'That's right.'

'How far has he got?'

'Oh, nowhere yet. But he's smart, and he's an operator. It's taken him twenty-four hours to make us import some help for him — two of his best PhD students, bristling with portable computers. Which reminds me, I have to find them an office with an electric plug in it, they should be so lucky.'

She hesitated. 'John? I'm sorry I went. I did think it was necessary, but I won't again.' McLeish grunted, oppressed and embarrassed, but she didn't press him. 'See you at six.'

* * *

McLeish put the thought of the evening ahead firmly out of his mind and applied himself to the coming interview with Jennifer Morgan. He caught up with Catherine Crane on his way down the corridor and walked into the canteen with her. It was an alarming and exhilarating sensation to escort a girl so beautiful that she cast a reflected glow on any man she was with. The sensation of being a much-envied top dog as custodian of this dazzling beauty was, he conceded, absolutely delightful, probably addictive, and not to be indulged here for fear of endangering both their jobs.

'Do you want me for Jennifer Morgan?' she asked, gracefully refusing an extra helping of everything from the man charged with doling out the vegetables.

'No, thanks.' McLeish had already decided without conscious thought that he would take Bruce rather than Catherine, and as he examined his reasoning he realized why. Jennifer Morgan had lived much of her life under threat from a more attractive sister and was likely to be on the defensive if he brought with him another very sexually successful young woman. He would take Bruce, and see if their joint masculine charm succeeded in relaxing her a bit.

* * *

'I never come here, it's ridiculous,' he observed to Davidson as they worked their way through a crowd of dazed Americans in the British Museum. 'People flock to it from thousands of miles away; I live here and I've not set foot in the place since I was a kid and Mum and Dad brought me to London for the day.' He stopped to peer admiringly at an illuminated manuscript in a glass case. 'Look at that!' Davidson bent obediently beside him and, like him, was gripped by the tiny, gold-illumined figures.

'I'll come back,' McLeish said earnestly to the case after a reverent couple of minutes, knowing he probably wouldn't, and bustled them both on.

They arrived at a tiny office off a dusty corridor which contained, largely, a desk and Jennifer Morgan peacefully contemplating a big blue-and-white ceramic pot. It was an excellent picture of an academic removed from present-day worldly considerations, McLeish thought, as they shook hands and she moved the pot carefully out of the way.

'Is that a good piece?' he enquired respectfully, and she looked surprised.

'It's quite nice, but I'm now sure it's a copy of a seventeenth-century original. It's not ours, but it's my turn this month to advise on the things the general public bring in for identification. I wasn't absolutely sure about this one at first — it's outside my period of expertise — so I asked if we could hold on to it overnight. I told the woman who brought it it was probably a copy, so she shouldn't be nursing great hopes.'

'People can bring things in, can they?'

'Oh yes. And do. Every now and then, of course, someone walks in off the street with a treasure. The trouble with ceramics is that they've usually been keeping something like car keys in it which damages the lustre, or they've chipped it. But you wanted to talk to me, Chief Inspector.'

McLeish, who had been harmlessly engaged in the process of putting a witness at her ease, was mildly chagrined to be called to order, but disposed himself and Davidson in the small, uncomfortable chairs and considered Angela Morgan's elder sister. She looked both more comfortable and more of a personality in her own office than she had in her parents' house, and McLeish saw that in many fields she would have held her own against an aggressive, lively, younger sister. This girl was also good-looking, though in a different style. Her hair was up today in a soft bun, which showed off her short, straight nose and classic rounded jaw. Evidently senior museum staff did not feel it necessary to wear the plain suits favoured by senior officials in the DTI, and she was dressed in a gently pleated pale-grey skirt with a neat round-necked pink shirt tucked into it, and round pearl earrings.

He noticed that she was sneaking another look at the pot which she had moved out of the way.

'Not sure about it?' he asked amicably, and she looked at him, amused.

'Yes, I am really. But it's nearly right. It's a pity.'

And we don't want anything nearly right in our museum, he thought, or possibly anywhere around us. 'Last time we met, the circumstances made it difficult for me to ask you very much about your sister, and I was hoping you now could help us a bit more.'

'Of course, if I can. Does this mean that you are not making much progress? In finding who killed her, I mean?'

'It's early days yet,' McLeish said automatically, but seeing the dispassionate look she cast on him he decided to abandon this line. 'No, we haven't made much progress. We've done a lot of work and maybe cleared some irrelevancies out of the way, but we have no real feeling for why she was killed, or by whom.'

'The answer to the first question being different in relation to the answer to the second question?'

'Yes, of course. But if you are starting from motive, as I am, it isn't obvious. Two people benefited financially from her death.'

'Me and Penelope Huntley, poor girl.' Jennifer spoke calmly, gazing out of the window, taking McLeish by surprise.

'Why poor girl?'

'Penelope? Because she was obsessed, eaten up with jealousy and miserable.'

'You knew her.'

'I met her at Bill Coombes's funeral. Then she came and did one of our courses here, and she talked to me a bit. I didn't like her but actually I do think she was badly treated. She thought of her uncle as her father, and he rejected her. Or that's how she saw it.'

McLeish remembered the appointment in Angela Morgan's diary.

'Did Angela know Penelope well, then?'

'Much better than I did, because of Bill, of course. I know she felt she couldn't go on seeing Penelope because she was so peculiar, but that was months ago.'

'Were they on good enough terms to have lunch together?'

Jennifer Morgan looked startled. 'I wouldn't have thought so.'

McLeish explained about the entry in Angela's diary and noted with interest that Jennifer Morgan seemed suddenly wary and withdrawn. '*You* don't know why they were to have lunch together? I mean Angela — your sister — didn't say anything to you about it?'

'No. We weren't close in that way, Chief Inspector — I mean, we didn't seem to discuss our social lives much. Of course she kept up with a huge acquaintance; it was part of her business to do so.'

'Did you have many friends in common?' He watched her hesitate, and spread his hands. 'I'm just trying to get a feel for what she was like, who her friends were.' He was sounding baffled and Angela's sister relented.

'Not really. We both knew lots of the same people, you know how it is with families, but her friends are — were — are — different. Mine tend to be academics or museum people, or of course people I knew at Oxford.'

'Was it at Oxford you met Mr Hawick?'

She looked at him warily, but he sat placidly and she decided to talk.

'Yes, it was. At a party at Exeter. He's ten years older than I am, but we were both at that college. I was one of the first girls to go there when it became mixed. He was being very funny — apologetically conservative, saying he couldn't quite get used to meeting women who'd been at the same college as he was.' She was sitting up straight and there was colour in her cheeks. McLeish tried not to breathe, but she fell silent.

'So it was you who introduced him to your sister?' he asked, knowing that it had not been.

'No.' The voice was without colour. 'No. Angela met him when she took a client to lobby him about something.'

'But you and he were already friends?'

'We had gone out a few times, usually in company with other people. It wasn't an affair, Chief Inspector, if that is what you were thinking. Angela and I usually liked different men. He invited her out straightaway.'

And you'd been hoping to sink into him, McLeish thought, with something uncomfortably close to pity. 'Did you mind?' he asked, ruthlessly.

'Yes, I did,' she said, surprising him again. 'I liked him, I still like him, and I thought he and Angela were not basically well suited. He's actually very academic, you know.'

Doesn't mean he fancies them academic, though, lovey, does it? McLeish thought. 'But they were going to marry just the same?'

She looked at him levelly. 'Oh yes. He was very much in love with her.'

'But not she with him.' McLeish was on to it like a big cat, and Jennifer, taken aback, smoothed her skirt nervously.

'I didn't say that. I'm sure she was . . . I mean she definitely wanted to marry him.'

'Someone else about, though, left over from the past?' McLeish asked chattily, and she flushed scarlet, clashing horribly with the pale-pink blouse. He watched her, alight with interest, as she pressed both hands to her cheeks.

'You are drawing quite unwarranted inferences,' she said, with dignity. 'She was happy because she was marrying an admirable man, then someone killed her. You should be trying to find out who did it rather than making insinuations about Angela.'

'We are trying to do just that, Miss Morgan. Do you have any views on who might have wanted to kill her?'

'Apart from me and Penelope Huntley, you mean?'

McLeish blinked, acknowledging an unexpectedly ferocious counter-attack, and she followed her advantage.

'I think it may have been someone she hardly knew.' She hesitated, but she was now well in control of herself. 'I expect everyone says this, but it must have been a stranger. She was very confident, you know, always thought she knew best, that no one would hurt her, that she could walk through fire. She never told anyone till afterwards but she hitch-hiked from the East to the West Coast of America by herself, one long vacation. She was twenty. She said to me that she didn't give it a thought, that if you didn't worry you didn't get into trouble. Dad encouraged her, of course.'

The echo of old resentment sounded in this recital, and McLeish had a vision of the younger, bolder girl confidently seizing things the older, quieter, more oppressed sister had feared to try for.

'So I wondered,' Jennifer Morgan was leaning towards him, 'I wondered if she had met up with someone she didn't know awfully well and let them buy her a drink, or taken them back to her flat for a drink, and they'd murdered her. She always said she knew whether a man was all right or not.' She was pink with the need to convince him.

'You're assuming it would have been a man?'

She nodded, wordlessly, and fumbled for a handkerchief.

McLeish sat back, feeling Davidson doing the same. He had always been worried about confident, sociable Francesca, who had odd acquaintances everywhere and would not have thought twice about going off for a drink with them or inviting them home. Of course, there were usually hot and cold running brothers round her place, but nonetheless . . . It was more than possible to imagine Angela Morgan, at a loose end without her fiancé on Saturday, meeting up with an acquaintance and offering him a drink or letting him buy her one, and finding out far too late that she was entertaining a psychopath.

Jennifer Morgan met his eyes.

'It is possible, isn't it?'

'It's possible,' he acknowledged. 'But the most likely murderer is someone she knew very well — that's how it goes, I'm afraid.' He paused, but she did not seem disposed to comment. 'I'd like to ask you something else. Mr Hawick has told us he received anonymous letters stating that Angela was still having an affair with Peter Yeo.'

She was looking at him, immobile, eyes wide, hands clenched.

'I understand she had at one stage been having an affair with him?'

Jennifer Morgan breathed out and her hands moved again. 'Yes. You said "Still"? Is that what the letter said?'

'Yes.'

'Poor Giles.'

'You assume it's true.'

'No, I don't.' The denial was a fraction slow. 'I meant, poor Giles, what a horrid thing to get.'

'Who do you think would have sent such a letter?'

'Well, can't you tell? Doesn't it have fingerprints on? Can't you tell from the writing?'

'No. The writer was careful.'

She stared at him, blankly, then looked away.

'Who are you thinking of?'

She dropped her eyes. 'Well, I don't suppose it'll make you any more suspicious of her. Poor Penelope — I told you, she is very mad on the subject of Angela. And it really didn't have to be true, you know, she would have done anything to upset Angela.'

'Even kill her?'

'I've always thought she was too mad. So did Angela. I mean, she wasn't frightened of her, she just didn't want any dealings with her. You don't need to look like that. Chief Inspector — I know I said Angela was reckless, but I *agreed* with her about Penelope. What if we were both wrong?' She was kneading her hands together and her voice was getting shrill. McLeish hastily tried to defuse the situation.

'We're still at the stage of looking at all the possibilities,' he said soothingly, 'and there's nothing so far to suggest Miss Huntley was involved. Now, can we just go over your movements on the last Saturday and Sunday week? This is a routine we're going through with everyone close to your sister, and I've only an outline of where you were.'

'When did she die?'

'Somewhere between Saturday morning, when she said goodbye to Mr Hawick, and about Monday morning. Not later apparently.'

'I was here for a bit on the Saturday morning, and I talked to one of the porters. Then I did some shopping — a lot of shopping. I went to Harrods and Harvey Nichols, looking for a cocktail dress, then I had a snack in a funny place — a pizza. I can't remember what the restaurant was called, but I could find it again, I'm sure. I went back to my flat about six o'clock and just had a quiet evening. I went on Sunday morning for lunch with Mum and Dad, and came down again first thing on Monday morning.'

McLeish looked sideways to see if Davidson had got all that and saw from the set of his jaw that he was not a happy man. Hardly surprising; this was yet another very difficult alibi to check.

'Did ye have any luck with finding a dress?' Davidson asked, twinkling at her, and Jennifer looked at him in surprise.

'No. I couldn't find anything I liked. I must have tried on twenty.'

'There'll be someone remembers you, likely?'

'I suppose so. There were a lot of people about, and I was just picking things out and trekking off to fitting-rooms with them. I mean, no one dances attendance on you anymore. At least not on Saturdays in Harrods.'

Davidson was heard to observe that they did in Ayr, now, but McLeish suppressed him and started to wind down the interview, uneasily aware that it was already five-fifteen and he was meeting Francesca at six. Jennifer said goodbye to them and returned to her work.

McLeish glanced back as he closed the door; she was looking into space past the doubtful bowl, hands laid flat on her desk, wide skirt trailing the floor by her chair. It would have made a picture, he thought, struck suddenly — the bare, uncluttered office, the girl sitting so still, and the bowl breaking up the flat space on top of the desk. 'But what was the artist trying to say?' his teacher-mother's voice asked inside his head, and he thought about that as he walked down the corridor with Davidson. Something about loneliness and hope: Jennifer Morgan looked like a prisoner, waiting for something or someone. He stopped in thought and realized what was bothering him.

'Bruce, she wasn't all that surprised about the anonymous letters, was she? She jumped, but it wasn't surprise.'

Davidson thought about that. 'She was pretty defensive,' he allowed.

'Could she have sent them herself?'

'Not her style, surely?' Bruce protested, seeking for words. 'Too much of an intellectual.' He knew as he spoke that he had really no idea; there might be no limits to what experts in Turkish ceramics might do.

'She's a woman as well as an intellectual,' McLeish pointed out. 'She still fancies Hawick, but there he was, hell-bent on marrying her sister because she was sexier, yes? Well, how would she stop that? She couldn't tell him face to face that Angela was still having it off with her guv'nor; Hawick would not forgive her that. She'd have had to do it some other way. First thing she checked, too — that there were no prints, that she hadn't slipped up.'

Davidson acknowledged that the hypothesis made a lot of sense. 'Do you want to go back to her?'

'Not yet. Have we got her prints?'

'Aye. I took them when I did her parents'. We can talk to her again when she signs her statement. You in a rush to get back?'

'I'm having a drink with Francesca at the Royal.'

'Good.' The commendation was both prompt and vigorous. McLeish looked at him in surprise but Davidson avoided his eye. 'I'd heard she was back yesterday,' he added, concentrating studiously on unlocking the car. 'She did the trick in New York, then?'

'Yes.' McLeish was disconcerted by the speed with which Davidson had smelt out some difficulty between him and Francesca. 'I spoke to her earlier today,' he added, intending to mislead.

'Ah, well. And you've the weekend coming up,' Davidson observed, evidently relieved. McLeish gritted his teeth.

He got himself dropped at the pub where he and Francesca usually met, and went in, observing gratefully that she had not yet arrived and that the place was empty of people they knew. He bought himself a beer, acknowledging as he did that he had no idea what he was going to say to her. He turned and there she was, in a rush as usual: short, straight hair ruffled by the wind and standing straight up at the back of her head. She looked thinner in the face and very tired, the dark-blue eyes sunk back into their sockets.

She came over to him, looking at him carefully as she stood on her toes to kiss his cheek. He kissed her back, inhaling the familiar scent of lilies of the valley, feeling clumsy and heavy, and incompetent. He got her a drink and took her over to a table in the corner, well clear of other customers, and felt rather than saw the quick, anxious look she gave him as they both sat down.

'You got Tristram home, then?' he asked for the second time that day, and she confirmed that he was even now installed in a suitable specialist institution.

'The Americans were glad to get rid of him in the end — they deported him, of course, but that was much the lesser of several evils.' She hesitated. 'As it turns out, I really wasn't needed. I mean, I suppose Tris and Jeremy found it comforting to have me there, but they didn't *need* me. The company's lawyers did it all, and I was just a spare wheel. Even if I had been more needed, I still shouldn't have gone and bitched us up.' She watched him, but McLeish could not manage to speak. 'How is the case? Not much advanced since lunchtime, I suppose?'

'Not a lot.' McLeish was feeling angry and foolish but could not work out where to start. He fidgeted crossly, sending an ashtray and a plate of crisps flying.

'Are you still furious with me?' Francesca regally ignored the weary attendant who came to pick up the bits.

'Yes. No. That isn't the point.' McLeish was horrified at himself but helpless. 'I've been thinking . . . I'd like some time on my own,' he said, hopelessly.

'You've got someone else.' Francesca went white and her blue eyes widened with shock.

McLeish got himself under control, took her drink from her and held one very cold hand firmly between both his own. 'Yes, I'm sorry. I don't know if it'll work.'

'Who is she?' The colour had started to come back to Francesca's face and the skin looked blotchy.

'Someone who works with me.'

'A colleague.' Her voice made it clear that she understood very precisely what she was being told; her own working relations were close and affectionate. 'That very beautiful girl I saw you with yesterday.'

He hesitated, belated worries about the whole thing getting back to his superiors besieging him, but she had made a statement rather than asked a question, and was looking at her glass intently as she struggled with tears. He watched her, still holding her hand. 'Let me get you another drink,' he said, distressed, having nothing else to offer. He glanced up to see how realistic this was, since the pub was filling up fast, and saw Catherine just coming in with a DI and two sergeants. His hands tightened convulsively in shock and embarrassment and Francesca looked up and followed his eye. She was always quick, he thought dully, as she looked across the room to Catherine and back to him.

'Is she meeting you?' She was weeping but angry, feeling for her gloves and handbag and shrugging on her coat.

'No, no. It's a coincidence, she didn't know I was here. Fran, don't go like that, for God's sake.'

She looked at him, the long bones in her face very prominent. 'You can finish my drink.' The stem snapped in her fingers and the glass tipped in her hands and she stared unseeing at the mess for a second before getting to her feet, nodding briefly to the barman's tentative greeting, and walking out of the swing door, straight-backed, leaving him pinned behind the flooded table.

CHAPTER 11

John McLeish walked heavily into his office a good hour later than he meant to, at nine-thirty a.m., and nodded to his secretary who was ensconced behind her typewriter. 'I'll get you some coffee,' she volunteered, hands stilled on the keyboard, and he realized he must look as worn as he felt. He had wanted to escape to the sanctuary of his office after the scene with Francesca, but had in the end gone home with Catherine as the only way of assuring her that he was not going to hold her to blame for her presence in the pub at the critical moment. The process of consoling her had been enormously pleasurable for him, as a small voice reminded him, but he was tired out this morning and would have liked to put his head down on the desk.

He looked over his coffee to see Bruce Davidson hovering at the door.

'We're not due at Mrs Yeo's till eleven, are we?'

'No. I've got some news on the letter that Hawick got: no prints.'

'Oh, thank you *very* much.'

Davidson scowled. 'Aye, well. Thought you'd like to know.'

McLeish watched him, puzzled. 'What's the *bad* news, Bruce?'

Davidson sat down, uninvited, and McLeish saw that he was both uncomfortable and angry. This was so unusual in the equable Davidson that he waited, unable to think what to ask.

'I just wanted you to know, John, that when I told Sergeant Crane where you were last evening, I had in mind that she would know not to join you.'

McLeish stared back at him, discarding various responses and realizing that Francesca's walk-out must have been widely reported. He arrived at what he hoped was a reasonable recognition of five years of working closely with Bruce Davidson.

'Francesca and I have been having trouble and that's not Catherine's fault.'

'Is it not?'

McLeish's head jerked up and Davidson backed off slightly. 'You'd no doubt have been better off without an audience, whatever.' He was still plainly outraged.

'And better off without all the gossip — has no one any work to do round here?' McLeish out of guilt was suddenly just as angry.

'We'll need to leave in an hour — I'll come back then.' Bruce Davidson walked off in a cloud of pique and disapproval, leaving McLeish shaken, and, as he reluctantly acknowledged to himself, rather flattered. He had not understood that the beautiful, desirable Catherine was both sufficiently possessive of him and jealous of Francesca not to have trusted him with her. What kind of man would start a serious affair with someone like Catherine and immediately go back to a longer-standing relationship? He was shaking his head, both disturbed and titillated by the whole thing, when the answer came to him. A long-married man might have done that — taken a night off from the most dazzling new girl to make sure that his foxhole was still there and that the home fires would be kept burning while he was off on an adventure.

Well, he was already half aware that there had been a married bloke in Catherine's immediate past, and now he knew more about him. Poor Catherine. He gritted his teeth as he thought of the scene in the pub last night with him pinned like a right nerd behind the table, then put it resolutely out of his mind and gazed inimically at his in-tray.

'John.' It was his secretary. 'The Commander wants you. Now. He knows you have an appointment at eleven.'

Commander Stevenson was looking particularly pared down and military, barking orders at his secretary. 'Right, McLeish. Sit down. Did you know Hawick is due to go to Washington next week?'

McLeish cursed inwardly. 'He did say something about it the first time I saw him, yes sir, but it slipped my mind. He said nothing yesterday.'

'Well, it was lucky Special Branch were good enough to tell me, wasn't it?'

McLeish forbore to observe that it was part of their job to deal with that sort of liaison.

'So. I've read your report, and put a copy up to the AC. You're nowhere near an arrest, are you?'

'No sir,' McLeish agreed, and the Commander glared at him.

'Well, you'd better get off your backside. My God, if Hawick did it we can't arrest him in the States.'

McLeish was moved, unwisely, to point out that in that event the Yard would simply wait till Hawick was in UK jurisdiction again, surely, and found himself blasted out of his chair. He realized, as he should have done in the first place, that the idea that he might have to arrest a Minister of the Crown anywhere was what was unnerving his superior.

'I like the Huntley girl for this one,' the Commander said firmly, when he had cooled down. 'Never neglect the obvious, McLeish.'

John McLeish agreed, through a worsening headache, to try not to do that, and detoured, via another cup of coffee and three Anadins, to find a woodenly correct Bruce

Davidson. They drove silently over towards the Yeos' Chelsea house, one look at Davidson's righteously sullen profile having decided McLeish not to struggle with his headache and run through Davidson's last interview with Claudia Yeo. They arrived on the Yeos' doorstep virtually without having exchanged a word. McLeish put a finger wearily on the bell set to the right of the neat neo-Georgian front door.

He was mildly taken aback by the woman who opened it to him. Davidson had described a woman who had let herself go a bit — well, this one had reined herself in again, in that case. Her hair was an elegant artificial dark blond with careful highlights, and her smart navy suit, worn with an immaculate white blouse and some chunky, matt-gold jewellery, had been carefully thought out. She was a bit plump, maybe, in an ideal world, but this was no distracted middle-aged woman; this one had all her buttons on and was well at the centre of her universe. She greeted him civilly, and only a touch nervously, and led them both to an immaculately tidy living-room, complete with fire and fresh flowers. Money spent here, McLeish thought, deciding which of the elegant thin-legged chairs would best support his weight, and seeing his dilemma reflected in a particularly pleasant oval mirror.

'Have the big armchair there, Chief Inspector, it's the one Peter — my husband — sits in.' Claudia Yeo was openly amused. 'The others are all right . . . they've never collapsed yet . . . but they are rather old. I'm not quite sure what you want to know. I told Sergeant Davidson all about my drink with poor Angela.'

'We are, of course, trying to establish just where everyone close to Miss Morgan was at around the time she disappeared,' McLeish said pleasantly. Another thing taught him by an early mentor was the use of the phrase 'of course' to legitimize whatever statement you might be making, as in: 'That was, of course, while mother was away in Broadmoor.' Mrs Yeo passed this particular sample without a blink, and described her movements on Saturday with only a few hesitations.

'Peter went to the office early, and I went shopping. We didn't have the children that weekend, you see, although usually one of them is with us, so I stayed out for lunch. I ate at Harrods, in the Dress Circle — that's what they call their lunch place. I didn't get back till well after six, then had a rest and a bath and joined Peter for dinner with some friends. I'll give you the name of the people if you want it.'

'Your husband — Mr Yeo — didn't come home first to change?'

'No, he had gone to see a film, and he rang me to say he would change at the office. He always has a spare set of clothes there, since he very often goes out directly from the office.'

For Sunday her account tallied with Peter Yeo's statement, McLeish decided, listening to it: they had spent the day together. No matter what Davidson was feeling he would have alerted McLeish to any discrepancies, even if he had had to ask a direct question. Unless one of the Yeos was lying to protect the other, any murders committed on Sunday would have to have been a team effort. For Saturday, however, neither of them appeared to be able to produce any independent witnesses to their movements. Mrs Yeo had managed to buy a suit — the one she had on, indeed. At Harrods, yes, rather early in the day, but she had been less lucky thereafter. She had put it on her account; the chit would be somewhere.

McLeish sighed, needing his lunch, but deciding he must tackle the question raised by the anonymous letter to Giles Hawick. He just wasn't feeling up to much in the way of a delicate touch.

'Mrs Yeo,' he began heavily, trying to lean forward in the big armchair, 'I understand that your husband and Miss Morgan had been business partners for some time?'

'Angela had been a partner for only about a year.' The correction was unexpectedly sharp. 'She had worked for the firm for about two years before that.'

'How did she come to join it, can you remember? Did she know your husband before she became his colleague?'

'Yes.' It was a very reluctant confirmation of something they already knew. 'She was working as a political adviser, and he met her then.'

'So he — and you — had really known her quite a long time? The thing is, Mrs Yeo, that Mr Hawick has just told us that he had received an anonymous letter some months ago suggesting that your husband and Miss Morgan were having an affair. Or rather that they were continuing an earlier affair.'

'How many months ago?'

McLeish was wrong-footed. 'I beg your pardon?'

She looked at him, patches of red showing under her make-up. 'I imagine someone will have told you by now that Peter *did* have a silly affair with Angela, but that was well over a year ago. He told me about it, and said it hadn't been serious and they were stopping by mutual consent. She had someone else she wanted.'

'The "someone else" that Miss Morgan wanted — did your husband say who that was?'

'No, but I'm sure it was Giles — Hawick, I mean. Well, I was not overjoyed about all this, as I'm sure you can imagine, so I was much relieved when it became clear she *was* going to marry Giles. We knew him before Angela met him.'

'So you don't believe your husband was still having an affair with Angela Morgan, as the letter suggested?'

'No.' She was tight-lipped and lying like the proverbial trooper.

McLeish watched unmoving, hearing Davidson's cough confirm his own view. 'Have you any idea who might have written such a letter?'

She looked at him, resentfully. 'I have no idea. Surely you can find out, by fingerprints or something?'

'There are no prints,' McLeish said grimly, remembering that Jennifer Morgan had taken exactly the same line.

'You don't think I wrote it, do you?' She put her coffee cup down sharply, spilling some in the saucer. 'For God's sake, Chief Inspector, I *wanted* her to get married so she wouldn't need to go on sleeping with Peter forever.'

'Would she have continued to work with your husband after she had married Giles Hawick?'

'Of course she wouldn't! Or not for long. Giles would have made her stop. I was at school with his sister — I've known him for yonks. He's always reckoned he's going to be Prime Minister by the time he's fifty. He wouldn't have let her go on working for a firm which earns its money by influencing government, he couldn't have afforded to. The party's very windy about that sort of thing, always has been.'

McLeish decided that on this point she was telling the truth. She had been confident that this marriage would have removed Angela Morgan from her husband's life. Equally, she had not been at all confident that Angela's affair with her husband was truly over.

'It must have been difficult for everyone, having her continue in the partnership?' he tried, cautiously.

'I wanted Peter to ask her to go last year, rather than make her a partner. But the firm was having a bit of a difficult time, and she put up a lot of cash — I suppose you know how she earned *that* — and Peter said it would be difficult to replace her. He thought she was marvellous, and not just in the sack.'

McLeish sat back, watching her pour more coffee, the lights in her hair bright in the February sun, very much in command of the high-ceilinged, pale, elegant room with its gilded mirrors and expensive ornaments. She looked well — in fact she looked blooming, and as she glanced challengingly at him he realized she looked like someone who has won an important prize after a long barren period of effort. Well, she had, hadn't she? She had, literally, survived the persistent threat to her marriage represented by Angela Morgan; she had her husband back and with him her confidence. And good luck to her — unless, of course, she had decided that the only way to get him back was to kill her rival. In which case, her conversation with Angela Morgan three days before she died might not have been an innocent chat about wedding presents but a completely different interview in which Claudia Yeo had threatened Angela Morgan. But with what? Exposure of the continuing affair to Giles Hawick carried with it the risk that he would simply pull out and not marry her, leaving the field to Peter Yeo. It was the same argument that militated against her being the writer of the anonymous letters.

'You've known Giles Hawick a long time. How do you think he would have reacted to a letter of that kind?'

Claudia looked at him, wide-eyed, the faint lines round the mouth and eyes showing clear under the careful make-up. She frowned, puzzled. 'But he didn't react — I mean you said this letter was weeks ago, didn't you? Well, the marriage was still going ahead, Giles was still devoted to her.'

Ten minutes later they were still no further on, and McLeish decided to call it a day.

'What did we get from that, Bruce?' he asked, hoping that Davidson and he were on speaking terms.

'She thought the affair with her husband was still on, and she's the one most likely to know. She's not the same lassie I saw last time; everything's come up roses for her.'

'But if the marriage *was* still on, she ought to have been all right then?'

'She has to have been more doubtful about that marriage than she's saying. After all, the girl's dead — it's even better than her being married to another bloke.'

McLeish thought of the lively face in the photograph and sighed. 'I wish to God Hawick could account for his time better on the Saturday. It's time we worked harder on the other end, Bruce: we need to see if we can find any trace of Angela that day. Neighbours?'

'Done all that — the notes are a bittie delayed, sorry. So far we've found no one who saw her at all round by her flat.'

McLeish thought about it, trying to guess what Angela might have done with her fiancé out of town. 'What about her office? Might she have been there?'

'No. Peter Yeo was there from mid-morning, remember?' Davidson objected. 'Or so he says,' he added slowly.

'And by himself, or so he says. Do that one, Bruce — talk to everyone round Yeo's office. Someone may have seen her. We'd be a lot further forward if we knew where she was that day.'

Bruce Davidson, to his relief, accepted this task with enthusiasm, and left him.

* * *

On a cold Monday morning at the DTI two young men in their early twenties, two mini-computers, Rajiv Sengupta and Francesca Wilson were all gathered in a room too small to accommodate them.

'Right. All plugged in? Regional Offices Employment stats for the last thirty-six months by Travel to Work Area in that pile; notified vacancies for ditto by ditto in that pile. When you've decided what you want to do with them, or when you want some more, please ring me or my HEO. Or Rajiv, I suppose.' Francesca was white with tiredness and had become very staccato and authoritative, cutting off questions from Thornton's two graduate students.

'Well thank you very much, that's an excellent start,' the braver and more sociable of the two said as cordially as he could, getting not a flicker of acknowledgement.

'I'll tell Professor Thornton where you are,' Rajiv said, lazily. 'I expect he'd like to know.' He observed with foreboding that this had totally passed Francesca by; she was deaf to him and everyone else at the moment. He drew her gently into the passage, leaving Thornton's team to fall on the papers.

'When did you assemble all those stats?'

'Oh, yesterday. Sunday.'

'Were you here late?'

'Yes. I don't quite remember how late.'

Rajiv looked at her profile, steered her into his office and gave her coffee, which she took without emerging from whatever place of darkness she was in. He watched her; he had taught her when she was a nineteen-year-old undergraduate and he had not seen her look so ill since the break-up of her young, ill-considered marriage when she was twenty-six.

'Fran, what is it? You and John quarrelled?'

'Yes. No. He's got someone else. Well, it wasn't working very well anyway, I suppose.'

Rajiv considered her seriously. 'Couldn't you get him back?'

'Like how? *I'm* supposed to beg and plead with him?'

Rajiv looked at her with simple exasperation as she sat upright and outraged, pride holding her spine up, skin blotchy beneath some hastily applied make-up.

'Anyway, it wouldn't work,' she said, quellingly, to her coffee. 'He's only just found this girl and he doesn't want to stop, does he? It's sex we're talking about here, Rajiv.' She contrived to make it sound like scarlet fever, but Rajiv recognized that she was as usual looking a fact in the eye. If a reconciliation were to come it would take time, and this proud, over-active creature drinking coffee as if it were hemlock would not give it time.

'Go home, Francesca. You have done more than your duty by those young men. Professor Thornton will be stunned.'

She put down her coffee and sighed, and Rajiv thought he had never seen her look so defeated.

'I can't. I'm chaperoning Jamie Brett-Smith — he's doing a guest appearance at the St Joe's Foundation Concert.'

'I know the child is your godson and a major talent, but does he not have a mother who could do this?' Rajiv objected.

'He does, but his father is ill again.' Francesca would not look at him.

'I have to say, darling, that I feel a passing sympathy for John. It cannot have been easy to fight his way through the undergrowth of your life.'

'Shut *up*, Rajiv.'

Francesca put her coffee down, got up clumsily and blundered out of his office, leaving him feeling both guilty and depressed. He decided to give credit where it was due, and telephoned Professor Thornton to tell him that contrary to all reasonable expectations his young men were installed, organized, and in receipt of enough raw data to keep them going for a couple of days. David Thornton welcomed this news cautiously and rang through to Giles Hawick, who was sounding bone-weary and harassed.

'I've managed to get the meeting put off till I'm back from Washington, David, so you've a bit of time. I know in my bones it's a nonsense assisting Huerter when Barton exists, but my DTI colleagues are putty in the hands of their officials. No, no more news about Angela. I don't know whether that's good or bad.'

He wasn't sure he was wholly in favour of Miss Wilson, David Thornton thought, as he wished Hawick luck in Washington. He had watched her performance that morning with something between admiration and irritation; she was so competent and so obviously suffering that he had not dared suggest any alternative to her method, for fear she would disintegrate. Trouble with a boyfriend, he had been quietly told, as if any reasonably experienced university teacher could not have observed that for himself. Glancing at his watch, he saw it was time he left if he was to get to his son's school concert.

Richard was the much-loved eight-year-old child of his second marriage and had not been born till David Thornton was forty-four. Thornton arrived in good time and the headmaster detached himself to greet him, in deference, he supposed, to his seniority. He exchanged civilities with the man, who assured him that Richard was happy and enjoyed his music; just as well, David Thornton reflected, given the demands of a choir school on its children. He was politely telling the headmaster how much Richard's mother regretted missing the concert, when he saw, perhaps ten feet away, young Miss Wilson, very much at home, emerging from one of the form-rooms.

'Sorry, Jonathan — I thought I saw a young colleague, Francesca Wilson. Surely she is not old enough to have a child here?'

'Francesca? Oh, you know her? No, she isn't a parent, she is looking after her godson, James Brett-Smith, who is doing two solos tonight. Have you heard him sing? No?

Then there is a treat in store. He left us last summer for Grantchester, but his voice is holding although he must be fourteen. We know Francesca very well here; all four of her brothers are old boys and two were the cathedral trebles for their year.'

He hailed Francesca, who was peering at him doubtfully across the room. 'I understand you know Professor Thornton? His son is in the first year.'

Francesca was looking somewhat better, David Thornton was relieved to see, restored by whatever she had been doing.

'Oh, I see. I thought I was hallucinating.'

'Having seen enough of me this week?' David Thornton enquired gently, and the headmaster looked at them uneasily.

'So, how is Jamie then, Francesca?' he asked, hastily.

'He'll be OK, he's just nervous. I was on my way to get him; he needs to run through his bits again.'

'You can have Room 8, Francesca. David, your lad is rehearsing, but of course you could see him for a minute.'

David Thornton said promptly he would much rather not disturb his son, but that, if allowed, he would love to watch young Brett-Smith practise. Francesca looked at him doubtfully, but accepted him, and he found himself in a small room with her and a spindly, tall, blond boy in a tidy, dark suit rather too small for him, who shook hands with the grave courtesy of the public schoolboy.

Francesca sat down at the piano and played the introduction to the Handel anthem, 'And he shall feed his sheep'. A competent pianist, Thornton thought, but she was having to concentrate to sightread the introduction.

'OK Jamie? From B.'

The boy, transfigured, opened his mouth and sang.

Now that was something else, Thornton thought with respect. A lovely flexible treble, every word audible, and real colour in the tone. A little tentative, though, on the top notes, which seemed strange for such an obviously experienced performer. He looked more carefully at Jamie, recognizing suddenly the changes of puberty — the sleeves of the shirt too short, too much sock showing below the trousers and the faint eruption of spots on the boy's chin. Of course . . . the voice was going. Thornton was transported back nearly forty years to the awful months when he had himself fought to keep his high treble and his place in the sun intact.

The boy stopped and looked anxiously towards Francesca.

'It's OK, Jamie. You're good for a while yet. Just think about placing that A — it's all in the mind.'

Jamie looked back at her, obviously worried, and she flipped back two pages of the music. 'I'll do the last bit of the alto, it'll give you a lead.'

The anthem was for two voices, of course, David Thornton remembered; the contralto sang first and then the soprano took over, high and clear like a trumpeter, on 'And he shall feed his sheep'. He listened with pleasure to Francesca's steady, slightly husky contralto. The boy Jamie came in strongly, an octave above, as she stopped, and he saw her grin to herself as she played through to the end. Jamie was still having trouble with the top notes, though — hiding the problem with a technique unusual in a boy so young, edging on to the note and filling it out when he was confident of it. The more credit to him, since Francesca was stumbling over the left hand of the accompaniment. She stopped abruptly.

'Sorry, Jamie. Not helped by the pianist, but if you can manage with me, you'll be fine with John Hathaway.'

'I'm fudging.' The boy spoke soberly.

'No one will know.'

'Can we do it again?'

'Of course. I'll try and get the left hand right this time.'

David Thornton, feeling an unusual need to do whatever he could do to help this enterprise, volunteered to accompany so that Francesca would be free to coach.

'Well, that would be very kind.'

Both of them were looking doubtful, but he was on sure ground, and took her place at the piano, flipping back to the beginning of the contralto aria. 'Sing it for me so I can get the feel of the piano,' he said firmly to Francesca, who opened her mouth to protest that she didn't know the aria very well. 'Come on. It'll be much better practice for James here.'

He spoke kindly but briskly, as if to one of his own stepdaughters, and felt her look sideways wonderingly, as she came and stood beside him. She sounded a little constricted as she started the aria, but he told her to relax in the same matter-of-fact tones, and was gratified to hear her ease up and open the throat. She's a musician, he thought with pleasure, listening to her careful phrasing and clear articulation; not quite enough breath to get through the long lines, she was having to sneak an extra one here and there, but a true alto with real strength in the lower range. She finished, holding the note and Jamie's clear treble rang out; he too had loosened up and the aria went much more fluently, the hesitancy on the top notes vanquished.

As they finished, Thornton looked up and smiled gently on them both, and James grinned back, liberated in relief. Francesca was not smiling, but she was transformed; her cheeks were pink and she was watching him wide-eyed, as if seeing him for the first time. She looked away from his mildly enquiring expression, and burst into action, fussing round Jamie and making sure he had his score.

'Thank you for accompanying — you're much better than me,' she said, formally, when she had dispatched Jamie, and looked at him again with that same incredulous air of discovery.

'It was a bit of a choice between music and mathematics,' he said, feeling some explanation was due.

She nodded, and said hesitantly that her father, who was also a better pianist than she, used to play for all of them.

Thornton paused, trying to phrase his question, but she saw his problem at once. 'He died. When I was eleven.'

'What bad luck.'

She nodded, and changed the subject easily, asking him which class his boy was in, and did he like it, and other civilities. Thornton explained his domestic situation.

'How old is Jamie?' he asked, as they crossed the road to the great cathedral, its cross lit up in the dark evening.

'Fourteen and a bit. I know we're on borrowed time.'

'Important that he doesn't go on too long.'

She gave him a sidelong, anxious look. 'I do know. I have four younger brothers, all of whom went on as long as they possibly could.'

'So did I, of course,' he said, ruefully.

'It's worse for Jamie because his father is ill, on and off, and Jamie's earnings make life a lot easier at home.'

'That's very difficult.'

'Same with two of my brothers who were successful trebles.' Francesca, who had not meant to explain any of this, found herself going on. 'We used to squander their earnings on rates and repairs and school fees after Dad died. It couldn't be helped, but it did mean that they felt failures twice over when their voices broke.'

'Do they all still sing?'

She looked at him with amusement. 'Perry is a major rock star, but I suppose you could have avoided hearing of him.'

'Not a lot gets through to my ivory tower,' he agreed placidly, and she laughed aloud, unaccountably happy. He was about to ask about the other brothers when he remembered that some trouble in America had deprived him of her help for his first days at the Department.

He sat down next to her in the row reserved for the more important school visitors and watched the audience file in, filling the cathedral. No wonder young Brett-Smith was nervous. It was a huge and probably knowledgeable audience and many of them would have come solely because he was singing; it was widely appreciated that that marvellous treble could not, in the nature of things, be there much longer. The choir was on first, with a tricky cantata, and Jamie was on second.

Thornton put his glasses on to pick out his Richard in the black ruff that denoted a probationary member of the choir. He looked very small but utterly concentrated and not at all nervous, and Thornton wished his wife could have been there to see.

'What a good boy,' Fran murmured to him. 'Didn't look to see you were there, just like they're told not to. The little ones usually do.'

'Oh, Richard is very conscientious.' He smiled at her, with pleasure, but she was watching the rostrum, tense and anxious, as Jamie walked up, to an audible murmur of interest. She chewed the nails on her right hand, unconscious of what she was doing, and without thinking about it he put a firm hand on her wrist, tugging it away.

'Sorry,' Francesca heard herself say, huskily, to his profile, her breath taken away by the authoritative, unthinking, intimate gesture. He nodded and let go of her hand, leaving her painfully conscious of his own hand resting casually on his knee, of his shoulder touching hers. Jamie was through the first bars before she heard a note. It was all right, she realized thankfully; he was getting the top notes; in fact, he was singing superbly. Thank God this concert was being recorded. By convention there was no applause but the silence that followed Jamie's elegant array of grace-notes as he landed square on the last note was its own tribute.

'That was all right,' David Thornton said in tones of temperate approval, and Francesca turned on him, indignant on Jamie's behalf, realizing belatedly from the faint glint in his eye that she was being teased. 'Very much helped by your biting your nails, of course,' he added.

She relaxed and smiled at him, overcome by a feeling of comfort and security that seemed to come from a long way back. 'You are being sardonic with me.'

'Are people not usually sardonic with you?' Thornton was smiling back at her, and she looked at him, dazed by an uprush of feeling. The headmaster, she realized, was signalling for her from further down the row and she leant courteously forward to receive his whispered congratulations.

The interval came round and she found herself barely able to offer an intelligent opinion. David Thornton had listened, she knew that; the man was clearly a musician. She hesitated, hoping he would not want to drift off, but he stayed gently by her as she greeted old acquaintances among the staff. He is married, she reminded herself, and old enough to be my father — and was stopped in her tracks by the memory of her own father playing 'Plaisirs d'Amour' and telling her brothers to shut up for a minute and let Frannie sing, she won't get the top A because she is a contralto, not a treble, for heaven's sake, will you little brutes pipe down — glancing sideways to encourage her as she sang.

The interval passed somehow. Jamie sang again — beautifully, Francesca observed with one part of her mind, while the rest was fully occupied trying to decide whether to risk biting her nails in the hope that David Thornton would hold her hand again. I am probably mad, she thought, what with jetlag and John, but I am not unhappy. Yet . . .

'Well, Jamie will always have *that* to remember,' she observed quietly to Thornton at the end of the cantata. There was a pause and she looked at him anxiously.

'Will he find that a consolation?' Thornton enquired without looking at her, and she gave the question thought. No, of course Jamie wouldn't; the better he sang the worse the loss he was facing. She considered the man next to her, recognizing the pedagogic method from her Cambridge days; you didn't tell an undergraduate they were talking rubbish, you mused aloud about whether some part of their hypothesis was right, leaving them to work it out. Not her own father's style, but a fatherly style nonetheless, not unkind, and not devaluing or attacking the young person addressed. He turned his head to her, drawn by her silence, and she looked back at him, helplessly.

'No,' she said, clearing her throat. 'I spoke before I thought it through.'

He smiled at her, touched and disturbed. 'You don't need to apologize.'

The choir re-formed itself to do the final piece of the programme, a short Mass, and this time it was David Thornton who watched Francesca as she sat listening, sombrely, to Jamie, singing easily now, rising effortlessly to a top B, the clear voice like a trumpet above the marvellously trained choir. She scrabbled for a handkerchief, but, having none, had to settle for a covert sniff. David Thornton found his own clean handkerchief and put it into her hands. The Mass came to an end, the lights went up, the headmaster leant over to congratulate Francesca again, and Thornton sat waiting to see what would happen.

'D . . . D . . . David?' He had not heard her stutter in the three days spent in her company; although he had told her to call him David, this was the first time she had attempted it. 'I'm going over to the school to collect Jamie — he has to get a train and he'll need feeding.'

'I'm going to walk over to see Richard, but I'm not allowed to take him out, or I would have suggested we all had a meal together.'

'Well, he is a bit little, isn't he?' Francesca said. 'If you would like to join Jamie and me, we should be honoured,' she went on tentatively. 'I have to put him on a train at Waterloo but I've arranged to feed him at an upmarket hamburger place first.' She hesitated. 'It *is* mostly hamburgers and perhaps that's not what you want?'

'I shall be very happy with a hamburger,' he assured her, and went to greet his son Richard. After ten minutes he kissed him goodnight, and watched with admiration as Francesca extracted an over-excited Jamie from his admiring juniors. He managed to find a taxi which whisked them all over to a small restaurant near Waterloo, where he watched with some awe as Francesca and Jamie each demolished a vast plate of hamburgers and chips. They were all talking so hard that in the end they had a scramble to get the train. Thornton, with a pang, observed as Francesca kissed Jamie that the boy was quite close to her own height. She stood waving till he was gone, and when she turned back she was looking bleak.

'Poor little brat,' she said, apologetically. 'Not much fun, and an awful lot of responsibility. I think he'll have to stop very soon — even if his voice would hold he's getting absolutely exhausted by trying to sing and keep up at Grantchester.'

'It does seem a lot to do,' Thornton agreed. 'Where do you live, Francesca, and would you like a drink, after all that?'

'I'd love one, and I live the wrong side of Holland Park.'

'So do I,' he said, surprised. 'Shall we go to that pub on the corner of Holland Park Avenue?'

'Lovely. But I must ring the school to make sure they meet Jamie off that train.'

In the event, by the time the taxi got them there, the pub was hideously crowded and Francesca was visibly fussing about the telephone call. She suggested, shyly, that if he didn't mind whisky he could have a drink at her house while she made the phone call. Thornton agreed, unwilling to impose on her but wanting to do whatever would make her feel comfortable about young Brett-Smith.

He was mildly taken aback by her establishment; he had expected a small flat, not a decent-sized house whose lower floor was given over to a well-designed kitchen-diner with expensive quarry tiling. He sat at the solid round dining-table, admiring the room and drinking a very good whisky while he listened to her talk to Jamie's housemaster who was all too clearly treating her as the substitute for Jamie's parents.

'I must go and let you get some sleep,' he said, when she had finished. 'I gather you stayed late last night to get things ready for my young men?'

She gave him a quick sidelong glance to find out what he knew as she sat down opposite him. 'Yes, a bit,' she said, suddenly looking very tired.

'You've got them all set up now. You could come in a bit late tomorrow.

'No, not tomorrow, I couldn't. I take it we did invite you to that nine o'clock meeting on Huerter? I certainly meant to.'

'You did. I'd just forgotten it for the moment.' He hesitated. 'Is the Treasury represented there?'

'No. It's solely a Departmental meeting. Treasury get their sixpence worth in rather later, at the official interdepartmental meeting. And again when E Committee meet. Treasury doesn't *have* to be represented tomorrow, we can all do their bit in our sleep. Or you could do it.'

He was taken momentarily aback by the swiftness of the attack, but he had not taught decades of the talented young without evolving some techniques for dealing with them. 'It will be enlightening to hear your people doing it.'

'I'm not sure that's what we want to do. Enlighten you, I mean.'

She watched him as he rose to put his whisky glass on the draining-board, having no idea what to do but most deeply not wanting him to go.

'Thank you for the drink. Till nine o'clock, then.' He smiled at her as she fetched his coat and it occurred to her that he was a little shy. So was she in this situation, she thought savagely — but on the other hand he would be with the Department for some time yet; no need to behave like a starving kitty. She took a step sideways, just as he had decided to try a courteous goodnight-kiss on the cheek, so that they all but collided on the way out.

'Sorry,' she said breathlessly, frozen to the spot. He gave her that careful, questioning look with which she was already utterly familiar, and she gazed back at him, helplessly. He took a step forward, and she stood still until he kissed her gently on the cheek, drawing back for a moment to see that this was what she wanted. Then he kissed her equally gently on the lips. She slid two arms round his neck and felt his arms go round her as she opened her mouth against his, with an overwhelming sense of coming home. They kissed for a long minute, then stopped to look at each other.

He pushed her fringe back from her face. 'Am I going to stay, or are we going to be sensible?'

'I couldn't bear it if you went.'

CHAPTER 12

'We've got nothing, and the local lads are laughing at us.' Detective Inspector Wylie was somewhat older than McLeish and sweating his promotion to Chief Inspector; he was clear that the task of checking Giles Hawick's alibi was not furthering his aspirations.

'We haven't found the people he met on Saturday. No one knows them, no one round here is known to have a Border terrier. If the couple exist, I don't believe they're from these parts. And you should have seen the looks I got at Regional Crime when I asked them to check dog licences issued in this area. Oh, they're doing it all right, or one of them is. You know, I expect, Chief Inspector, that dog licences are not filed by type of dog — I mean there is a space on the form but, funny thing, they file them by owners' names.'

McLeish allowed, meekly, that this piece of lore had escaped him. 'Better than filing them under the dog's given name,' he pointed out. 'I mean, I might have had to go back and ask Mr Hawick if he'd spoken to the animal.'

A reluctant laugh came down the line, and McLeish was emboldened to ask about Saturday night and Sunday.

'We've taken the climbing hut apart and we may have his prints there — I'll know later. I've no idea how to find the young couple he ran into. There's quite a lot of them locally. I could of course do a house-to-house, asking for anyone who'd been for a walk and who'd met a Minister of the Crown disguised as a hiker.' Wylie was sounding just this side of openly insubordinate and McLeish acknowledged silently that he had set the Inspector the task of finding the proverbial needle in a haystack. What you needed was a bloody great magnet, like an advertisement in all the local papers. Well, no doubt Mr Hawick would find that preferable to being arrested, but that was not yet the choice before him.

He decided to rally Inspector Wylie to the cause. 'I know it's a bugger, Ian, but it's important, and as you know it was old man Stevenson himself who wanted it done. Do your best, ask around, and remember that when you come back you and I will have to explain to those on high why we didn't get any further. He's really bursting his braces over this one.'

McLeish rang off and doodled on his blotter, thinking hard. The phone rang again.

'John? Forensic has no prints at all on the car. All wiped.'

McLeish decided he needed to hold this conversation face to face, and summoned Davidson. Catherine arrived with him, apologetic but determined. 'Can I come in, too? I've got an hour before I see Penelope Huntley.'

McLeish, who had been with Catherine the night before, welcomed her stiffly, uneasily, conscious of Davidson's sharp, hostile observation.

'Well,' Davidson began, 'we know that the car was outside Angela's flat on the morning she disappeared — I did tell you; it's in that note on your desk — but we haven't found anyone who saw it later on Saturday.'

'So either Angela took it, or someone else. Or, of course, they both did.'

'Aye. And then someone drove it back to London and left it in Malplaquet Terrace. Several people remember it being there on Sunday. No one remembers it on the Saturday, but the owner of the house nearest to it was away over the weekend and he would have been the one most likely to notice because he had to take a wee bit trouble to avoid it.'

McLeish sighed. 'The easy bet is that the murderer drove the car. But why use her car at all?'

'Because he was smart and knew about forensics. If he'd used his car he might have left something — or picked something up — which could be traced to him.'

'Or perhaps it was just chance — he didn't have his own with him,' McLeish said, gloomily. 'But then why not ditch it in Cambridgeshire? He obviously knew the place, so he could have put it somewhere where we'd never have found it.'

'He needed it to get back to London in.' His sergeants spoke simultaneously, and McLeish nodded agreement.

Bruce Davidson clarified a point: 'It took us long enough to find it in London: he knew where he was putting it. I've looked at the house-to-house — half the people in that wee terrace have a country place as well, and were away. On Saturday dinnertime, and for the evening meal, both those restaurants do a big trade and the road's full of strange cars. You could do anything you like in that road on Saturday or most of Sunday, provided you didn't try breaking and entering. They've all got burglar alarms, half of them wired to a central service.'

'So the murderer was in London Saturday night?' Catherine ventured.

'Not necessarily. He needed to get *back* to London for a reason, yes — but what he wanted may have been to catch a train, if it was Giles Hawick. A train to get him to Derbyshire so he could get into the climbing hut and give himself an alibi.'

His sergeants contemplated him, looking for the holes in this thesis.

'What if he left London early on the Saturday, with Angela in the car, then killed her, and pushed her body down the embankment? Then he took the car back to London and caught a train, got into the hut, at whatever time; slept there; and went on walking on Sunday.'

'Why didn't he take the car on to Derbyshire?' Bruce objected.

'Would have led straight to him, wouldn't it?' Catherine Crane was on the point at once.

'We need to look at the trains, Bruce — see could he do it?'

'Disguised as what? Lots of people know his face from the telly.'

'Come on, it wouldn't take much. A scarf, a hat, whatever — on a late-night train.'

'What about Ian Wylie, John? This might be a slightly better job for him,' Catherine suggested, and Bruce Davidson looked at her sharply. 'I'd do it, Bruce,' she protested, 'I just thought since Wylie was looking at Mr Hawick's alibi, he'd want to.'

He hadn't found time to chat to Bruce about Wylie's reactions, McLeish remembered irritably, but he had talked to Catherine. And Davidson was alert enough to realize conversations were taking place to which he was not party. He could ill afford to add career rivalry to this mix. 'I'll sort that out,' he said, firmly. 'Had you not better go and see Penelope?'

Catherine looked at him, obviously surprised by this brusque dismissal, but accepted it meekly and went, her departure attended, unreassuringly, by Davidson's thoughtful gaze.

'Bruce.' McLeish called him to order. 'I don't see why he would have done it: Hawick, I mean. I think I need to understand about this Barton case.'

'You could ask Francesca.'

McLeish looked up to meet his eyes. 'No, I couldn't.'

'Och, well.' Bruce Davidson relaxed; not exactly happy with the information but pleased to receive this confidence. 'You could ask your man himself, nae bother.'

'I could, couldn't I? You free, if I can get in to see him today?'

'Aye, I am.' Bruce was looking a lot brighter at the realization that he was getting places where Catherine Crane wasn't. 'What about Mr Yeo?'

'Yes, I must talk to him too. I've got a date in an hour. You free? Good.'

* * *

Catherine Crane found herself an hour later on Penelope Huntley's doorstep, wondering, as she rang the bell for a second time, whether the girl had forgotten their appointment, and what it was she was taking or doing to be so impossibly lethargic. Just as she was about to press the bell for a third time the door jerked open and Penelope Huntley, hair in a towel, beckoned her in. 'Sorry, I was tidying up and I needed a shower and thought I just had time.'

Catherine Crane blinked and acknowledged that she was in fact a few minutes early.

'Coffee?'

Catherine agreed she would like some, and followed her hostess into the kitchen, pleasantly surprised by what she found. The last time she had been there the place had been a tip: unwashed crockery, grease all over the Nescafé jar, not a clean spoon to be found. The place could still do with a coat of paint but it didn't smell, it wasn't dirty, and the spoons were clean and where you would expect to find them. Catherine, immaculately, fastidiously neat herself, half knew that she was threatened by dirt and untidiness because of the crowded council flat where she had spent her childhood.

Penelope Huntley herself looked a great deal better as well. Her nails were short and bitten but clean, her spots appeared to be much improved, and the wet hair she had released from the towel was at least washed even if in need of a good cut. Catherine stood drinking her coffee, looking round for clues to this transformation, and saw on a shelf beside the Nescafé and the tea — no longer in a half-used packet but in a jar labelled for the purpose — a bottle of pills, the label still bright and clear: one of the more powerful anti-depressants.

She considered her witness thoughtfully, accepting her invitation to move into the living-room. This room looked quite different as well; the curtains were open, and while there would never be quite enough light filtering in from the little area, itself well below pavement level, to illumine the room without recourse to artificial means, it all helped. And the curtains were new, the fresh material contrasting sharply with the old, desperately shabby sofa and chairs. The whole room smelled slightly of ammonia and the chairs, which Catherine examined carefully before deciding where to sit, had been cleaned so that the old grease-spots were only shadows on the fabric. And the room was tidy; no clothes, old newspapers, or dirty cups on the surfaces, just a magazine and some books.

'The bedroom's still a shambles,' Penelope Huntley said, startling her further. 'I'll get to that next.'

Catherine drank her coffee, lost for comment. The girl she had seen a few days ago would not have noticed her reaction to the flat or anything else much, so sunk had she been in her own misery. Surely an anti-depressant could not have worked that fast? Penelope Huntley fished a cigarette packet out of her bathrobe and offered it; the index and second fingers on the right hand were still deeply stained, so reform had obviously not progressed that far. But Catherine, politely refusing, remembered that a week ago this same girl had not even thought of offering this courtesy to a guest.

'I like your new curtains,' she said, cautiously.

'Mum bought them.' Penelope was sounding sullen but then added, unexpectedly, that it was nice of her, they weren't quite to her taste, but then she was going to sell the flat, and the new curtains did make it look better.

Catherine seized her opportunity. 'Have you found another flat?'

'Yes, I have. Saw it yesterday and I've made an offer. It's not round here, it's near Holland Park. My solicitor says I can afford it now.'

Catherine, remembering that this girl had inherited £200,000 from her uncle eighteen months ago, reflected that she could certainly have afforded something better than her present flat then; she must have been very angry to have settled for a small, inadequately lit basement flat in Brixton. Unless she had had a pressing need for cash for some other purpose?

'Are flats round here expensive?' she asked, chattily.

'Not that expensive. But I had a big overdraft which Uncle Charles was going to pay off. So when he died, of course, I had to do that out of what he left me. I thought I'd better keep a bit of cash.' Her mouth drooped downwards and for a minute she looked both frightened and discouraged. 'Of course it's different now I've got more of my money.'

She looked at Catherine in sudden alarm and it occurred to Catherine that it was the first time that morning she had remembered who and what Catherine was. A bit simple perhaps, thought clever, gathered Catherine, finishing her coffee — not mad, not really, just didn't quite see the consequences of what she was saying or doing. Childish, that was it; pouting and miserable and vengeful when injured, merry and cheerful when the sun shone, even if it had taken a death to bring out that sun. But all this was beyond her experience, Catherine decided calmly; she'd have to talk to one of the Yard's psychiatric experts.

'I'll have to get my legs waxed,' Penelope Huntley said, peering at long, thin, white legs, thickly overgrown with dark stubbly hairs. 'Maybe I'll ring up now.

'I'm certainly not sorry she's dead,' she went on, happily, reminding Catherine again of a six-year-old. 'So, it was the Saturday she died.'

It was not a question and Catherine Crane cursed herself. Never, never, never underestimate the intelligence of a witness; never let yourself be riled; and keep to yourself what you know, she thought, feeling young and incompetent, and uneasily conscious that John McLeish would think she had handled this badly.

'That has not yet been established, but I've no doubt it will be by forensic means,' she said, coldly and mendaciously, knowing perfectly well that the medical evidence was not going to improve in any way. She took a deep breath and went back to where she had been, observing with exasperation that Penelope Huntley was openly squinting round to read the magazine lying on the table.

'Miss Huntley, why had you arranged to have lunch with Miss Morgan if you disliked her so much?'

'I was going to have one last go at asking her if she would give me back some of my money.' Penelope Huntley was still trying to see an elusive paragraph.

'What do you mean *your* money?' Catherine Crane snapped, and the other girl looked up at her in surprise.

'The money she had a life interest in. My solicitor said she could agree to give up her life interest so that I would get some money now. She'd been saying no, although she didn't need the money. My mother said that she thought it would be better if *she* went and asked Angela. She actually liked her, you know.'

The note of angry, wondering resentment momentarily gravelled Catherine, who had found herself increasingly a champion of Angela Morgan's. It would give her great pleasure, she thought viciously, to put this sullen, loopy, great gawk into prison if she had had a hand in Angela Morgan's death.

'But you thought you knew better?' she suggested.

Penelope Huntley did not answer, just looked at her, the dark brown eyes dull. For a moment Catherine felt chilled, and was reminded sharply of a woman she had arrested, who had killed two of her neighbour's children, hidden them under a mattress in a loft, and gone out to her regular Bingo session, apparently untroubled. Psychopathic, a psychiatrist had said briskly, so that woman was now in Rampton, not Holloway.

Catherine, realizing that the other girl was simply not going to answer, was forced to move on, having been sufficiently disconcerted to sound ineffective and portentous. She had read Davidson's note of the interview with Jennifer Morgan and decided to try the question of the anonymous letters on Miss Huntley.

'What did they say exactly?' Penelope Huntley asked, with every sign of returning animation, and Catherine said, unforthcomingly, that the letters had accused Miss Morgan of having a continuing affair with another man.

'Well, that was true — of course she and Peter Yeo were still lovers. I told you she was a bitch.'

'You seem very confident that she and Mr Yeo were lovers at an earlier stage?'

'I know they were.' The answer came unhesitatingly, and Catherine Crane looked at her carefully. The girl pushed the drying hair from her face and reached for another cigarette. 'I used to follow her,' she said to the packet. 'I wanted to know what she was doing.'

'This was before or after your uncle's death?'

'Oh, after.' The girl was surprised enough to look her in the face. 'I was *stupid*. I mean, I didn't realize she was sleeping with Uncle Bill. I thought he was too old.' She stubbed out the cigarette, one-third smoked, got up restlessly and made for the kitchen. 'No fool like an old fool, they say,' she said savagely over her shoulder, the cliché sounding like a curse.

'So why were you following her?'

'I wanted to make her give me my money, of course.' Penelope Huntley sounded as if she was dealing with a rather slow child. 'I found out that she was going to bed with Peter Yeo and I told her I would tell Mrs Yeo.'

'And what did Angela — Miss Morgan — say?'

'She laughed. She said I would find that Mrs Yeo already knew.' Penelope was looking resentful and defeated at the memory of this conversation. 'Then she said that obviously she wasn't going to discuss breaking up the Trust against a background of threats, and thought we'd better stop talking altogether. The cow!'

A very good negotiator, Angela Morgan, Catherine thought enviously. She had managed to laugh off a threat that, if it had been acted on, must at the least have made her life difficult. More than that, she had managed, without engaging in counter-threats herself, to keep the possibility of liquidating the Trust held over Penelope Huntley's head. Of course, she thought, sobered, an alternative hypothesis was that Angela Morgan was tough enough and confident enough of her own power not to care what Peter Yeo's wife knew or thought. Unlike her own situation with Dave, she thought grimly; if anyone had told *his* wife he was playing away he would have gone straight back to her. As he had done, when she had faced him with choosing between them. Perhaps she had been no worse a negotiator than Angela Morgan, but was starting from a radically different position.

Seeing that she had been silent long enough to make Penelope Huntley uncomfortable, she followed up her advantage. 'So in the end you decided to write a couple of anonymous letters to Mr Hawick?'

The girl stared at her. 'No, I never thought of it.'

'Oh come on. Angela had called your bluff; we know from her solicitor that she had refused to answer your letters or see you about the Trust. You got angry and wrote to her fiancé.'

'I never thought of it,' Penelope repeated, wonderingly, sitting bolt upright.

'Why not?' Catherine needled. 'How would she have known the letters came from you? He might not even have told her about getting them.'

'But I thought she'd stopped going to bed with Peter Yeo when she got the other chap.'

The two women looked at each other and Catherine decided slowly that, despite Penelope Huntley's obsessive dislike of Angela Morgan, it was just possible that she had not believed she could be sleeping with both men simultaneously. She considered Penelope Huntley again, acknowledging to herself that she could have done with John, or even Bruce Davidson. This girl was sufficiently peculiar in her responses to make her doubt her own perceptions. And there were huge gaps in her alibi for both Saturday and Sunday.

'You're not moving immediately, I take it?' she asked pleasantly, aware that she was sounding threatening. 'We will need to talk to you again.'

'No. Not for a few weeks.' Penelope Huntley got up to show her out, hair now dry, falling lankly to her shoulders.

'I'm going to have it cut a bit,' she confided, apparently unmoved by any threat. 'All the ends are split.'

Catherine, whose hair was trimmed once a month for a special price in an expensive West End shop, suppressed the thought that several inches would have to be removed, and said goodbye, conscious that despite her insouciance this strange girl was in a state of high tension and a sort of suppressed excitement. As if she had managed to get away with something.

Catherine very nearly walked into the traffic trying to work out what it was she had missed.

* * *

John McLeish, Davidson at his side, walked heavily into the tiled reception area of Yeo Davis, and failed to return the smile of recognition he got from the pretty girl behind the desk.

'Mr Yeo, please,' he said, giving their names, and followed her upstairs, feeling old-fashioned and unsmart in his decent Marks & Spencer grey suit. Bruce Davidson, he was pleased to see, was, as usual, unmoved by his physical surroundings and fully occupied in chatting up their escort.

Peter Yeo sat behind his giant desk absorbed in something he was writing, and McLeish watched him with interest as he surfaced from his work like a diver coming up for air. This one was not just a flash salesman — he knew how to concentrate and was openly impatient at having been interrupted. He shook off his preoccupation civilly enough and sent for coffee, changing the order for tea as he caught Davidson's eye. Treats everyone like a client, of course, McLeish observed, and followed his lead in making small talk for a couple of minutes, till the tea was served.

'I wanted to see you again because I now understand that your relationship with Angela Morgan was extremely close,' he plunged in briskly. His man was ready for him.

'I don't know who told you so but at one time — before she met Giles Hawick — that was true,' he said pleasantly.

'Several people appear to have known.'

‘I’m afraid they probably did. Angela never bothered to be discreet,’ Peter Yeo agreed, politely.

‘But the affair came to an end when she met her fiancé, Mr Hawick?’

‘There was a certain amount of overlap, I expect.’ Peter Yeo sounded amused and entirely in control. ‘I was very sorry when it ended, if that is what you are asking, but given that I was already married one had to assume the end would come some time. When Angela found someone she wanted to marry.’

‘She didn’t want to marry you?’ McLeish asked, trying to match Yeo’s tone, and the man hesitated.

‘Oh well, you know how it is — are you married, Chief Inspector? No? There was a certain amount of discussion, and at one time I think Angie did hope I might divorce Claudia for her. And, to be perfectly honest, there was a time when I considered it. But not for long; I knew it wasn’t really on, I mean, we’ve got children and we’ve been married eighteen years. Not something just to throw up.’

McLeish considered him, reluctantly disarmed by his frankness. ‘So the affair had ended, what, a year ago?’

‘More or less,’ Peter Yeo said, demurely, but faced with McLeish’s best wooden gaze decided to go on. ‘Yes, for all practical purposes. We did get back into bed a couple of times. I took it she was having problems with Giles.’

‘Did your wife know about this affair?’

For the first time Peter Yeo looked uncomfortable, the easy, sophisticated man-to-man approach deserting him. ‘I’m afraid she did. We never quite talked about it, but she very much opposed Angela’s being made a partner. I pointed out, you know, that she was very thick with Giles Hawick, but Claudia was very uptight about it.’

‘What did she do about it? Take a lover, or threaten to leave you?’ McLeish succeeded in sounding both bored and impatient, and watched as a slow flush worked its way up the older man’s neck.

‘Neither of those. Claudia doesn’t want a divorce and other men aren’t her style.’

McLeish raised both eyebrows conspicuously, and wrote very slowly in longhand.

'You don't seem to believe me,' Yeo said angrily.

'What did she do, then?'

'She sulked.' Yeo's voice was full of exasperation and reluctant admiration. 'And she let the children know she wasn't happy — no, I don't think she told them Daddy was having an affair, but she made it clear that Daddy was being unkind to her — so they sulked, too. I spent a fortune on a skiing holiday for everyone. That helped a bit.'

Just an ordinary story of middle-class adultery? McLeish, trying to see in it the familiar pattern of a police marriage going adrift, realized that the contexts were much the same. A burgeoning young business concerned entirely with ideas and personalities had much in common with police work; it must be all-absorbing, stressful and damn difficult to explain or share with people who weren't in the trade. The wives of the Yeo Davis partners probably did have a thin time, just as policemen's wives did, with their husbands working all hours in the company of young women as fully involved in the job as they were. Of course, a partner in Yeo Davis could afford to make up for his absence and apologize for his infidelities by treating the family to a skiing holiday. Most policemen in similar circumstances would be lucky to be able to fund a weekend in Skegness.

'But nonetheless,' he said, aware that Peter Yeo had started to fidget under the pressure of his silence, 'you decided to offer Miss Morgan a partnership?'

'My partners and I decided. We are a partnership, Chief Inspector, not a company. There is a difference; this is very much a people business, and you can't operate a hierarchical structure. You have to proceed by agreement.'

McLeish, who had spent all his working life in a people business with a rigidly hierarchical structure, considered this proposition with interest, then pulled himself firmly back to his main line of enquiry.

'I wanted to ask you about the partnership agreements. Miss Morgan's solicitor gave me a copy of the agreement, and told me she had put a substantial sum of money into the partnership, but all this is a bit new to me and I'd be glad if you would explain how it all works.'

'Yes.' Peter Yeo looked at him measuringly. 'Well, the key thing about a partnership is that all of you are equally responsible for any debts incurred or contracts taken on. There is no shield between you and the outside world as there is with a limited-company structure.'

'Is that not a disadvantage?'

'Yes. However, a partnership is much more flexible as a structure; new partners can come in and other partners retire without having to have complicated arrangements about selling shares. And the whole tax structure is much easier to deal with, as I explained before.'

'But if the partnership gets into debt you all have to pay up — you can't just close it down?'

'That's quite right, Chief Inspector. It's actually like being a Name at Lloyd's.'

Got a bit carried away there, had Mr Yeo, and brought in a bit designed for another audience, McLeish thought, amused. Not many policemen are Names at Lloyd's; in fact, he'd be pushed to think of one. 'Miss Morgan's solicitor gave me your last year's accounts, but I'm not sure I have understood them,' he said, trying to look like an honest, dim copper. 'I expect they're out of date, anyway.'

'What have you got? No, only about a year; we are just doing the next lot now.'

'I could see your auditors, I suppose, but it might be quicker if you would take me through them.'

Peter Yeo gave him a wary look, and made to take the booklet from him, but McLeish flattened a large hand over the side of the page and looked at him hopefully. Peter Yeo hesitated for a second, then produced a duplicate booklet from his right-hand drawer.

'Right. Why don't we start with the profit-and-loss account? At page 7.'

John McLeish turned obediently to page 7, confident that he would find there was a problem in Yeo Davis's accounts. The Met had not given him any accountancy training but he had been around Francesca and her DTI mates for over a year, and had used his ears and eyes and asked the odd question when anyone had looked as if they had time to answer. '*Start with the balance sheet, always*,' the Department's best accountant had advised. '*That's where the bodies are*.' So if Yeo was turning straight to the profit-and-loss account, they weren't yet in the graveyard. '*Profit is a statement of opinion*,' he heard the shrewd authoritative voice go on inside his head. '*The only facts are cash and assets. And only assets if you've seen them with your own eyes and had a recent valuation*.'

At all events, the partners of Yeo Davis seemed to believe they had made a profit of £300,000 on fees of £3.2 million. Moreover, in support of this view they had actually drawn £240,000 of that profit between the five of them. Nice going, McLeish thought respectfully, £50,000-odd a man, *and* not paying all that much tax on it if he had remembered Peter Yeo's previous comments correctly.

'Some partners earn more than others, of course,' Yeo said firmly, seeing him reading these interesting notes. 'It's a complicated formula, but I drew £80,000, my next two partners £50,000 each and the other two £30,000 each.'

McLeish remembered that Angela Morgan had been told she would be able to draw £30,000 minimum. Well, if Yeo Davis had made more profit in the current year, *that* ought to be all right. And they had also left some in the business.

He thought about the sums more carefully, flipping back to the balance sheet at page 3, trying to remember what the DTI's expert had told him to look for. If it was a business that had stock, then your profit depended on having got your stock valuation right. If on closer examination you found you had six years' supply of the left-handed widgets, then you had to ask yourself what they were really worth. Well, this lot didn't have stock. They did appear to have something called goodwill but he had been told to ignore that. All right, what else? The debtors, of course. There were a lot of them, totalling £500,000. According to the hardened DTI practitioners, you always had to decide whether debtors were actually going to pay. Yeo Davis was apparently flourishing, but those debts did seem high.

'How old are these debtors?' he asked, in Francesca's brisk tones, and Peter Yeo just managed not to gape at him.

'Not old at all.'

'Are they lots of different small debtors or are there some really big ones?' He didn't get an answer immediately, and after a few seconds looked up inquiringly at Peter Yeo.

'A lot of it must have been the last part of the Regina account which we had just submitted.'

McLeish remembered belatedly the Notes to the Accounts: '*Worth reading those before you read anything else at all*,' the DTI's man had advised. He found the right page. 'It seems that Regina owed you £400,000 of that lot.'

'Yes, that is right.'

McLeish remembered, from what felt like months ago, Angela's ultra-modern solicitor wondering aloud what consultancy firms needed cash for. 'Is that account now paid?'

'No. We're having a little argument with the customer.'

It was in the accounts for a period ending fourteen months ago, McLeish reminded himself. And the partnership profit was £300,000. So if that account was never paid, then, blimey, the partnership had made a loss of £100,000 rather than a profit of £300,000. But the partners had drawn their £240,000. He considered the balance sheet again. 'Cash at Bank' appeared to amount to £8,500, but on the debit side sat a bank overdraft of £200,000. They had borrowed against the Regina bill, quite a lot they'd borrowed, especially at an interest rate of, what, 14 per cent? Angela Morgan's £100,000 must have been very useful.

He looked up cautiously at Peter Yeo, who was studiously not looking at him, lost apparently in contemplation of the telephone. 'You expect to get that bill in soon?' he asked.

'Most of it, yes.'

'What is the problem?'

'A fairly standard one for firms like ours. We were hired to help them resist a takeover. They lost, and we hadn't been quite careful enough about making sure our bills were paid as we went along. We had five people on that job full time for six months, *and* we ran up a lot of expenses. Of course, the firm who took them over also takes over their obligations but there is always an argument. And the partner who was in charge of the account here has left.'

Real difficulties then, McLeish thought, especially since the successful party probably hated Yeo Davis's guts. He remembered the case now, dimly; it had been a particularly hard and dirty fight, the repartee in the 'and-anyway-your-chairman-only-likes-little-boys' class.

'How much of it will you get?' he asked bluntly.

'Oh, most of it.' Peter Yeo looked him in the eye, head slightly tilted back, and McLeish, returning that over-candid look, yearned for two minutes with a good lawyer. Well that could be arranged, too.

He changed the subject and took Yeo carefully back over his relationship with Angela, noting with interest the care with which the man was avoiding an assertion that the affair had been totally over. So it hadn't, and this careful customer was not going to put himself in a position where he had lied to the police — he was just being very economical indeed with the truth. But by the time that Yeo's secretary had put her head round the door at least three times, McLeish was getting no further, so they left Peter Yeo with courteous thanks.

Deciding that his most urgent need was for a pee and some tea — Peter Yeo had not offered any more after the first cup, clearly feeling that he might never get rid of them if he did — McLeish and Davidson sat down in a small workmen's café, grease clinging to every surface, where he explained the significance of the unpaid Regina account.

'What do you reckon, Bruce?'

'It was a gey bad time for her to be marrying. Or rather it would have been a bad time if she'd wanted to leave the firm. They'd used her cash to pay the partners, nae bother. And mebbe she would have felt she had paid in too much, anyway, if that bill was bad.'

'And if she'd wanted to leave, she'd only have had to give six months' notice. Because she died, they've a year to pay up.'

Bruce Davidson scowled at his rock cake. 'Yeo's not the only one in bother, though, he told you. They're all obliged to find the cash.'

'You mean they all got together to do her in? Come on, Bruce.'

'Mebbe not, then,' Davidson agreed and gagged on his tea.

McLeish looked at him, seeing how pale he was. 'You all right?'

'I've a bittie cold.'

And a fever, McLeish realized. 'Go home, Bruce, for God's sake, sleep it off a bit. I'll drop you.'

He did that, alarmed by the lack of protest from his colleague, and insisted on seeing him into his small flat across the river and getting a couple of aspirin into him. And buying some basic food and drink — it was all too clear that Davidson spent his waking hours between the job and the pub. He then took himself back to the Yard, reporting as he went that Davidson was a non-starter for the next day, and surveyed his desk, buried under a heap of paper, dispirited.

The phone rang and he picked it up, relieved not to have to tackle the mess immediately. 'Alan Toms, John. You've got our Catherine.' The voice at the other end was as cheerful and nasal as he remembered it.

'Yes, she joined us a few months ago,' he said, cautiously, when he got his breath back.

'Well I hope you're looking after her.' Alan would be a Super, perhaps a Chief Super by now, McLeish decided, and well entitled to the paternalist line he was taking as he enquired after the details of McLeish's own career and personal life. 'I hear you're spoken for, yourself?'

'We were all wondering here why you'd ever let Catherine go?' McLeish said, firmly ignoring the question.

'Oh, I wouldn't have, lad.' Toms was sidetracked immediately. 'I'd have got rid of the bloke sooner, I can tell you. Usual thing — she'd got tangled up with one of my DIs, married but playing away. He didn't want to leave his ball-and-chain when it came to it. I'm not sure I'd have stayed with mine if I'd had a girl like young Catherine offering for me. But there you are. So she said she'd rather have a complete break. You look after her, find her a good bloke to marry.'

McLeish, through what felt like a serious obstruction to his breathing, promised to try to do that and went on to inquire about other colleagues.

Toms gossiped obligingly but returned, at the end, to Catherine, who had obviously found a niche in that shrewd flinty heart that no one else had discovered. 'I'd have kept her because she's a lot better, as well as a lot prettier, than her bloke,' he said earnestly. 'She did the decoy stuff for our rapist — you remember him? We had the lads there, of course — but you know how it is . . . came the crunch, she was on her own. Fought him off, hung on to him till the dozy lot we had in CID got there. I put her up for the Police Medal but I suppose she was too pretty. Got a Commended, though.'

McLeish thanked him, put the phone down two minutes later and gazed unseeingly at the door of his office. So it *had* been a married bloke who had let Catherine down, and, like Angela Morgan perhaps, she had decided to put it all behind her and find someone unattached to marry. Only, unlike Angela, she had got herself out of her ex-lover's vicinity. He decided he owed himself a drink and just at that moment found a note from Catherine saying that she and 'some of the others' were in the Victoria.

CHAPTER 13

'Well, the feeling of the meeting seems to be that Ministers should take a robust view.'

'You mean rescue Huerter and its nine hundred jobs, and let Barton whinge on, Bill?' Francesca asked cautiously, on behalf of the group.

It was a week since the last meeting on Huerter had been held, and March rain was sheeting down, further obscuring the scummy windows of the DTI's headquarters. All the overhead lights were on in the cramped room, mercilessly illuminating a table at which eight people would have been comfortable, but around which fourteen were huddled, papers spread on every inch. Francesca, sitting three places away from David Thornton, between Rajiv and the young accountant responsible for producing the case paper, shifted awkwardly, kicked Rajiv, apologized, and added further to the confusion by banging the table with her knee so that everyone's coffee jumped in its cup.

'Francesca, do sit still. Yes, that's what I mean.' Bill Westland caught David Thornton's mildly inquiring look. 'If our Ministers accept the recommendation, they will of course have to defend their view to Treasury colleagues.' He looked down the table at Francesca who was wearily biting the thumbnail on her left hand.

'Francesca? You can write the submission, but it goes through me, please.'

'Of course it does, Bill,' she said reproachfully. She flicked a glance towards David Thornton. Bill Westland, without moving a muscle in his face, took the point and observed, to the entire meeting, that it was by no means clear that DTI Ministers were going to accept officials' advice on this point; the submission would have to make it clear that a decision was required quickly but it would be premature to brief Treasury officials before he had had an opportunity of taking Ministers' minds. Eleven civil servants to whom the whole procedure was second nature looked at him blankly, while Francesca carefully poured coffee from her saucer back into its cup and David Thornton gazed serenely at the water pouring down the window.

The meeting broke up in a welter of separate conversations, the five with responsibility for getting a recommendation to Ministers in good order that night forming a private huddle of their own. David Thornton watched Francesca, who formed the centre of that group, for a minute, decided she was immersed beyond rescue, and left quietly. Westland watched him go, broodingly.

'Quite right, Frannie,' he said, to the huddle. 'Do you think he got the message or is he racing to alert Treasury now, even before we get to our Minister?'

His goddaughter hesitated. 'He seems to me lazily efficient — I mean, he doesn't go out to meet trouble, so he won't tell Treasury unless and until he knows our Ministers are prepared to stand and fight. But I bet you anything he's going to organize those two graduates of his right now to gather defensive material, as it were. And as Hawick is going to Washington soon, I suppose Professor Thornton might have a word there first.'

Bill Westland considered her gloomily. 'That sounds right. You've probably spent more time with him than any of us, of course?'

'I expect that's true.' She did not meet his eye and returned to organize contributions to the submission.

* * *

At New Scotland Yard an equally unwieldy meeting was going on in McLeish's room, with ten people crowded round a table meant for six, while he reviewed the Morgan case. For a week there had been no progress worth having, as the meeting had just agreed. Exhausted, they had decided to make one more collective attempt to focus on the most likely candidates.

'You make Mr Hawick the favourite, then, sir?' the young detective constable asked, hopefully.

'Not necessarily,' McLeish said, watching Catherine Crane out of the corner of his eye. She was looking abstracted and was drawing idly on a corner of the paper in front of her. 'Anyone else think different? Bruce?' He looked towards Davidson who was still pale but looking a bit better.

'I like Mrs Yeo for the job. She got what she wanted out of Angela's death. What about Penelope Huntley, though?' Davidson looked pointedly at Catherine, who roused herself to answer.

'I just don't know,' she said, tiredly. 'I'd like some company on the next interview. She can't be eliminated because she doesn't have an alibi. And she *isn't* quite normal, though I just can't explain why not. I don't think I know.' The table regarded her with surprise and McLeish hastened to intervene, deciding that what he and she both needed, and soon, was a good night's sleep if one or both of them was not to topple over in the corridor.

'Jennifer Morgan, anyone?'

'I'd want to murder my sister if she took my boyfriend off me.' The group all turned to look at a young, dark, athletic-looking woman detective constable, attached to them the day before by the Commander who was, in desperation, pouring manpower at the case. '*And* the death got her some useful cash.'

Catherine smiled at her faintly and McLeish reflected that she probably found it difficult to imagine having a sister capable of taking a boyfriend away from her. She was looking extremely beautiful, the clear, slightly freckled skin and bright blond hair making everyone else in the room look grey and old.

'All right,' he said. 'We'd better meet again tomorrow, same time, same place. Let's all do some work.'

He rose dismissively and the meeting filed out, Catherine last and hesitant.

'I *would* like to try an idea on you, John. And Bruce, if he's got time.'

Tactful, thought McLeish, relieved, not wanting to fuel Davidson's suspicions or to make him feel he was being excluded. The three of them sat down again, pushing coffee cups aside.

'I've been thinking about those anonymous letters Giles Hawick got. We had a case in Tottenham where the writer didn't just write to one person, they wrote to several.'

McLeish and Davidson looked at her.

'No one else seems to have got any,' McLeish said, slowly.

'She's right though, John,' Davidson observed, ungrudgingly. 'We should have seen it. There's likely someone else has had a letter and isna saying a lot about it.'

'Who then?'

'Well, who else had an interest in that affair? I wondered about Claudia Yeo — I've not interviewed her, but it is her husband we're talking about.' Catherine had gone rather pink and was digging into the papers with her pen. McLeish watched her, all his senses sharpened. Had someone done that to her lover's wife, he wondered; was that what had precipitated the crisis?

'Yes.' Davidson spoke on an exhaled breath. 'We mebbe missed a trick there, John. Look at it. Hawick was apparently paying no mind to the first letter he got — well, the marriage was still on, wasn't it? So, whoever it was has to think of someone else. So he or she, most likely, stirs up Mrs Yeo to make a fuss and force Giles Hawick to take notice.'

'She did get a letter, you're right!' McLeish spoke with conviction, replaying in his mind that curious hesitancy under questioning and the relieved briskness with which Claudia Yeo had dealt with questions about the letter to Giles Hawick. He beamed at Catherine with simple pride; it was a sound point and would move them on. 'We'll go back and ask her about it, as soon as possible.'

His secretary appeared. 'There's a DC Christiansen on the line for Bruce. Says it's urgent.'

McLeish blinked, then remembered who it was; yet another detective constable detached, resentfully, from his own preoccupation and allotted to the Morgan team in the last couple of days. I'm losing my grip on this lot, he thought, sobered.

'Oh, well done, lad,' Bruce Davidson was saying, grinning into the phone. He covered the mouthpiece and turned to McLeish: 'One of my lot has found a Paki newsagent near Miss Morgan's office who says she bought a paper from him around ten and then went into her office on the Saturday morning!'

'Christ! Is he sure? Did you show him a photo?'

'No need, sir. He says the newsagent knew her. He didn't know we wanted to know where she'd been on Saturday. He talked to the chap himself.'

'Is he sure about the time?'

'Apparently. He was waiting for a delivery.'

McLeish called for Peter Yeo's statement. He had got to the office about ten-thirty, Yeo had stated. No one else had been there.

'We need to see both Yeos — Peter, then Claudia.'

Half an hour later, McLeish's secretary Jenny reported that this simple plan was frustrated conclusively by the fact that both Yeos were out of London for the day. Peter Yeo would be available early the next day, if that would be helpful, but Claudia not until late in the afternoon of the next day.

'Fix both for tomorrow, will you, and don't make it sound desperately important. Sorry,' he added, catching Jenny's patient look. 'I know you wouldn't.'

* * *

'Francesca? Is your office full of young men?'

'Yes, it is.' Francesca hoped she was sounding brisk and business-like for the benefit of the young men who were sitting around her, but she was not at all sure she had succeeded; a sense of childlike excitement and happiness filled her when she heard David Thornton's voice.

'I'm having a drink with Giles Hawick in the House at six-thirty, so I'm a bit occupied this evening. We could meet later, or tomorrow?'

'I was going to have a drink with Jim Waters, PS to the Chief Whip,' she lied promptly. 'So I could find you at the House?'

'All right.' Thornton sounded cautiously amused. 'How will you know exactly where we are?'

'Jim'll fix it,' she assured him. She got rid of her meeting and turned to the task of persuading her fellow civil servant, seconded from the DTI to the Chief Whip's office, to buy her a drink in the House of Commons.

Jim Waters received her request with no more than a raised eyebrow, confident that there was a good deal he was not being told but bearing her no grudge. A canny, shrewd Scot, whose father had been a miner, he had found his niche when he was twenty-seven as a Minister's Private Secretary. It had been a matter of time only before he had been seconded to the Chief Whip's office, where he had spent ten years under three different governments and five Chief Whips, and from which no one had any plans to dislodge him. He liked Francesca and had long ago decided that whatever she did she would emerge in some key part of the curiously linked machinery by which the country was governed.

He decided to exceed his brief that evening and once he had bought her a large gin and tonic, he edged her gently towards the back of the small bar, nodding greetings as he went, to join two men sitting in unusual isolation. 'Evening, Minister,' he said quietly over Francesca's shoulder to Giles Hawick and his rather older companion who was not an MP.

'Hello, Jim.'

Jim observed with interest that rather than looking grateful to him for achieving so neatly the meeting she had surely intended, the redoubtable Francesca was looking young and shy.

'Do you know Professor David Thornton?' Giles Hawick, who appeared wretched, had pulled himself together to meet Francesca. 'I recognize your name — you've just ruffled a few feathers in my Department about PESC. What did they do to you?'

Francesca, Waters was relieved to see, recovered rapidly from whatever it was that had ailed her.

'There are those of your officials, Minister, who utterly fail to grasp that the DTI cannot predict the incidence or the spend on selective financial assistance. I've never been able to decide whether it's genuine, or tactical, stupidity.'

Giles Hawick smiled at her, momentarily roused from preoccupation and misery. 'Oh dear, oh dear.'

Francesca considered him. 'I am so terribly sorry to hear about Angela,' she said bravely, and the other two men held their breath. 'We were at school together.'

'Of course, she must have been a contemporary of yours.'

'Almost exact. Did you meet her at Oxford?'

Jim Waters let out a long breath as Giles Hawick answered, obviously released by being able to talk about his lost love. He put another drink unobtrusively beside Francesca, noticing as he did so that Members who had been leaving a space around Hawick were now moving closer, and that two more had joined the group. Glancing sideways at Hawick's companion, he was interested but not surprised to see that he was watching Francesca with open, amused affection, instantly suppressed when he caught Waters's eye. Moved by the intense curiosity about people that made him so successful in his job, Waters engaged Thornton in conversation, listening at the same time to Hawick who was now talking generally to an enlarged group.

'So, Francesca,' Hawick could be heard saying with something like animation, 'are you going to tell me which of my civil servants is being so obstructive?'

'Oh no, Minister, I am sure that would be wrong.' Francesca, pink with gin, somehow invested the last word with a capital letter. She smiled at him, sparkling. 'In any case, obstructive people are everywhere in your Department — they're trained that way.'

There was an appreciative burst of laughter from the group. One of the backbench audience patted Francesca's shoulder and declared in tones only slightly slurred by drink that he now saw why people wanted to be Ministers. Giles Hawick, looking human for the first time since the tragedy, Waters thought, grinned at her in acknowledgement. Not attracted to her, Jim Waters observed, automatically, pity that, but cheered by her. Well, as it turned out, she had *not* been seeking a quiet word with a Treasury Minister, it was this Thornton she was after, bloke well old enough to be her father.

'How's your policeman?' he asked her, into a gap in the conversation.

'John?' she enquired stagily, as if there might have been several of them. 'I haven't seen him recently.' As always when she was nervous this came out with a clarity and pitch worthy of the Royal Shakespeare Company, and he noticed that both Hawick and Professor Thornton were receiving the information with as much interest as he was. So was one of the hovering backbenchers, who offered her another drink. She refused, blushing, and looked hopefully over to Thornton, who was finishing up his drink and saying something valedictory to Giles Hawick. Jim Waters, deeply interested, diverted the backbencher with a civil question about the last debate, smoothly extracting himself from the conversation in time to escort Francesca and Thornton to the nearest exit as if he had been there to do nothing else.

'Thanks, Jim,' Francesca said quietly, one professional to another, as he found her coat. He touched her shoulder in acknowledgement. 'Let's have lunch,' he suggested. 'I'll ring you.'

He disappeared back into the fray and Francesca watched his stocky back with affection.

'I take it that was a Royal Command?'

'About lunch? Yes. He wants to know what I'm doing.'

'With me?' Thornton sounded wary, and Francesca stiffened.

'With Giles Hawick. It's Ministers he's interested in.'

'Rather than middle-aged university dons.' Thornton accepted the snub with amusement and she blushed. 'Are we eating?'

'Either that or I fall over,' Francesca said, recovering. She hesitated. 'Are you coming home with me?'

'I thought that was why you'd come to fetch me. Or were you there to see that I wasn't saying anything untoward to Giles?'

'I was there anyway,' she said defiantly, and he locked an arm into hers, grinning.

'Of course you were.'

She looked suspiciously at his profile, but he was concentrating on hailing a taxi.

They ate in Francesca's kitchen, and she dealt with the accumulated messages on her answerphone while he sorted out papers, listening with half an ear as she talked to Jamie Brett-Smith's mother.

'I'm sorry, darling. Don't worry about Jamie, I'm there. He'll want you, of course, if you can possibly come, but I can cope.' She looked harassed as she came off the phone.

'All right?'

'No. Jamie's wretched father, who is schizophrenic, isn't taking his pills again. It'll be the usual thing, he'll get dottier and dottier until they have to certify him, then he's in for a bit while they straighten him up, then they let him out, then it starts all over again. It reminds me usefully that there are worse things than being an orphan.' She wrote savagely on the wall calendar, looked at her list, sighed, and dialled another number. 'S'me. How was Tris? So I should hope. Another four weeks? Just as well you're rich, Perry. I'll go next week, yes, but after that it's Charlie's turn. Yes, I'm all right, thank you. No, I haven't — I don't know what he's doing. No, it's OK, really Perry. I've got friends here, now. Yes, I will.'

She put the phone down and started to bite her nails, and David Thornton went over to stop her.

'Is this the brother in hospital?' he enquired, holding her hands firmly. She looked at him gratefully.

'Not a real hospital. A bin. Nothing to be done.'

'No, indeed. High time you cut him loose. And yourself. You're not his mother.'

'They never cut themselves loose, do they? I mean, if you're a mother you're stuck with it.'

David Thornton thought of his wife and his stepdaughters. 'I'm afraid that may be so,' he said, interested.

'You'd not seen it before?'

'Not quite.' He realised that Francesca was rigid with tension. 'What is it?'

'It's maybe not marriage I'm frightened of, but children.'

'Not surprising. You've already got four. Five, if you count Jamie.' Thornton was casually authoritative and she winced.

'Let's go to bed.'

He followed her up the stairs, deciding it was none of his business; people found their own solutions. But as he made love to her he realized that she was in distress, that her mind was elsewhere. He exerted himself to get her attention back, without success, and looked down at her strained face with exasperation. 'What *is* it?'

'I don't know. Not you. You I need. I love you.'

Thornton felt himself recoil involuntarily and knew she had felt it, too.

'Sorry, darling. I also need a cup of tea. I must be tired.'

He accepted the offered olive branch. 'I'll get you one.' He eased himself carefully out of her and padded downstairs. When he reappeared with a neatly laid tray, he was relieved to find Francesca composed and reading.

They drank the tea companionably, and by mutual consent decided to go to sleep instead of trying to make love again.

Thornton woke, restless and needing to pee two hours later, and realized as he slid back into bed that he had woken Francesca as well. Reaching for her tentatively, he got a prompt, fierce response. He rose to the occasion, both alarmed at and stimulated by her need. Afterwards he looked down at her thoughtfully, and she smiled at him, easy and relaxed.

'No need to look so hunted.'

'Was I? Sorry.' He reached over to the light, snapped it off, and settled himself comfortably beside her. 'I didn't mean to,' he murmured.

'It's not as if you're the only man I love.'

'No, of course not,' he said drowsily. 'There are all those brothers.' He tucked in a loose piece of sheet and drifted towards sleep.

'And Peter,' the clear voice said, consideringly, ten seconds later.

'Who's Peter?' he said, jerked awake, startled and jealous.

'You've met him: Peter Andrews, in Textile Division — tall, blond chap. Does my PQs if I get stuck. And Jim Waters, whom you just met.'

David Thornton opened his mouth to speak, realized he was being effectively put in his place, and pulled her hair. 'How many other candidates are there?'

'Henry Blackshaw of course. And Rajiv, sometimes. And Martin Bailey.' She was apparently giving the list careful consideration, and he squinted at her in the darkness with affection and anxiety, recognizing a very fast defence-mechanism.

'I am greatly fortunate, then, to have got to the top of this list.' He thought for a minute and decided to risk it. 'Why me?'

'Oh, because . . .' She gave the question thought. 'You remind me of my dad — no, that can't be right, you're not like him at all — but there is something there.' She lay for a moment in the darkness. 'I know who it is, it's the father of my best friend — at school. He was a don too. He was lovely; he liked me and encouraged me. Indeed he did that for a whole group of us anxious little girls. I loved him and that whole household. There were no younger brothers in it, no worried widowed mother, I had no responsibilities.' Francesca was no longer with him, she was away in a lost world. 'I used to sit under the dining-room table there and read, or we used to play games. He wrote little plays for us to act in. Or played cards with us.'

David Thornton waited, not liking to move. 'Where is he now? Do you still know him?' he asked into the silence.

'He died, too. When we were all sixteen.' The beautiful voice was totally without inflexion. Thornton, realizing he was on difficult ground, fought to stay awake. 'What rotten luck. Do you want some more tea?'

'No, it's all right.' She sounded forgiving and remote. 'It's time we got some sleep.'

He was conscious as he fell irrevocably asleep that he had failed her, and was cheered to see when he woke, reluctantly, to the alarm, that she must have slept at least some of the night. Not enough of it though, he realized, watching her as she organized breakfast for them both. The dark-blue eyes were sunk back in her head and the eyelids were reddened. He managed to distract her with the lead story in the newspaper — a political crisis in the Opposition — and was profoundly relieved to get a trenchant and amusing analysis of what was actually happening.

* * *

In Ealing, John McLeish was also waking slowly to another day, in his own bed and by himself. He ate a scrappy breakfast — the milk, six days old, had soured, and he had to improvise with orange juice on his cereal — then surveyed several days' worth of letters. The flat looked reasonable, thanks to his share of a Filipino daily help found for him by Francesca. Apart from the difficulty of preventing Maria from ironing everything including his Y-fronts, the arrangement worked splendidly and had been a major help in his life.

As he put plates into the dishwasher — another innovation forced on him by Francesca, who had behaved as if she had been required to cook on an open fire in the drawing-room when she found he was still washing up by hand — he thought about the morning ahead. Despite the appalling amounts of manpower being deployed on the case, not a lot of progress was being made. Giles Hawick was still there in the frame and until he could eliminate him or convict him, McLeish feared he would find himself supervising ever-increasing numbers of hard-pressed, fed-up detectives.

He had agreed to see Peter Yeo at eight-thirty, because Yeo had another meeting at ten. Not that Yeo was going to get anywhere near that second meeting unless he came up with a pretty satisfactory explanation of how he had managed not to see Angela Morgan when they were apparently both at the same office, McLeish thought grimly, but Jenny had been told to book this as though it were a piece of routine, and that was what she had done.

He picked up Bruce Davidson outside the office, and they were received by Peter Yeo himself, immaculately suited as usual, with an elegant Italian shirt and large silver cufflinks that just escaped being vulgar. He was his usual courteous self, plying them with good coffee, but the politeness concealed anxiety, McLeish was interested to see, as the square, neat hands fumbled the milk jug.

'We have received information that makes it clear that Angela Morgan was at these offices on the morning of Saturday, the day she disappeared.'

'Who from?'

'A reliable witness, who knew her.'

A thick silence fell, neither McLeish nor Davidson moved a muscle, coffee steaming unregarded in front of them.

'I should have told you.' Peter Yeo was rubbing his hands together unconsciously, the cufflinks catching the light. 'I had my reasons, as I expect you can imagine.' He tried for a frank man-to-man smile, but froze as he met John McLeish's level look. 'No, not that sort of reason — I didn't kill her, for God's sake. We had arranged to meet that morning.'

'Why?'

'Why do you think?' Peter Yeo was sweating at the hairline and very pale.

'In order to make love?' John McLeish, feeling like the Speaking Clock, was nonetheless determined to get the facts on record.

'Yes.'

'In previous statements you said that your affair was over.'

'And it *was*, Chief Inspector.' Yeo was all but leaping across the desk in his desperate need to convince. 'This was the last goodbye, if you like. And it was Angela's idea, not mine.' He looked into McLeish's face carefully. 'There's a sort of tradition — Brigade of Guards stuff, really — that chaps before they marry sleep with all their old girlfriends one last time. Sort of a wedding present from the old girlfriends, yes? Well, Angela was just reversing that tradition; she told me so. I wasn't going to say no. We always got on well and particularly so in bed.'

He would have to check with Bruce Davidson, McLeish decided. Nothing of this accorded with his own experience. He sat watching Yeo, who was pressured into speech by his silence.

'She left about one o'clock, Chief Inspector. I'd thought we might go and have a boozy lunch somewhere and maybe spend the rest of the day together. But she said she needed the time, so we drank the Fleurie and ate some quiche which was in the fridge. And the rest of the day I did exactly what I told you I did.'

McLeish reminded him wearily that concealing evidence was a serious offence. 'In this case, too, it's caused us to waste a lot of time.'

'I really am sorry. It was stupid of me. To be honest, as I expect you can guess, I'd had all kinds of trouble with Claudia about Angela, and I didn't want to start it all up again.' He hesitated. 'I really don't want Claudia to know about this. Does she have to? It would upset her very much, and it just doesn't seem necessary.'

'And besides the wench is dead' McLeish thought, suddenly angry, watching the prosperous citizen opposite him.

'We have no reason to suppose this version of your activities that Saturday is true either,' he said levelly, and watched Yeo reach shakily for his coffee.

'But you know Angela was here,' he said, gulping coffee.

'We have a witness to her arrival, yes.'

Yeo stared at him, over his cup. 'But not to her departure. I see.' He finished the cup of coffee, looking steadily into it. 'May I talk to Claudia before you do?' he said, to the coffee cup.

'I'd like you to come to the Yard with us now, so we can take a revised statement from you.'

McLeish leant forward to finish his own coffee and saw out of the corner of his eye that Bruce Davidson was tidily putting away notepad and pencils.

'I must just square a few things here.' Yeo looked at his face. 'Are you arresting me?'

'Not yet. But I've got at least twenty people on this investigation and I'm not prepared to waste another minute of their time. Or my own.'

Peter Yeo looked at him and decided not to go on. 'I'll just talk to my secretary, if I may.' He rose to go out.

'Call her in, please, and give her any instructions you need to.'

Peter Yeo opened his mouth to protest, then closed it as he realized what was being said to him. He called in his secretary, still in her winter boots, and told her that he would be gone all day and that everybody should get on without him, with the exception of one meeting to which he was critical and which she should rearrange for later in the week. He was unable to help a glance towards McLeish, who was unreassuringly writing the day's list of things to do, totally ignoring the other occupants of the room.

'Thank you, Lisa. I am at your disposal, gentlemen.'

As a piece of bravado it missed its mark. McLeish, intent on his train of thought, simply grunted, while Davidson sat tight, indicating that he moved nowhere without his senior officer.

Peter Yeo watched the top of McLeish's head with mounting alarm. 'Can I ask my lawyer to sit in?' he asked. 'When I give a statement?'

'When you give a revised statement, you mean. Certainly, if you feel the need.' McLeish did not lift his head from his list, confident that this quelling statement would have the desired effect. As usual, he decided that his list was several people's work. And just for once he had people falling over themselves to do some work on this investigation.

Yeo, his poise destroyed as McLeish had intended, came with them quietly and without further mention of legal help. At New Scotland Yard, McLeish left Davidson to escort him to an interview room and raced upstairs to see Stevenson and tell him that the picture might be changing.

'This doesn't let Hawick out though, does it?' Stevenson said heavily, having thought about it.

'No. It does bring Yeo into the frame, though.'

'Does, doesn't it? I'll let the AC know, it'll cheer him up. Hawick's flying to Washington today. You want to arrest Yeo?'

'Not on what we've got, sir. Not unless he coughs up something more on a formal statement.'

Two hours later McLeish conceded that Yeo's formal statement left them no further forward than they had been first thing that morning, just better documented.

'Keep him there,' he instructed, briskly. 'Give him some food — let the girl get her lunch — type his statement up slowly, and keep him off the phone. Come on, Bruce, we've got half an hour to get to Mrs Yeo.'

He thought for a moment, when they arrived, that she had been warned and had decided not to see them; there was no answer to the bell and the house looked deserted. But at that moment a big Volvo, gleaming in dark blue, drew up and bumped on to the forecourt.

'I'm so sorry! The traffic is awful.'

McLeish went down the steps and courteously assisted Claudia Yeo and her packages from the car, noting as he did so the car telephone fitted between the front seats. He hoped that his people had managed to stand between Peter Yeo and a phone, but noted that he could not be confident that the Yeos had not been in communication. Claudia was not looking particularly tense or suspicious — indeed, her attention seemed to be primarily on domestic details, including the annoying fact that the milkman, ignoring the note she had left out for him the day before, had left too much milk. McLeish, reminded of his own domestic situation, just stopped himself from volunteering to buy a couple of pints from her. Pulling himself together, he got them all sitting down in the pretty drawing-room.

'Events have moved on a little since we fixed this appointment with you, Mrs Yeo,' he began carefully, glancing to see that she was not holding her cup as he spoke. 'Your husband is at Scotland Yard at the moment. He has now told us that Angela Morgan was in fact with him at the offices of Yeo Davis on the morning of the Saturday when she disappeared.'

Claudia Yeo stared at him, open-mouthed. The colour literally drained from her face, leaving her careful make-up looking yellow. 'Have you arrested him?'

That was not the question McLeish had been expecting. He knew from long experience that people in shock asked apparently utterly foolish questions, and on that basis Claudia Yeo's response should have been something on the lines of 'What were they doing?' or 'Why was she there?' But she had asked a quite different question, and one very much to the point: how much danger was her husband in?

'Not at the moment,' he said, unhelpfully. 'But he gave us a false statement the first time, and I have no reason to suppose this second statement is any more reliable.' He saw her fingers clench round the edge of the table. Her colour was coming back, and she pushed a stray piece of hair behind her left ear, drawing his attention to the fashionable, heavy gold earrings. She got up, abruptly, and walked away to the kitchen. He and Davidson looked at each other, momentarily disconcerted, but she came back immediately carrying another jug of coffee.

'I knew Angela was there,' she said, pouring coffee carefully, not looking at him.

'How?' McLeish was on to it at once.

'I followed him. I thought he was going to meet her, and so was actually relieved when he went to the office. I was just going to go away when I saw her arrive.' She looked McLeish in the eye. 'So I waited around. I thought about going in — I think I might have, I wanted to know whether they were making a fool of me.'

'But you didn't?'

'No, and I'll tell you why. I wasn't the only person hanging around. I'd just decided I bloody well *was* going to go in when I saw Giles Hawick. He was standing on the other side of the road, looking up at the windows.'

'Are you sure?'

'Of course I am. I know him well. So I decided not to go in. I didn't want an audience for another bloody awful quarrel with Peter. We've had enough of them about that bitch.'

'Did he see you? Mr Hawick, I mean?'

She hesitated. 'I couldn't be sure. I ducked back round the corner pretty smartly, I can tell you, but I wasn't expecting to see him and for all I know he might have seen me first.'

'You didn't wait to see what happened?' McLeish watched her as she struggled for an answer. 'Better not to lie,' he observed, drily. 'I'm feeling pretty unconvinced by you and your husband right now and it won't take much to put you right at the top of my list.'

'Are you threatening me?' She sat bolt upright, a formidable woman in her own right, her surroundings a statement of power and privilege. McLeish was unimpressed.

'No. Unless you or your husband killed her. If you didn't, stop messing us around and tell the truth.'

'The truth is that I didn't hang around. I thought if there was going to be a major row I wanted to be as far away from it as possible. So I went shopping, as I told you — I didn't want to be at home if Peter came back after an embarrassing scene. So I don't know what happened. But Giles *was* there.'

'He is a family friend, I think you told us?'

'But he's not my husband, Mr McLeish. I didn't think I was misleading you by not telling you; Peter said it was Giles you suspected. But if you're trying to pin this on Peter, I'm not going to keep quiet about Giles. He was *there*, I'm telling the truth.' There were tears in her eyes and red blotches over her cheekbones.

'Have you not talked to your husband about all this?' McLeish was frankly incredulous.

'No, I haven't. He was a bit late for the dinner on Saturday, rather thoughtful, but very affectionate, and I just wasn't going to rock the boat. And the next thing I heard Angela was missing, and the rest you know.' She inspected McLeish's expression. 'Look,' she said, leaning over the table, 'I've made an awful fuss twice before and it hasn't got me anywhere. Peter's just a better poker player than I am, and he's got less to lose. I'm forty-two and I've seen divorced girlfriends of mine trying to find someone else. All the spare men of our age want a twenty-three-year-old bimbo, not older girls like us. *And* they can pull them. So I was going to hang on and just hope that Giles would take little Miss Morgan away, and give her a hard time.' She glared at him, then mentally replayed the last sentence and clapped both hands to her mouth. 'I didn't mean that. I'm not saying Giles killed her.'

McLeish, who had been waiting his chance, nodded to Davidson, who got up and left the room. The noise of the front door slamming followed immediately.

'Where's he gone?'

'To telephone.'

'You could have used ours. Oh, I see, you didn't want to. What has Peter told you? Didn't he see Giles that day?'

'We'll have to ask him. As far as we know at the moment, your husband is the last person to have seen Angela Morgan alive.'

‘Oh *no*!’ Claudia Yeo turned white. ‘Look, he may be a bit of a stupid shit sometimes, but he isn’t a murderer.’

On the heels of this tribute Bruce Davidson returned, nodding to McLeish.

‘Did you speak to him?’ Claudia Yeo asked, turning the full power of her attention on him. Davidson hesitated.

McLeish said firmly: ‘Mrs Yeo, I’m going to want to collect a revised statement from you as well, so I would be glad if you would come back with us.’

‘Can I see Peter?’

‘When we have both your revised statements signed.’

She looked carefully into his face. ‘You’re not arresting me?’

‘No.’

Davidson cleared his throat, and McLeish realized he had been about to forget a key line of questioning. ‘One thing I did wonder about, Mrs Yeo. What made you suspect the affair was still continuing?’

She started to speak, hesitated fatally, and turned slowly scarlet.

‘Was it an anonymous letter?’

‘Yes, it was. Just like the one Giles got, apparently. I mean, letters cut out of a newspaper. Much the same words.’

‘Why didn’t you tell us?’

‘Because it might have made you suspicious of Peter. But I can’t make it much worse now, can I?’

McLeish indicated that this was correctly perceived, and picked away at her, establishing that there had been two letters, one received three months ago and a second about ten days before Angela Morgan’s death. No, to her regret she hadn’t kept it, she had just torn the beastly thing up and put it in the dustbin. But the contents had nagged away at her.

‘So you decided to check?’

‘Yes. I didn’t really think Peter had *that* much work to catch up on at the office.’

They let her wash and redo her face, and change into a suit that she evidently considered more appropriate for visiting New Scotland Yard than the slightly baggy tweed skirt in which she had arrived. Freshly made-up, wearing rather too much good jewellery, an expensive brown suit and a pale beige silk shirt, she looked both smart and formidable. Any neighbours wondering about her movements would probably have concluded that he was her chauffeur, McLeish decided, sourly, as he held open the back door for her, having snatched up the bag containing the remains of his lunch. He stood back from the car as she settled herself, and raised both eyebrows at Davidson.

'Hawick's gone, John. Plane took off half an hour ago. Anyone wanting to talk to him will have to do it in Washington.'

CHAPTER 14

'So how was Tristram?' Charles Wilson asked absently, watching with love what he could see of his sleeping baby daughter.

'Pathetic.' Perry Wilson was sounding truly exasperated. 'I saw him on both Saturday and yesterday. He was complaining that the Americans had been tipped off and were victimizing British groups.'

'I take it that's true, but who should blame them?' Charlie spoke in an elder brother's disapproving tones.

'Course they watch the groups. Tristram knew that, he's just whingeing. Never mind him, have you seen Frannie? I talked to her on the phone but she won't let me buy her dinner, or even a present.'

'She's been here once to see the baby. She cried. John's gone you know, he's got someone else . . .'

'That I'd understood. But what's she doing — I mean why won't she talk to us?'

His elder brother sighed, then smiled involuntarily as the snuffling baby found her fingers and stuffed them in her mouth.

'Well, she's pissed off with us, isn't she? She had to go to New York, and that caused the break. And from the way Tris is behaving we might as well have left him there.'

Silence fell between the brothers. Perry said, reluctantly, that perhaps it was a bit late for this piece of thinking. 'But what is she *doing*?' he demanded, fretfully. 'Why can't I go round and see her?'

'She doesn't want us, does she? Not even you, unbelievable though you may find it,' Charlie said.

'No,' Perry agreed, after a resentful silence. 'No, she doesn't want us. I'll go and see John?'

'Perry, for God's sake!'

'No, all right. Bloody hell. Blast Tris.'

* * *

Jennifer Morgan was sitting in her small office, gazing unseeingly at another doubtful pot, her well-trained mind refusing to apply itself at all. This would pass, she thought desperately. She just must resist the urge to tell anyone; nothing was going to make her feel any better.

The phone rang and she spilt her coffee. As she struggled to clean up the mess with shaking hands and an inadequate amount of Kleenex, she found she had agreed, hypnotized, to see John McLeish, who was, he had said, in the area.

She only just had herself under control and her desk clean when McLeish arrived, looking enormous in her small office. He sat down, and she found herself unable to look away from the bright, watchful, dark-brown eyes.

'I'm afraid you've missed coffee,' she said, unhopefully.

'No matter. I've come to talk to you again about these anonymous letters.'

'Oh?'

'Mrs Yeo also received two letters.'

Jennifer Morgan felt her hands getting hot, and gritted her teeth.

'I wondered if you could help us any more?'

Soft-spoken for such a big man, she thought, in a late attempt at critical analysis as she stared at him, frozen, and saw his eyes narrow.

'It was me,' she said, helplessly, with a feeling of appalled relief.

'And the letters to Giles Hawick?' McLeish sounded completely matter-of-fact, like a man putting letters into a crossword puzzle.

'Yes.'

'How many did you send? Two to Mrs Yeo, two to Mr Hawick. Any others?'

'No, no,' she rushed to reassure him. 'Just those four.'

'Why?' he asked, gently, and she realized that there had been a considerable silence in the room since she had last spoken.

'I wanted to stop them marrying,' she said drearily. 'I thought if Giles just understood what Angela was like, he wouldn't want to marry her. But he didn't seem to take any notice, he didn't believe it; so I wrote to Claudia Yeo. I thought she'd go to Giles and *make* him understand that Angie was still having an affair with her Peter. But nothing happened.'

'Until Angela was murdered.'

She looked back at him, speechless, her own worst fears articulated. 'I feel sick,' she said faintly, and put her head down on the desk until she felt slightly better. Lifting her head slowly, she realized the man had not moved at all, but was sitting waiting for her to go on, the brown eyes very cold.

'Giles *couldn't* have done that! If he had believed the letters he would just have walked away, he wouldn't have lost control.' She was gabbling in her need to convince him. The face opposite her was impassive, and she despaired.

'I know he wouldn't,' she said hopelessly. 'She was my sister — do you think I would have risked telling him a thing like that if I had thought he was violent-tempered enough to hurt her?'

'I don't know,' McLeish said, evenly. 'Depends perhaps how much you wanted Giles Hawick back.'

This indifferent assessment galvanized Jennifer. 'You stupid man, don't you see? With Angela dead, I'll never have a chance with him again! How can he ever marry a person who reminds him all the time of someone who was killed like that?' She stopped, exhausted, but saw that she had got through; something of the coldness had gone and he was looking interested.

'So you did not intend to stimulate either Mr Hawick or Mrs Yeo to murder?'

'Not only did I not mean to, I don't believe I did, even accidentally.' Emboldened, she glanced at him and found herself frightened again; his was the impersonal look of the hunter.

'*I* didn't kill her,' she said, horrified. 'I couldn't do anything like that, even though I hated her for taking Giles away and then treating him badly.' She felt sick again, but swallowed resolutely, praying that she would manage to hold out, while John McLeish waited for her to break.

'I'd like you to come back to New Scotland Yard with me to make a statement, now,' he said eventually, judging that she was not going to say anything else, not yet.

She looked round her office blindly, located her coat, and tried and failed to work out what message she could possibly leave with the departmental secretary. There was, she thought, nothing at all to be done, she would just have to endure. She stepped out into the plain, chilly corridor with John McLeish at her heels.

* * *

'Catherine, that was your admirer Ian Wylie on the blower. Sounds rather pleased with himself, but he'll not tell me about it. You're to call him back.'

'Thanks, Bruce.' Catherine Crane, looking beautiful and tidy in the cluttered canteen, like a lily on a dung-heap, Davidson thought, followed him out, hustling him along.

'If it's good news, it'll wait, lass. Wylie wanted John first off, mind,' he added, maliciously.

'Then it will be good news,' Catherine Crane said serenely, sitting on her desk to use the phone. 'Ian? It's Catherine Crane. What's up?'

'You'll not believe it,' the voice at the other end of the phone assured her. 'The folk with the Border terrier — you know, the ones Mr Hawick saw? We've got them, and they place him on the track there at five o'clock on the Saturday, just when it was getting dark. He wasn't hurrying, either.'

Catherine Crane congratulated him warmly before going on to the details, and Bruce Davidson, listening in and watching her, reflected that he would have asked Wylie for chapter and verse long before he uttered a civil word of congratulation. Catherine's way worked better, you had to concede.

'But how did you find them, Ian?'

'You'll laugh. The bloke is a copper, isn't he? Sergeant in the uniformed branch here, near retiring age, so takes all his holidays and doesn't bust his braces with weekend work. He and his lady wife walked the dog, same like usual, on the Saturday, and on the Sunday morning they put the dog in kennels, got into the car, and took a plane to Tenerife on one of those three-weeks-for-the-price-of-two oldies' deals. Never read a newspaper in three weeks. Just come back, haven't they, and found every policeman in Derbyshire looking for a Border terrier and a late-middle-aged couple.'

'Are they sure it was Hawick they met?'

'Yes. Or they were when they saw the pictures. They thought he was a TV actor at the time, only they couldn't think who he was. Fancy, they said to each other; wonder who he is? Got it immediately from the photos. Cor, stone the crows!'

Catherine Crane was laughing in sympathy. 'Oh, Ian, what a set-up! I'll get DCI McLeish to call you; he'll be really pleased.'

Bruce Davidson watched as Catherine tranquilly chatted on, sardonic but admiring of the technique. She had made quite sure of Inspector Wylie's co-operation on anything she might ask for ever again by the generosity of her thanks and the flattering implication that but for him the couple would never have been found.

'Doesn't put Hawick really in the clear though, does it?' he observed stubbornly as she came off the phone. 'He could have done it, killed her earlier on the Saturday, then rushed up to Derbyshire.'

'Hardly likely, though,' Catherine said, firmly, and Davidson was agreeing, reluctantly, when John McLeish arrived in the doorway, bristling with energy.

'Jennifer Morgan's downstairs. I was right. She wrote the letters. Come on Bruce.'

'John, wait!' Catherine Crane rushed after the two of them, explaining about Ian Wylie's lucky find. He was gratifyingly pleased, but his attention was plainly on the interview with Jennifer Morgan, and she felt a little piqued as he and Bruce Davidson clattered off, chatting animatedly. Looking round to see what she could do, her eye fell on the Huntley file. She frowned at it. The position on Penelope Huntley was distinctly unsatisfactory; she had not succeeded in eliminating her from the enquiry or in making her any more convincing as a suspect than she ever had been. Penelope had had a very strong motive, was taking no trouble at all to disguise her dislike of the dead girl, and had no alibi for the time when the car must have been dumped, or for the most likely time when Angela, dead or dying, had been pushed down the embankment in Cambridgeshire. It was all very well for John to get excited because he had found the writer of the anonymous letters, but that didn't mean he had also found a murderess.

Catherine brooded about Penelope, reading the files, then realized that, despite heavy work put in by the teams, no one had been to see her bank manager. It was well worth establishing how strong Penelope Huntley's financial motivation had been, and it would be a bank manager who had the best eye on that. She rang him up and made an appointment for that afternoon. Her start was delayed again by phone calls, but a good hour and a half later she was ready to go.

She was hesitating outside New Scotland Yard when she saw Peter Yeo emerge from the tube station and watched him, amused. She would have put money on his not knowing where the underground was or how it worked. She was also surprised to see him anywhere near New Scotland Yard; it had been clear from last week's session that he was very much under suspicion, and that John McLeish had been hesitant about letting him leave after he had made a revised statement. She nodded to Yeo, in a reserved way, as he noticed her, and watched him pause, then alter course to speak to her, the good manners still much in evidence. But he was showing signs of strain, she thought, suddenly alert. He looked even more stressed than when she had last seen him.

'How are you?' he asked, with that misleading air of personal interest, and Catherine replied that she was well, merely deciding whether to go by tube or take a taxi.

'I took the tube today; there's a water-main blown on the Euston Road and the traffic is chaos. Where are you going?'

Catherine told him Brixton before she had thought properly, and his face, surprisingly, lit up. 'To see the Huntley girl? The more I think about it, the more I think she must have been involved. I mean, she gets the money and she's not very well balanced.' He looked into Catherine's professionally unyielding face and sighed. 'Well, at least you're still interviewing her. Look, I've got ten minutes and the tube is amazingly fast, if rather unpleasant. You want coffee?'

He sounded unhopeful and Catherine surprised herself by accepting. He was a suspect, of course, she told herself, stirring her coffee, but that wasn't the point. He was a bit like Dave, and like Dave had apparently stuck with his wife and kids when the crunch came. There was something about marriage she must not have understood — Dave's wife was not particularly attractive, and he didn't spend a lot of time at home, and it was obvious that she didn't treat Dave with the same care and affection that Catherine herself had. But he had stayed with her, even when someone who loved him and had a lot more to offer had appeared.

Having invited her for coffee, Peter Yeo did not seem to have much to say. He was obviously fully preoccupied with whatever was happening in his own head, and Catherine, knowing instinctively that he might be ready to tell her something, decided that silence might be the best way of forcing out whatever it was. She gazed out of the steamy window and saw, in cameo, Jennifer Morgan emerging from the Yard's main door, looking exhausted, Bruce Davidson by her side. She looked away quickly, but Peter Yeo had seen them too.

'What's Jennifer doing here? She looks terrible. I thought you'd questioned her already.'

Catherine stayed safely and, she hoped, ominously silent, but Peter Yeo was galvanized. '*Of course* — she had an even better motive. Cash *and* Giles Hawick.'

Catherine Crane considered her coffee, startled by the crudity of Yeo's need to find another suspect. She had seen that kind of behaviour before but had not expected it of this smooth customer.

'Is that right? Is *she* now the favourite?'

'You can hardly expect me to comment on that, Mr Yeo,' Catherine said, coldly.

'No, sorry.' The man made a visible effort to pull himself together and snatched at his coffee, eyes not moving from where a wooden-faced Davidson was handing Jennifer Morgan into a cab. 'Did you find out who wrote those letters?' he asked, every ounce of his attention bent on Jennifer Morgan as she climbed awkwardly into the taxi. 'The ones to Claudia and Giles?'

'We are continuing with our inquiries,' Catherine said, jolted, in what she hoped were her best non-committal tones. Risking a glance sideways at Peter Yeo, she found his attention was not with her at all; he had finished his coffee in one gulp and was biting on a lump of sugar from the bowl.

'Quick fix,' he said, seeing her eyes on him. 'Must go, thank you for your company.' He whisked himself over to the counter to pay, and she watched him fascinated. The exhausted, stressed man she had met a quarter of an hour before was gone; Peter Yeo was back on form, colour in his face and head up. He flipped a hand at her, and was gone, moving fast towards the Houses of Parliament, leaving her sitting feeling that she had stepped on something that wasn't there. What was it she had missed? Had the man simply been cheered by the fact that enquiries were continuing around other potential suspects? Had he assumed from last week that the police thought him guilty beyond a doubt, and been given new hope by realizing they were still considering other people? He must surely have known that if the police had been confident enough, he would not now be a free man?

Catherine gave up; people under stress reacted oddly and it was probably a waste of time to look very carefully at their behaviour. At this rate, it would be tea-time before she got to Brixton, and she should get on.

* * *

Eight floors up, John McLeish and Bruce Davidson were considering Jennifer Morgan's statement. She had admitted formally to four anonymous letters, one sent three months before to Giles Hawick; one two weeks after that to Claudia Yeo; a third letter to Giles Hawick three weeks ago; and a fourth to Claudia Yeo ten days later, just before Angela Morgan's death. She had told them, sodden with tears, that Giles had appeared to take no notice at all of the two letters she had sent to him, so she had written to Claudia on both occasions after about a week's gap.

The first letter to Claudia *had* elicited a result, as the policemen knew from their interviews with the Yeos. A fierce row between the Yeos had ensued, but Peter's affair with Angela had evidently continued. Giles Hawick, by his own account, had taken no notice at all of the first letter, believing it to be the work of the jealous Penelope Huntley. But though there had been no outward signs of any difference in his behaviour, the letter must have triggered his suspicions about his fiancée — he had not received the third letter when intended, but he had still followed her to the office. Claudia *had* received the fourth letter, and had acted to check its truth, and perhaps acted to deal with the threat to her marriage.

'Poor lass,' Bruce Davidson had said, shaking his head over the shaky signature. 'She'll never forgive herself for this lot.'

'Bruce!' John McLeish knew he was tired but Davidson's lapses into sentimentality, though rare, always annoyed him. 'Poor lass nothing. At the best she didn't have the guts to put herself on the line and tackle the situation directly. At the worst she wrote those letters and when no one did enough about them she killed her sister.'

'Never!'

'Don't tell me people don't kill their sisters over a man, Bruce. Even in Ayr.'

'Especially in Ayr, now I come to think on it. Aye, but this lassie hasn't what it takes to do that.'

'It could have been accidental — the death I mean. Angela could have stumbled and fallen back?'

Davidson shook his head. 'I don't see it John. I don't see Jennifer being able to manage it without falling apart. I don't see her moving the body. Look at her today, over a few letters.'

'It may have been more than a few letters that was distressing her, Bruce.'

Davidson considered him, shaken. 'But you let her go?'

'Yes. There is no real proof, and there are still others in the frame, even if Hawick *is* looking less likely. He's back, by the way. We're seeing him this afternoon and it is going to be embarrassing, given that he never told us he was by Angela's office on the Saturday morning. I told Himself, and he very decently offered to come with us but I thought we'd just keep it at my level.'

* * *

A good decision to have taken, Davidson thought admiringly as he listened to McLeish explaining to Hawick that the couple he had met in Derbyshire that Saturday afternoon had been traced. The junior Minister was still looking ravaged, but better, even jetlagged as he was.

'I'm very glad. I've been realizing how difficult it was going to be to find them — and how difficult for all of us if we couldn't.'

'Indeed. And particularly difficult because while you were away we turned up a witness who claims you were in the vicinity of Miss Morgan's office on the Saturday morning.'

The man visibly jumped, Davidson observed, and equally visibly considered whether a quick bit of bluster would work, but that impulse died in the face of John McLeish's politely enquiring expression.

'Who is the witness?'

'Someone who knows you personally and was in no doubt about the identification.'

'Yes. Yes, well I *was* there.' He flung out of his chair towards the window. 'I'm sorry, I'm finding this very embarrassing.'

John McLeish sat in impressive silence and Hawick collected himself. 'I was having doubts about Angela, Chief Inspector. I really had not taken the anonymous letter very seriously, but you know how it is . . . once you've been alerted to something, even if you don't believe it, well, you keep your eyes open. Claudia Yeo was at school with my sister, and was a girlfriend of mine when we were in our early twenties, so I knew her quite well. I saw her at a party about, what, three weeks after I got that letter, and she was looking terrible. She was trying to get me to say Angela should leave her job, taking the line that surely it would be a conflict for me having Angela in a firm specializing in government relations, and that although, as anyone would tell me, Peter would miss her very much, it must be the right thing from everyone's point of view to have Angela do something else. She certainly managed to imply that Peter and Angela were still involved sexually without actually saying so.'

'Did you talk to Miss Morgan about it? I am sure you can see this is important.'

Giles Hawick considered him with something between dislike and respect. 'Oh, I do see, yes. Well, I didn't tackle Angela about it directly, I have to confess. I did tell her, however, that I wanted her to get out of government relations work, go into straightforward financial PR or another branch of the business where my contacts and friends could be useful to her but where there would not be so much likelihood of a conflict of interest.'

'But you didn't talk about Peter Yeo?'

'No, I didn't. I should have, of course. Angela would have known there was a hidden agenda. I suppose I hoped she'd hear what I was saying.'

'But she didn't?'

'I don't know. I stopped thinking about it — very easy to stop thinking in politics, one's so busy. Claudia Yeo rang me up about a week before Angela died, I suppose. She asked me to have a drink with her, and when we met she had two very quickly. Then she asked me if I was really getting married, because she'd been talking to Angela and had got the impression the whole thing was cooling off, and that Yeo Davis were making plans for next year in which she played a very major part.'

'What did you say?'

The Minister laughed sourly. 'Well, it was very awkward — I said that we'd both been too busy to discuss much what would happen after the wedding but everything else was on course. And I got rid of Claudia before she could tell me anything else.' He sighed. 'But when I thought about it afterwards, I realized I couldn't just dismiss it as Claudia stirring things up — she was obviously having real trouble with Peter. So I decided I would tackle Angela but, you know, *not* just before I went away on a walking weekend. So I never did raise it with her but — I'm not proud of this — when she said she would do some shopping and might go into the office I decided to go and see if Peter Yeo was there, too. I know his car and he always leaves it on a meter outside the door.' He fell silent.

'So you went there. At what time?'

'Must have been about ten-thirty to eleven. I got the eleven-thirty train. Peter's car was there, so was Angie's. Then I felt a bloody fool because I realized it didn't actually prove anything — no reason she shouldn't have gone to the office.'

'Might they not indeed have been more likely to meet for other purposes at Miss Morgan's flat?'

'Oh no. Of course you don't know, how should you? The woman living in the flat opposite Angela was at school with my sisters and Claudia. I can't imagine that Peter Yeo would have been prepared to visit Angela there on a regular basis. Not if Claudia was already suspicious.' He caught McLeish's eye. 'There's a lot of people in Parliament with these problems, Chief Inspector.'

Not just in Parliament, John McLeish thought fleetingly before returning to the matter in hand. 'What did you do then?'

'I thought about going into the office; then I thought that that was silly and undignified. If I was suspicious of Angela I should speak to her directly, and I'd decided not to do that. So I went to Derbyshire.'

He swung his chair towards the window, then got up with a jerkily, badly co-ordinated movement and snatched a Kleenex out of the box on his desk. McLeish and Davidson waited.

'Who was it saw me? I suppose you're not going to tell me. Somebody *did* see me, I take it?'

'Oh yes.'

The Minister considered him. 'Did you get any further with the anonymous letters?'

'I was coming on to that. Jennifer Morgan has told us that she was the writer both of the ones you received, and two received by Claudia Yeo.'

Hawick gaped at him, his poise gone for a moment. '*Jennifer* wrote them? Are you sure? I mean, she's terribly upset by Angela's death — are you sure she isn't just confessing to anything?'

'She isn't confessing to her sister's murder, sir, just to writing anonymous letters. She has told us that she thought Angela's marriage — to you — would be a disaster and she could not think how else to stop it.'

Giles Hawick looked at them wordlessly, then looked away, and finally rested his elbows on the table, hands laced across his forehead. 'Oh God. Poor Jennifer. Where is she now?'

'She left Scotland Yard about two hours ago.'

Hawick's head came up. 'Was she much distressed?'

John McLeish was about to say that naturally she had been when he realized what Hawick was suggesting.

'Chief Inspector, there seems to me a real danger that she will over-react.'

John McLeish, cursing himself, looked round for a phone but Hawick forestalled him.

'For God's sake, let me do one difficult thing right. I *will* ring her — could you just wait outside for five minutes?'

'Sir, just see if she answers, then I'll go. Otherwise we'll send someone round.'

He heard the phone answered and pushed Davidson out of the room with him, feeling like a brutal, unimaginative apparatchik. He waited, trying not to bite his fingernails, for a long five minutes until Hawick buzzed for him to come back.

'She's all right, but I'm going over there. She needs convincing that she is still part of the human race.' He was organizing coat, gloves and papers as he spoke.

'She must be considered still as a suspect in her sister's murder,' McLeish reminded him.

'If she did *that*, then the need is even greater.' Hawick spoke with conviction and McLeish remembered that his grandfather had been a Methodist minister. He stood back, respectfully, words about signing statements dying on his lips. All that could happen later, much later.

* * *

Catherine Crane was getting on very well indeed with Penelope Huntley's bank manager, a lively, shrewd young Yorkshireman who was putting in two years in the salt mines at a Barclays branch in Brixton.

'Well, I found her a bit peculiar, between you and me. And she certainly spent money like water, not that you ever saw much result for it in her clothes. She always looked as if she'd thrown them on — not like you, Sergeant, if I may say so.' He considered her longingly, wondering if he dared suggest a quick drink after work, before remembering he was due at the Clapham Rotary. 'Look, I'll show you. Her mortgage is with us, too. Her uncle — a Mr Coombes — helped her to buy the flat which cost her — what? £70,000, three years ago. She had about £50,000 on mortgage, which was far too high in relation to her salary, but he guaranteed the payments. Perfectly all right with us. So the flat went up in value and she borrowed even more: another £20,000 — again, all right with us, since uncle was guaranteeing payments. Then uncle died and left her £200,000. I expected her to trade up.'

'But she didn't?'

'No. She was really angry, and . . . well, you know all this. She paid off her £70,000 of course, and the small overdraft. Then she gave up her job and took a set of expensive holidays. Made a fair old hole even in £130,000, I can tell you. She started using a lot of cash, too; she told me it was for parties. Well, it was her cash, wasn't it? I watched it shrink. We keep the share certificates here as well, and I did the schedule before you came — there's about £40,000 left. And the flat of course — but property prices haven't risen that much round here.'

'If she hadn't come into another lot she'd have been stuck in that flat?'

'Well, she owned it outright. No mortgage to pay. She could have traded up easily if she got a full-time job.' They looked at each other, two children of working parents, both mortgaged heavily. 'I mean, I didn't sympathize — I'd never throw away money like that — but I was sorry for her. She'd expected to be really rich.'

'She isn't doing too badly now,' Catherine pointed out.

'No. And of course if she had got a full-time job instead of working only when she felt like it she would have been fine. But she wasn't trying, and I wasn't looking forward to having to say in a year or so that I couldn't lend to someone with no income.'

But he had never needed to, Catherine thought. Penelope Huntley had been saved by Angela Morgan's death, had got herself out of a downward financial spiral and been able to start again. She sat thinking about the girl who had felt herself so comprehensively rejected by her substitute father and wondered what would have happened if her position had not been redeemed by Angela's death.

She thanked the young bank manager, went out into the crowded street, and walked slowly towards the supermarket where Penelope claimed to have been shopping at six-thirty on that Saturday three weeks before. She turned in, found the manager, and apologetically but unhesitatingly went over the ground with him again. No one there had remembered Penelope Huntley, but they were always crowded at that time on a Saturday and they had been short-handed — sorry they were sure, dear, not to be able to help, just like they had told the other sergeant.

Catherine decided she had had enough and needed to sit and drink coffee and think. She was sufficiently tired and discouraged to walk into the nearest place available, a small, run-down, workmen's café, occupied principally by a large jukebox, a discouraged Irish proprietor and a predominantly Jamaican clientèle. Catherine collected her coffee and sat, as forbiddingly as she knew how, at the end of the bar, feeling for her notebook. She realized that her immediate neighbour, a black man in his twenties with dreadlocks, was moving in on her, and hunched one shoulder defensively.

'Hoo,' he observed to no one, 'what's a beautiful whitey girl like you doing down here? They bad men in this place.'

Catherine ignored him, but he continued, and she started to feel a fool. 'I'm a police officer trying to get a break before I go back to work, that's what I'm doing,' she snapped, noticing two of the clientèle start to edge towards the door.

'What you investigating, pretty lady?' the man asked. She turned to look at him properly and realized that the brown eyes were steady and intelligent.

'I'm checking an alibi,' she said, deciding to take a chance. 'There's a girl we want to clear . . . to stop wondering about. She says she was round here just over three weeks ago, on a Saturday. We can't find anyone who remembers her.' She showed him the pictures.

He took them and held them up to the inadequate, harsh lighting. 'I know her! She called Penelope. What day she say she here?'

Catherine told him, amazed, and he startled her further by pulling out a pocket diary and consulting it, working his way back, considering the closely written pages.

'The group was recording that day, round the corner here. We broke around six p.m., the technician need to eat. We came here — the food no good, but it convenient. I see Penelope here; she just having a coffee and she bin shopping, lots of bags.'

'Are you quite sure?'

'Certain sure. We don't do no recording on a Saturday except that day. Tell you how I know — it was the day after my birthday and I was embarrassed to see her; I thought I could have ask her to the party and I hadn't. She a bit draggy, but I was sorry for her. So I paid her coffee and gave her a jolly-up but she real sad.' Too depressed, indeed, even to remember this critical encounter, thought Catherine, unable to believe her luck. She looked doubtfully at the dreadlocks and decided that John McLeish must be able to overlook appearances and see, as she had, an eccentric but intrinsically reliable man beneath this unpromising exterior.

'If I ask you properly, will you give us a statement? If you're really sure? This could be important.'

'You promise I don't get her in no trouble?'

A very confident lad this one, Catherine thought, fleetingly. The average black man in London is worried about getting *himself* in trouble with the police.

'I promise. You're getting her out of trouble.'

'What trouble?'

Catherine hesitated. 'The worst.'

The young man considered her soberly. 'You too pretty to be a real police lady. I'll give you a statement but I won't go near the pigs in the station here.'

'Deal.' Catherine put out her hand, and he took it, laughing. 'You come with me now and I'll buy the taxi,' she said, briskly following up her advantage, and they left together with every eye in the café on them.

CHAPTER 15

'OK, OK, here we go.' Francesca put the phone down and beamed at Rajiv, who had poked his head round her door. 'We're on! Ministers have approved assistance to Huerter, all we have to do is flatten Treasury. A letter needs to go to Giles Hawick at the Treasury now, seeking agreement.'

'It won't get by without a meeting,' Rajiv said conclusively.

'Never,' she agreed. 'I'll find out when the next E Committee is.' She picked up the phone to talk to a colleague in the Cabinet Office and learn when the next scheduled meeting of the Economic Affairs Committee of the Cabinet was due to take place. 'Yes, it is Huerter,' she confirmed, unsurprised to find that the Cabinet Office knew exactly where the next storm was coming from. 'Our Ministers have approved. There'll be a letter round this evening, but I wanted to tell them when "E" was, with the covering submission, since there's bound to be opposition. We *can* get to that one, just, if you bend the forty-eight-hour rule a bit. We can't wait the extra week because the company is in deep shit, sorry, major financial problems . . . Clear it by correspondence, Julian? Not a chance. Look, I'll call you when I know the letter is leaving.'

She put the phone down, shaking her head. Matters on which two departments are utterly opposed are never cleared by correspondence, and she considered for a moment whether the chap in the Cabinet Office, a secondee several years her senior from DTI, was quite as good as everyone had thought.

She shared her doubts with Rajiv, who looked at her thoughtfully and wondered aloud what the party political situation was in the constituencies around Huerter and Barton? Francesca frowned at having forgotten to check, and he supplied the information from memory. Huerter was located in a strongly held government seat; the constituency next door, home to Barton's, was also strongly government-held; the two to the north and west were Opposition seats, one soft, one less so. It was not obvious either way, as Francesca observed on reflection, so they gave it up and she settled down to draft a letter for the relevant DTI Minister to send to his Treasury opposite number, which would recite smoothly the reasons why the DTI felt assistance at a level of £8 million should be granted, and would go on formally to seek Treasury's consent, as the Act required for any assistance above £1 million. The letter would be copied round the other Economic departments, signalling the start of a battle between Treasury and those Economic departments who saw advantage in supporting them, and the DTI and its adherents.

Francesca spent a peaceful hour writing a first draft, then passed it to Rajiv, who made a few amendments and gave it back to her, observing that further alterations would be a waste of time; several senior hands were going to feel it necessary to fiddle with the words of a document of this importance. Giving the letter to his secretary, for speed, she decided she had earned her lunch. On this thought she looked up to see David Thornton in the doorway of the office.

'David,' she said with pleasure, then realized that he was looking uncomfortable and distant.

'Yes. Would you like lunch?'

'Yes, please,' she said, refraining from pointing out that it was not yet twelve-thirty. 'I'll get my coat. Oh, thank you, Jean.'

She took the draft letter from Rajiv's secretary, remembering that in this tussle, which she had been enjoying up to that moment, she and David were on opposite sides. She decided to head into the wind. 'David. You know, I take it, that our Ministers are recommending assistance to Huerter. Would you like to see the letter I have drafted?'

He considered her, frowning. 'Oh, Huerter. Well, it was inevitable, wasn't it, that DTI Ministers would want to do it? Let's go out — that is if you have time?'

Francesca abandoned the draft for checking and onward transmission, ignoring the secretary's questioning look, and followed David Thornton down the long corridor and out of the building into Victoria Street, casting a sidelong look towards St James's Park tube station and New Scotland Yard. They were sitting next to each other in a comfortable pub before she realized that Thornton had not looked her in the face since arriving in her office.

'Sorry,' he said, abruptly and plunged off to fetch them drinks. He came back with two gin and tonics, and she tasted hers doubtfully while he drank half of his as if it were water.

'I had a telephone call from New York this morning,' he said, still not looking at her, after a long minute. 'Sarah is coming back rather sooner than she had planned. Tomorrow, in fact.'

'That will be nice for you, and Richard,' Francesca managed to say, feeling sick. She watched the slice of lemon floating next to the ice at the top of her drink and prayed not to weep.

'It means we shall not be able to meet as often,' Thornton said painstakingly, and she took in a deep careful breath, feeling the start of the familiar process of distancing herself from the intolerable.

'Of course,' she said, politely, 'you'll be busy.' She risked a look at him to find that he was staring at the table in embarrassment.

He reached a hand across the table and seized her wrist. 'I'm sorry. I don't want to stop. Can we go on, even if we have to be rather more flexible?'

It's the sort of thing women write to agony aunts about, Francesca thought, his hand warm on her wrist. Those letters which explain how the writer has been having an affair for five, seven, ten — inconceivable numbers of years — with this married bloke who keeps saying he is going to leave his wife, and you think, that woman is insane, how *could* she have wasted so much time? Well, now I know; if David were a different bloke, if the proposition he is putting to me were only a little less stark, I too might waste a lot of my life because it always feels like coming home when I am with him.

Francesca sat up straight, and turned her wrist in his hand so that he let go.

'Much better now, don't you think?' she said, trying to sound sensible and worldly, and deciding that with this man it did not matter that she had failed and that tears were steadily filling her eyes. 'I wouldn't be able to stand it,' she said, finding relief in the uncompromising truth.

He looked away, uncomfortably.

'Not your fault,' she said, baldly. 'I'm having a bad patch.'

'I'm sorry.' Thornton looked at her with relief. 'You don't want that drink, do you? I'll get you something else, and something to eat.'

'You can drink it.'

'I'm drinking too much. But I probably will.' He smiled at her and went off to the bar and she sat straight-backed, saying goodbye again to what had seemed like a haven of love and comfort. Enough of this, she thought: I am tired of being peripheral. *I* want to be the wife at whose homecoming all mistresses and other diversions are instantly and unhesitatingly abandoned. I am meant to be someone's cherished wife, daughter-in-law, mother even — if I must — but of central importance to someone. Not a mistress. And not a sister anymore.

She sat still, nursing this clarity of vision and managed a smile for David Thornton as he came back, a slightly stooping, burly, fifty-year-old, his large hands steadying a tray of drink and food.

'It's time I got married,' she said, as if they had been discussing the matter.

He followed her thought. 'Yes. I married late, as you know. It did me a lot of good, and I am happier for most of the time than I was before.'

'And you have a son.' It was, as it always had been, easy to say anything at all to him.

'And you might have a daughter instead of all those brothers.'

'That would be good.' Francesca finished her sandwich and washed it down with bitter lemon, holding his hand for comfort. It felt all right, she thought, in a curious way; sad but companionable. They looked at each other for a long moment, and she leant over and kissed him on the mouth, unheeding of her audience.

'Bye, David,' she said, feeling the tears well again.

'I'll come with you,' he said, and took her back to the Department, holding her hand as if she were a child, bracing himself to ignore any comments from his own generation.

Quite unnecessary to have worried, he thought dazed, five minutes later — they could have arrived entwined and half-dressed without arousing any comment at all. Bill Westland, Rajiv and three young men in urgent conclave, fell on Francesca without apparently noticing his presence or that she was close to tears. The letter, it appeared, required substantial redrafting and even her godfather had not been willing to do this without consulting her as the originating draftsperson. Standing unregarded just inside Westland's office, David Thornton tried to pick up what was happening.

'Treasury *aren't* going to oppose? Why not? Bill, are you sure you've got this right?'

'Thank you for your support, Francesca. It is not my judgement that is in issue, but David Llewellyn's. As the responsible Minister he tells me he has talked to Giles Hawick and they have agreed that Treasury will support. Which means it has no need to go to Cabinet, so it needs a different letter.'

'One expecting the answer yes, rather than your draft, darling, which anticipates objection,' Rajiv pointed out, helpfully. 'He wants the same points dealt with, of course.'

'Only differently. Yes, I do see.' Francesca had recovered. 'But what happened? Have his other troubles so unmanned the poor Giles Hawick that he can't cope with a battle, or what?'

This, which seemed to David Thornton like an eminently sensible question, and one to which he would have liked an answer, was greeted by the assembled senior officials as a major failure of taste, and five minutes later he followed Francesca, bloodied but totally unbowed, from the room.

'It must be political,' she said to him as to an old and trusted friend. 'Come with me.' He followed meekly, and watched her dial a number that she obviously knew well. 'Whip's office,' she explained, as she waited for an answer. 'Jim, darling, have you thirty seconds? You are good.' She explained succinctly what had happened and Thornton could just hear the man at the other end of the phone laugh.

He sat down, unable to hear any more but watching Francesca look amazed, then angry, then finally, reluctantly, amused. 'Bloody hell, Jim. So all the loyal efforts we've been making to put together the best possible case for assisting Huerter are irrelevant. The point turns out to be that some fool backbencher in the next-door constituency but one, with a not very exciting majority, is about to have to resign for reasons so unspeakable you aren't prepared to disclose them. I suppose that the government not assisting Huerter, while in accordance with its policy, wouldn't be the best start to a by-election campaign?' She scratched her head, visibly brooding. 'If it had been the constituency MP for Barton who had been found in bed with half the local football team, or whatever, the decision would have gone the other way? All right, you can explain to me another day. Thanks, anyway.'

She put the phone down and scowled at Thornton. 'How was I supposed to know *that*, may I ask?'

'I wonder if the MP in question is resigning in order to ensure assistance for Huerter?'

Francesca looked at him carefully and Thornton felt an enormous pang of regret as he watched her decide that he was being sardonic with her. 'I'll miss you.'

'And I you,' she said, briefly. 'Now I must do that letter. And tell the chairman of Huerter, if Bill hasn't. And, come to that, I might ring up Yeo Davis just before the announcement. They'll be sick as parrots.'

Looking back from the door, he saw her as he was always to remember her, rather flushed, hair spiked up, reaching with relish for a telephone, escaping into her own sphere of competence.

* * *

Catherine Crane was feeling as near piqued and neglected as she ever allowed herself. John McLeish had been obviously pleased when she had reported her discoveries of yesterday, but had now vanished without a word from his office. She felt abandoned, and was convinced that John's secretary was being a great deal less co-operative than she might be.

'I'm sorry, I don't know why he has gone off to Baldock, Sergeant. I agree, it must have something to do with the Morgan case — he was following a line of enquiry that he had initiated — but I'm afraid I know no more than that. Of course you could ring up the station there. He is with a Chief Inspector Standish.'

Ta very much, I don't think, Catherine Crane said inwardly, in a swift unexpected return to her childhood; John *would* be pleased with that, wouldn't he? She had made one major contribution: she had eliminated Penelope Huntley from the investigation. She had pulled her weight.

The afternoon had opened up before her — her paperwork was well up to date, no one would think the worse if she did some essential bits of personal administration, and she wasn't going to sit like a lemon in the office all afternoon. Just to show John McLeish how things should be done, she left a message with her shared secretary that she was moving around but would ring him at five p.m.

Two hours later she was at the top of Malplaquet Terrace, the cul-de-sac in which Angela Morgan's car had been found, telling herself that after all she had never seen this place, so busy had she been on other bits of the investigation, and a fresh eye might be helpful. What she hoped of course was that she might, by going over the ground again, bring off a coup. She walked slowly past the busy shops down to the big houses at the end of the road, hesitating as she tried to remember the number of the house near which the car had been found, then noticing that the chalk marks drawn by the forensic squad still showed faintly. She stood on the other side of the road considering the patch of road between two driveways where the dead girl's car had been parked, and let her mind go blank.

As she watched, an old lady crept, crab-wise, down the steps of the next-door house. A Jamaican workman, carrying a thermos and a plastic bag, strolled whistling past on his way towards the last house in the road. And across her field of vision walked a woman, tantalizing familiar. It was Claudia Yeo, Catherine realised with a jolt of excitement as she got a good view of her profile, which was slightly masked by a large silk headscarf.

Catherine stopped breathing and stood half hidden by the tree, momentarily frozen in fear of alerting the other woman as she hesitated by the pavement. After a petrified five seconds she remembered that Claudia Yeo had never met her, and knew she must move — it would be the sight of an unmoving watcher which would alert Mrs Yeo. She forced herself to walk to the end of the road, then to turn back, looking frustrated, as if she had been unable to find the house she wanted. As she turned back to face towards the top of the cul-de-sac she saw Claudia Yeo turn as well, look anxiously at her watch, and walk briskly up the road, in heavy, elegant, flat shoes. Catherine drew in a deep breath, felt her heart thump and her eyes clear in the happy certainty that there was only one thing to do — to follow Claudia Yeo wherever she might be going, and pray that there would be an opportunity to ring and tell someone — anyone — where she was and what she was doing. As she walked she tied on a drab headscarf; while not conceited about her beauty she knew that she was instantly recognizable to anyone who had got a good look at her, and that she needed to cover her bright blond hair and as much of her face as possible. She had to stand uncomfortably close to Claudia Yeo as she queued to pay her fare on the bus, but the woman was plainly unconscious of her surroundings, bent entirely on some internal calculation.

* * *

'Oh, Christ. Are you sure, Andy? This could just be Huerter whistling in the dark.'

Peter Yeo listened, forehead rested on his hand, as Andy Barton assured him, amidst a set of expletives, that even a businessman of the calibre of Huerter's chairman would not have got a message from the DTI completely backwards.

'But we *knew* DTI Ministers were going to recommend assistance, Andy. Are you sure that the message did not just say that? Our information, you see, is that Giles Hawick at Treasury intends to oppose.'

'Well, maybe he just isn't interested, Peter. And Angie, God rest her, isn't here to keep him up to scratch.'

Peter Yeo, experienced as he was, felt his breath taken away at the crudity of this analysis, but recovered his poise sufficiently to urge Andy Barton to do nothing drastic until Yeo Davis had had a chance to consult their other sources. Having got Barton off the phone, he assembled his partners for consultation.

A thick silence met his exposition of the problem, and it was with deep reluctance that he caught his finance director's eye.

'Means we can kiss goodbye to a five-hundred thou fee, if it's true, Peter.'

'I had realized, Tim,' Yeo snapped, relieving his pent-up tension. 'We need to find out if it's true or if it's just one of those panic rumours.'

'What about that girl at the DTI? Francesca Wilson?'

'I've met her once only,' Peter Yeo said, recollecting with unease the bright, enquiring, sardonic look she had fixed on him. 'I know she's the Principal responsible but I have a feeling she'll be stuffy.'

'I know Hawick's PS,' Mike Laister volunteered. 'But I'd rather not ask him unless it's absolutely critical.' He caught Peter Yeo's eye. 'Of course it's jolly important to us which way the decision has gone, but I think Michael would reasonably object that we'll all find out, either way, very soon.'

The voice of reason, as often, served only to inflame, and Peter Yeo said, through his teeth, that if something had gone horribly wrong, it was fundamental that Yeo Davis should bloody know before the customer — would Mike, for God's sake, go and pull that particular string?

The meeting waited in funereal silence while Mike banged out of the room on his errand. It was broken only by the sound of Tim Reagan punching a calculator and entering revised figures with a squeaky pencil on the draft balance sheet. Peter Yeo gritted his teeth but held himself in until Mike returned. One look at his face told the group the news.

'Fucking hell!' Yeo shouted. 'How did that happen? What's *wrong* with Hawick?' He stopped short, silenced by the expressions on his partners' faces, and made an enormous effort. 'All right, sorry, gentlemen all, evidently it *has* gone wrong, these things happen. Now, let's do what we can by way of damage limitation. Mike, get as much as you can on why it went wrong; Tim, make sure you've got everyone's time sheets. I'll need to talk about the fee when I ring him again.'

Two of his partners left the room, fast, but Tim Reagan sat tight.

'Regina's offered us £50K in settlement this morning. Counsel advised taking it and be thankful. He doesn't fancy our chances.'

Peter Yeo stared at him. 'If we do that, and there's no success fee from Barton, what happens?'

'We write £350,000 off the bottom line this year. That means we make about £50K this year. Before partners' drawings.'

'What have we drawn, do you know?'

'£257,000, give or take, as of this morning.'

Peter Yeo looked at him, taken aback by the speed of the response.

'We're £200K over at the bank on current overdraft. Plus, of course, the building loan,' the financial director further volunteered.

'What do we do?'

'The Bank won't let us overdraw any more, not when we tell them about Barton and the proposed Regina settlement. And we have to.'

'We could refuse to settle with Regina.'

'And get a note on our accounts? Doesn't help.'

There was a long silence which both men were reluctant to break.

'It just isn't realistic to ask anyone to refund money they've drawn,' Peter Yeo said, defensively.

'It's what we ought to be doing,' Tim said primly, and Peter Yeo remembered that this one had always reached the end of term in faraway Cambridge with enough of his grant left to get him through the vac.

'I don't see where next month's drawings are to come from, though, even if all our clients pay this month's bills inside a week.'

They contemplated that unlikely prospect and settled down to work out what could be done. At the end of a hard two hours it was finally clear to Peter Yeo that even if all partners drew nothing next month, Yeo Davis's cash flow was such that the bank would have to be made party to their difficulties. At the very best, all that could be hoped for was that the bank would allow substantially reduced drawings by the partners. That didn't sound too bad, Peter Yeo reflected, through a headache sitting persistently above his right eye, until you reminded yourself that all Yeo Davis partners and their wives had been confidently expecting a substantial surplus to share out at the year end, rather than a reduction in what they were already getting. His finance director watched him covertly and decided that the rumours about his relationship with Angela Morgan and his marriage had been absolutely true.

Peter Yeo, feeling the day had gone on long enough, climbed exhaustedly into his big car. In the general agitation in the office no one had remembered to feed the meter, so two plastic-covered wads of paper flapped across his windscreen as he drove off, causing him narrowly to miss a parked car.

The journey home was, as usual, full of cars containing other wearied men trying to get home as fast as possible, and he arrived wishing only for oblivion, or alternatively a double gin and tonic and a quadruple Anadin. He was momentarily relieved to find that Claudia was apparently still out since he did not want to see another human being. It was only half an hour later, when she had still not returned and both panaceas had started to take effect, that he let himself examine again the nagging, cold fear that now seemed to be with him more and more of the time.

* * *

'John.' Catherine Crane heaved a sigh of relief. 'It's me. I'm in a phone box in Markham Street. Mrs Yeo is in a café over the road.'

'Markham Street, Chelsea?'

'SW3, yes, sorry.'

'Two minutes from her house. What are you doing there?'

Catherine told him, quickly. 'I'd no idea this was where she lived,' she said, watching Claudia Yeo's unmoving profile. 'She came straight here from Malplaquet Terrace. She's just sitting in the café, not even drinking coffee. John?'

'I'm here. I'm organizing some help. You stay where you are, don't let her out of your sight.'

'What if she moves?'

'Stick with her.'

Catherine felt the hair at the back of her head prickle and remembered that John McLeish had been called away so suddenly earlier that day that he had not even told her where he was going.

'She isn't moving yet. Where were you, John?'

'At a carwash in Baldock. I worked out the murderer's route home, and the Cambridge force found the place. Angela Morgan's car was washed there, the bloke on duty remembered the letters on the number plate. His girl's initials are also AJM, as it happens. He wondered, he tells us, how he could get that nameplate without having to buy the BMW it went with.'

'Who was driving it?'

'He couldn't make anything of the photos. But he was quite sure it was a bloke — a big, heavy one. Not a lady, no way, he was clear. Catherine?'

'So it wasn't Mrs Yeo?'

'Not unless she brought a heavy to drive the car. And hid under the seat herself while they were in the garage. She still there? We can't place Yeo; I put a man on him, but the bugger hasn't rung in. Hang on, yes, he has. Yeo's at home already, Catherine. He must be in the house.'

Catherine looked out along the darkening street, hoping to see Yeo's watcher, but failing. Instead she saw a movement in the café. 'She's on the move, John. Do I let her go in? Into the house, I mean?'

'Sorry, I was assembling some more help. We haven't got enough to arrest Yeo, Cath, so we have to let her go in. I'm on my way. You just hang around outside. The bloke on Yeo is called Thomas.'

Catherine put the phone down unceremoniously and shot out of the phone box twenty yards behind Claudia Yeo, who was walking slowly. Catherine caught her breath and steadied herself, letting the other woman get further ahead. Claudia put her key in the door, and Catherine saw her head come up in response to some sound within the house. Looking cautiously round for Yeo's watcher again, she spotted him dawdling on the other side of the road.

Claudia Yeo shut the door behind her and pulled off her coat, feeling intolerably tired. Every movement was an effort, and reaching up to put her coat on a hanger felt like climbing up on the cross. She looked once again at her watch and went into the kitchen, where she found the ice-bucket with the lid off, a half bottle of tonic and a bottle of gin, both uncapped. She looked longingly at them, then replaced the tops, pushed in the switch on the electric kettle, and waited for her husband to come downstairs.

The phone rang, sharply. Claudia looked at it, willing it to stop, but she could hear splashing from the bathroom and Peter shouting to her to pick it up, would she please, he was in the bath for God's sake.

'Yes, he is here. Yes, I'll tell him.' She wrote down the number and stared at it, then sat down again to wait.

Her husband came down ten minutes later, wrapped in a dark-blue bathrobe straining against its tie belt, his hair still wet. 'I've had *the* most bloody awful day, I need another triple gin and tonic, and after that I've got some bad news.' He swung round to face her. 'How was your day?'

'Awful. I have bad news as well.'

'Oh, Christ.' He poured himself a massive gin, and loaded ice and not very much tonic into it. 'Do you want to go first? Gin?'

'No. Thank you. Peter, listen to me. This afternoon I went to Malplaquet Terrace. I wanted to see where Angela's car had been dumped. And when I got there, I knew. I mean, I knew the place. We went out to dinner there with those awful people — you remember, Aubrey something; you wanted him as a client? — and we talked about parking and he said that provided you didn't block someone's driveway you could leave a car there for ever. You remember all right?'

He was looking away from her, and for a moment did not speak.

'Oh Christ,' he said, about ten seconds too late, 'whatever has got into you? I don't even remember who the awful people were. I didn't have anything to do with Angela's death.'

'Oh God, Peter, do stop. We've been married eighteen years and I know you. Did you have a quarrel? You left her car in Malplaquet Terrace because you knew the place and knew no one would find it quickly.'

Yeo swallowed his drink in one gulp and reached to pour another before managing an artificially patient smile. 'You've certainly been having a bad day, haven't you, darling? Look, could we stop this? I've got some really shitty news for you and you'd better hear it while I'm still sober. Who was the phone call from, by the way?'

'Chief Inspector McLeish. He wants to see you.' She was sitting inert, in complete emotional exhaustion.

'What have you told him, you stupid bitch?' The colour came flaming up in Yeo's face as he stood straddle-legged, red in the face and shaking.

'Nothing,' she said wearily, 'nothing at all. But he's clever and he's after you. What are you going to do?'

He stared at her across his glass and suddenly drew back his arm and threw it at her, so that it glanced off her forehead and bounced on to the parquet floor where it shattered.

'Oh God, Peter, that was one of Granny's.' Claudia Yeo, momentarily totally distracted, struggled out of her chair, holding her head.

'It was an accident,' he said stupidly, staring at it. Claudia, on her knees picking up the pieces, stopped and looked at him, dry-mouthed.

'Angela was too,' he said, sitting down. 'I met her at the office that Saturday and we had lunch and went back to bed and got up again around two. I said I'd drive her up to Kirton: it's only an hour from the office. I needed to talk to her about business and I'd have plenty of time to get back to the Middletons. We were both a bit pissed, and I was bursting by the time we were getting close to Angie's parents' house. I didn't want to use the loo at her parents' — didn't want to talk to them, or explain what I was doing driving her, so we drove off the road and I had a pee. So did she.' His voice trailed off. Claudia, on her knees beside the shards of her grandmother's glass, did not dare interrupt.

'Then she told me she couldn't do anything about Huerter,' he said, painfully. 'She said she was having trouble with Giles and she'd probably have to leave the partnership. And whatever happened she dared not press him about Huerter.' He was sitting staring at the fire. Claudia waited, deaf to the street sounds and conscious only of the sickening thump of her heart, and her husband's grief and sense of loss.

'We had to have that "success fee",' he said, finally, into the silence. 'That's what I was going to tell you — we might even go bust without it. I was still a bit pissed, and I hit her once, but she was pissed too and she must have caught her heel and she fell backwards on to this bloody great rusty plough which was standing there.' He stopped again, his face twisted, and Claudia got up in a rush and reached for him. She felt his arms go round her convulsively. 'It was an awful noise,' he said, holding her fiercely. 'Her eyes went crossed and you could see her head was all out of shape, and she was breathing in this dreadful, strained, noisy way. I didn't know what to do. Then she stopped breathing.'

Claudia, holding her husband in her arms, felt his whole chest move in shuddering heaves.

'Then you tried to hide her?' she said, mechanically stroking his back.

'Yes. I panicked, I knew she was dead or dying, so I pushed her down the side of the embankment. I thought no one would find her for ages — the pheasant-shooting season was over and no one bothers with pigeon on that estate. I drove back to town — the car was filthy so I got it washed in case they could trace the body by the type of mud, and I dumped it in Malplaquet Terrace. I changed and showered at the office, and decided to risk waiting till Monday to take everything to the cleaners. The shoes I got rid of straightaway — they were caked with mud and I thought it safer. I threw them in the Thames. Oh God, Claudia, what have I done? I wish I were dead, too.'

'No, Peter darling, don't. I need you.'

'I'm sorry, God, I'm sorry.'

Suddenly the tears came, blocking her throat uncontrollably. They wept together, in each other's arms, ignoring the phone which rang and rang, until Claudia, without letting go of her husband, nudged it on to the floor. They stood locked together, slowly calming each other, until a whining sound from the phone forced them back to face the world's demands.

'It'll go on doing that.' Peter Yeo, face blotched with tears, replaced it and was turning back towards his wife when it rang again, and the doorbell shrilled simultaneously. The Yeos looked at each other, two competent, sociable people, united even at this moment in the need to find a way of dealing with whatever neighbours had chosen this moment to call.

'Upstairs,' Claudia said, under her breath and they both crept upstairs, where Claudia picked up the intercom and snapped into it: 'Who is it? I'm in the bath. Oh, Mr McLeish . . . can you hang on while I get dressed? Or better still, come back in ten minutes?' She felt her heart thump and her voice go shrill.

'Is Mr Yeo not home yet?' John McLeish was sounding tense, she thought.

'No, I don't think so, or he'd have answered the door.' She listened to the sound of water running in the bathroom and fought for calm; every minute she could keep the police at bay gave Peter a better chance.

'I'll just wait, then, for a few minutes till you're ready.'

Claudia put the phone down, tense but triumphant, and looked up to see her husband emerging from the bathroom with his jacket and tie. He held out his arms and she went to him.

'You're a good girl,' he said, shakily. 'Give us a kiss, then.' They embraced and she understood that he was calm again, his face and hair still damp from his wash.

'Claudia.' He stopped kissing her, moved his hands to her shoulders and made her look at him. 'This is going to be bad. The business is in a mess, and I mean a real mess, so there isn't much income. But this house is worth a lot, and we've got some investments.'

'Peter!'

'Darling, there is nothing to be done. I'll have to tell McLeish what happened. He either knows already, or he's close to it. I thought he'd got it yesterday, he just couldn't prove it. Come on, that's my good girl.' He held her as she burst into tears again. 'You did well. I had the time to realize that I couldn't go on, that we'd never manage to keep going, having to keep a secret like this. I thought I could when it was just me, but actually I don't think I could have, even then.' He held her away from him. 'Come on, darling, I'd rather let him in than have them force their way in. I looked out the window just now and there are two blokes round the back, and the girl I told you about, Sergeant Crane.' He held Claudia while she quietened, listening to the silence outside.

'Sorry, sorry. Let me wash my face, and I'll come with you.'

So they went together to open the door and admit John McLeish who for a split second looked startled, then understood immediately.

'I have Sergeant Davidson and Sergeant Crane with me,' he said gently.

'I'll come with you,' Peter Yeo said.

'We'll come with you,' his wife corrected him.

* * *

At well past midnight, when Claudia Yeo had been sent with a police driver to stay with a sister for the night and Peter Yeo had been bedded down in a police cell, Catherine Crane walked slowly down the yellow-lit corridor, past darkened offices and stopped at the door of her own office. She frowned at her desk; the in-tray had filled with papers since lunchtime, but why was the top one in red? She walked round her desk and saw that it was not one but three messages, all marked urgent, all asking her to ring Detective Inspector David Smith at whatever hour of the night she wished.

She sat down heavily and spread the pieces of paper in front of her, her heart thumping. Then she rang the number that had been given to her and the phone was answered on the second ring.

'It's Catherine.'

EPILOGUE

John McLeish swung his car into the green space beside the church, next to a BBC van. He climbed out and stretched, realizing how exhausted he still was; despite forty-eight hours out of the office, mostly spent asleep, the hour's drive had tired him. He stood in the raw, bright sun, shivering slightly in the wind that swept across the fens straight from Moscow, considering the sizeable parish church before him: fourteenth-century, with a lot of later additions, he decided. The lines of the building were obscured by yards and yards of cable, apparently suspended from the flying buttresses. McLeish picked his way past a throbbing generator and five men eating sausage rolls from a mobile canteen, and hesitated at the church door, taking in the scene. He slid quietly into a pew halfway up the nave, a good ten rows behind a group of people all engaged in furious argument.

'Hold it right there, please Jamie. Little to the left, so you pick up the mike in the pulpit. Somebody get that bloody cable out of shot — excuse me, Vicar.'

There was a pause while Jamie Brett-Smith moved to stand unselfconsciously still, four feet from the pulpit, and two cameras swivelled towards him. 'All right. Last song, just "Bless this House" then it's a wrap. You look a little unfinished, Jamie, somehow. We don't want to keep the frock for this, do we, but what about a bow tie?'

Jamie was seen to look enquiringly at someone in the row of spectators, and McLeish saw a familiar dark head come up sharply.

'Absolutely not. Too naff!'

This definite judgement was delivered with all Francesca's confidence, and as usual took no account of her audience at least fifty per cent of whom were sporting bow ties.

'What else do you suggest, darling?' The question was plainly rhetorical, but Francesca, McLeish could see, was giving it careful thought.

'His choir smock? If that does not appeal, how about an ordinary tie and the school jacket, worn unbuttoned? That at least will be unremarkable.' The clear voice was totally assured, and the producer was heard to say *sotto voce* that he had, in his pathetic way, been aiming for something remarkable, but no matter. Agreement appeared to have been reached and Jamie pulled on a tie and shrugged himself into a dark jacket. He glanced towards the organist, waited out the introductory bars and launched, high and clear, into 'Bless this House'. He sang like a lark, and the audience sat in a stillness that could be felt.

McLeish was unsurprised to see that one of the cameramen, attention never wavering from his job, had tears rolling slowly down his face. Francesca, he could just see, was hunched forward, her head held stiffly, as Jamie went confidently for the top note. And the voice cracked, producing only a thin, stretched sound.

He stopped immediately, the spell broken, and looked anxiously towards the front row.

'Take it again from D, Jamie.' Francesca sounded tense. The boy missed the note again. Relax, girl, McLeish urged silently — that boy vibrates to you, always has. There was a small silence while Jamie stood rigid and miserable, touching his throat, looking anxiously to Francesca.

'Tea break?' she said briskly, and he saw her profile as she glanced along the line to the producer, who nodded reluctant approval.

'Ten minutes.'

Francesca went straight to Jamie, and McLeish watched as the two of them disappeared through a door in the north transept.

'The voice is breaking, that's the problem,' the producer observed in a high drawl to the rest of the row. 'Lucky if we get through today. Better not book him for any more, Sally. When it goes, it goes.'

McLeish hoped silently that no one was going to say anything like this in front of Jamie and shrank as close as he could to a pillar, nodding politely to a young woman who was prowling the aisle and was hesitating as to whether to challenge him. He waited, unmoving and patiently, until there was a small stir in the front row, and Jamie and Francesca appeared again, both genuflecting and making the sign of the Cross as they passed the altar. One forgot that Francesca had been brought up High Church, McLeish thought disapprovingly, his Presbyterian hackles rising.

This time Jamie got right through the song, triumphantly hitting the top note, filling it in as he got there, and ending only a little husky. He stopped, let the camera track him to the link reporter, and, looking about six years old, beamed at Francesca in the front row. She was slightly off centre, so McLeish could just see her in profile as she grinned back at Jamie in a moment of perfect complicity.

Then she rose and signalled, and the boy followed her through the side door, her arm going round his shoulders as they went out. McLeish noticed again how he had shot up, the top of his blond cockatoo haircut now only just lower than the top of Francesca's dark head.

McLeish waited a decorous two minutes while, true to his upbringing, he said the Lord's Prayer without bending the knee, then he moved swiftly through the purposeful gangs of BBC technicians silently tugging at cables and dismantling equipment like people taking down Christmas decorations. Emerging into the bright light of day, he saw Francesca and Jamie leaning on an ornate tomb, deep in conversation, heads bent against the cold wind. Jamie was crying, and Francesca's arms went round him, easily and tenderly. McLeish stopped in his tracks and shrank into the porch only a few feet from them.

'I can't go on with singing, can I?' the boy said painfully into Francesca's shoulder.

'No, pettie, it's over. It happens, and if you go on you'll strain the vocal cords. Gin isn't all that good for them.'

The boy giggled, and observed it was as well that she had known that trick, he would never have got through without it.

'Well, I had to use it for Perry and Tris. I should know.'

Francesca found a handkerchief and gave it to him. 'Jamie, if your voice didn't go, all sorts of other things wouldn't happen and you'd never be a grown-up man.'

'What sorts of things?' Jamie enquired innocently, blowing his nose.

'Get on with you, you bad thing you.'

'Anyway, what's so great about growing up?' The boy, remembering, stroked her shoulder apologetically.

'There are bad patches,' she acknowledged, grimly. 'But it's still better than being a kid and being pushed around without anyone telling you what's happening.' She contemplated some of the bleaker passages of her own childhood, looking over Jamie's shoulder to seek some relief from her thoughts, and started as she recognized John McLeish in the shadow of the church porch.

Jamie turned, following her gaze, and beamed with pleasure, stopping awkwardly as he recalled that McLeish was no longer a Wilson familiar. McLeish strode heavily towards them, noticing how Francesca backed against the tomb as if preparing to defend it against all comers. Jamie looked uneasily from one to the other and ranged himself beside Francesca as McLeish stopped.

'Frannie?' the boy said anxiously, ignoring him.

'It's all right, Jamie. You go back in and make sure you've got all your stuff. I'll fetch you from the church.'

Francesca spoke as steadily as she could and patted his arm as she dispatched him, giving him a little reassuring wave as he turned anxiously to look back at her. Then she looked reluctantly to John McLeish, at the familiar solid jaw, slightly crooked nose, and determined straight mouth. He has come to tell me it is truly over, she thought steadily: he has come to say he is marrying that beautiful girl, and I cannot bear it. I have lost my chance of becoming the central concern of a good man, and I did that myself.

She felt the stone cold at her back, remembering other unbearable things that in the end she had endured and survived, and found the strength to move away from the supporting marble.

'How are you, John?' she said, pushing her hands hard into her pockets to keep herself from shivering. 'What are you doing here?'

'I've just finished the Morgan case.' He looked at her, waiting to find a way of going on, getting no help from the impassive shuttered face beneath the short dark hair.

'I saw, of course, that you were in court with Peter Yeo last week.'

'Yes. He is pleading guilty to manslaughter.'

'Not murder?'

'No. He didn't mean to kill her. I'm not sure what he meant, but he didn't want to lose her.'

Francesca moved involuntarily, her eyes lifting to his face.

'It's not quite as easy as that, but that's it at its simplest. He didn't want her to marry Giles Hawick or leave the firm — he had good financial reasons for that — and she was going to do both. He hit her, and she fell backwards on to a bit of agricultural machinery.'

'How did you find out?'

McLeish decided that he would have to finish this before he could say what he had come to say. 'I had him high on my list, but there wasn't any real evidence. In the end he just cracked up, as people do if you keep the pressure on.

Your lot helped — I mean, when the government decided to assist Huerter after all. Yeo Davis lost a big success fee from Barton. That brought the house of cards down. All the partners had to face up to drawing very little, or even paying some of the cash back. Yeo got home on the heels of this news to find his wife had become suspicious. And we were there too; Catherine Crane on her own initiative had followed the wife. She did very well.' He stopped, content to have got Catherine's name spoken between them.

Francesca looked steadily back at him. 'Is that what you came to tell me? That Catherine did a good job?' Her skin had gone blotchy as it did in the cold, and she looked pinched and wretched, and his heart turned over.

'No. I came to say I'm still here if you want me.'

Francesca stared at him, then felt blackness come down on her and she spread her arms to keep her balance, fighting not to be sick. 'Oh, John,' she said, as the blackness receded. 'Yes, I do want you. I'm sorry, it was my fault. I know I have to give the boys up.'

He let out his breath with a grunt and hugged her to him, feeling the familiar ribcage as he put his hands under her coat.

'There are conditions,' he said, after a minute, pulling back to look at her. 'Are you listening? We get married soon, and we start living together as of now. And you don't have to abandon the boys altogether, but you let them go. You leave them to grow up.'

Francesca looked back at him, hair standing up straight, her face very serious. 'I've got a condition, too — you won't like it, but I don't believe we'll manage without it.'

'What is it?'

'You have to work differently. I know you love being a detective and working all the hours God sent, but I don't believe we can make a go of living together on that basis. I'm going to find the whole thing difficult enough, anyway.'

'I agree.'

Her eyes widened. 'You do?'

'Yes,' he said, smugly. 'I do. This morning I told Stevenson I would accept a promotion into the Uniformed Branch. I am going to be a Superintendent at Edgware Road. Office hours, or not much worse.'

She regarded him with simple amazement.

'Will you like it?'

'It's a good job. One of the best uniformed jobs for me.'

She looked at him, unable to believe that what she had wanted was so suddenly achieved. 'What about Catherine?'

She was shivering now and he took her in his arms again, wrapping his coat round her.

'Gone back to the bloke she had before me, who decided to leave his wife. That's not why I'm here. It might have taken me a bit longer if her bloke hadn't come back, but you suit me better.'

That rang true as well, she thought. This man would always tell her the truth. With his arms round her, she was assailed by an inconvenient but unavoidable thought. 'So now we go and get a licence, tell our families, and get on with it,' he was saying, squinting down at her and disconcerted to find her looking anxious and guilty. 'What is it?'

'Well, darling John, I do absolutely know what you mean about the boys and I do agree, but the thing is I promised to get Jamie back to school and it's not been a good day for him and he needs feeding, and actually Grantchester isn't the right school for him, and his dad's having a bad patch again, and his Mum can't cope, and I think *I'll* have to move his school.' She looked up at him, pale but determined, and he looked down at her with love.

'Oh I knew I'd signed on for *Jamie*.' He kissed her. 'Come on, let's collect him and his gear and take him to a chippy somewhere. Need we move his school tonight, or could it wait till tomorrow?'

She laughed with relief and turned in his arms, calling to Jamie, who was studiously reading the notices inside the porch. And so they went off together, Jamie awed into silence and Francesca also very quiet in the front seat, until McLeish put a hand firmly on hers. 'We'll be all right.'

Jamie, reassured, leaned forward and slapped a tape into the player between the front seats and, liberated by relief and a man-sized slug of gin, flawlessly sang 'Jesu, Joy of Man's Desiring' as a hymn to the future, while they sped through the darkening countryside.

THE END

THE JOFFE BOOKS STORY

We began in 2014 when Jasper agreed to publish his mum's much-rejected romance novel and it became a bestseller.

Since then we've grown into the largest independent publisher in the UK. We're extremely proud to publish some of the very best writers in the world, including Joy Ellis, Faith Martin, Caro Ramsay, Helen Forrester, Simon Brett and Robert Goddard. Everyone at Joffe Books loves reading and we never forget that it all begins with the magic of an author telling a story.

We are proud to publish talented first-time authors, as well as established writers whose books we love introducing to a new generation of readers.

We won Trade Publisher of the Year at the Independent Publishing Awards in 2023. We have been shortlisted for Independent Publisher of the Year at the British Book Awards for the last four years, and were shortlisted for the Diversity and Inclusivity Award at the 2022 Independent Publishing Awards. In 2023 we were shortlisted for Publisher of the Year at the RNA Industry Awards.

We built this company with your help, and we love to hear from you, so please email us about absolutely anything bookish at feedback@joffebooks.com

If you want to receive free books every Friday and hear about all our new releases, join our mailing list: www.joffebooks.com/contact

And when you tell your friends about us, just remember: it's pronounced Joffe as in coffee or toffee!

ALSO BY JANET NEEL

WILSON & McLEISH MYSTERIES
Book 1: A FATAL BLOW
Book 2: A FATAL FALL
Book 3: A FATAL ENCOUNTER

Printed in Great Britain
by Amazon

37596787R00158